Runaway Horses

Alfred Silver

Pottersfield Press, Lawrencetown Beach, Nova Scotia, Canada

Library and Archives Canada Cataloguing in Publication

Silver, Alfred, 1951-
  Runaway horses : a novel / Alfred Silver.

ISBN 978-1-897426-49-4
  I. Title.

PS8587.I27R85 2013   C813'.54   C2013-900230-8

Cover design by Gail LeBlanc
Cover image iStockphto.com

The author would like to thank the Nova Scotia Department of Communities, Culture & Heritage for assistance in writing this book.

We acknowledge the financial support of the Government of Canada through the Canada Book Fund for our publishing activities. We acknowledge the support of the Canada Council for the Arts, which last year invested $157 million to bring the arts to Canadians throughout the country. *Nous remercions le Conseil des arts du Canada de son soutien. L'an dernier, le Conseil a investi 157 millions de dollars pour mettre de l'art dans la vie des Canadiennes et des Canadiens de tout le pays.* We also thank the Province of Nova Scotia for its support through the Department of Communities, Culture and Heritage.

Pottersfield Press
83 Leslie Road
East Lawrencetown, Nova Scotia, Canada, B2Z 1P8
Website: www.PottersfieldPress.com
To order, phone 1-800-NIMBUS9 (1-800-646-2879) www.nimbus.ns.ca

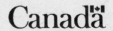

There are only two forces that can carry light to all the corners of the globe: the sun in the heavens and The Associated Press down here.

– Mark Twain

I
≡

Seana McCann stopped and leaned on her shovel, knee-deep in the earth and at the bottom of her lungs for now. She said breathlessly to Percy, "I know, I'm pathetic – you could dig twice as fast and need no pick and shovel. But you never could dig where anyone wanted you to, could you? Just where you wanted to."

Percy didn't raise his head off his paws, but did raise his soft chestnut eyes. He was black and tan just like her, or so her father'd declared the day he brought Percy home. It was said the Black Irish got their colouring from Spanish sailors shipwrecked from the Great Armada, though some said it was gypsies – especially of someone like her father, who travelled from horse fair to horse fair. Or he used to, back in Ireland.

Seana took her hands off the shovel for long enough to arch her back and stretch her arms up and back, trying to flex some life back into stiff-sore muscles and bones. No time for long rests, her mother and little brothers wouldn't be gone all day. She stabbed the shovel into the floor of the hole and jumped on its shoulders with both feet. The shovel blade went down about three inches and then stopped dead with a jarring crunch, sending a jolt up through Seana's knees. Damned Nova Scotia ground – or at least the piece of it her family'd ended up on – was nothing but gravel and tree roots. Her father used to say that on good Irish farmland you could dig down four feet and not find a stone; her mother would roll her eyes. Mam wouldn't've given Da any argument, though, that a digger in Ireland wouldn't hit so many tree roots – there weren't as many trees left in Ireland.

Despite stones and tree roots, now that Seana'd started she had to finish it today. And it couldn't've been put off much longer any-way, in a couple or three weeks the ground would be frozen too hard to dig. There were autumn teeth in the wind crackling brittle leaves off the branches that weren't already bare.

She set the shovel aside and picked up the pickaxe. There wasn't much room to swing it, since the hole was less than four feet long and about two and a half feet wide, and too deep now to stand out-side and dig. Boxed-in, Seana managed by standing in one end of the trench and bent-armed swinging the pick down at the other end: bite the pointed pick head into the earth, pry up on the handle to loosen the ground, repeat and repeat and repeat, then back to the shovel... Didn't help that her hat kept falling down over her eyes. It was an old, old felt hat of Da's and didn't exactly fit, but it did help keep the sweat from dribbling down her forehead, and she'd stuffed her hair up under it to keep it out of the way.

While she dug, Seana thought of the day Percy first came to live with them. The first summer in the McCanns' new home in New Scotland, Seana'd sometimes got to ride behind her Da on his trips into the village. In a farmyard halfway along the road, there was a mostly black dog chained to a post. Whether he was ever let off his short chain, Seana didn't know, but he was always there when she passed by with Da. And when she'd asked Da if the dog was chained to the post whenever he rode by alone, Da had just nodded grimly.

One day about mid-summer Da came home with a black and tan dog running beside his horse. Da shrugged at Mam, "He just followed me home, I didn't encourage him," though when Mam'd unwrapped the piece of meat Da'd brought home from the butcher's, she glanced at him sideways. Percy was a mess, his shaggy hair all matted and coming out in tufts, and underneath his fur there was just skin and bones. But he quickly filled out on table scraps – he'd eat anything – his coat grew glossy and the rats who'd been bothering the henhouse disappeared, as did whatever'd been nibbling on the vegetable garden at night. He lost his habit of cowering whenever someone reached a hand to pat him. And nobody stepped foot on their property without Percy letting them know.

Not that they got many visitors in those early days. But one afternoon a rough-looking man rode in on a horse built more for a plough harness than a saddle. Percy had backed up against Seana's legs and there was a difference in his barking this time, as much a snarling growl as a bark. Da seemed to hear the difference, too, for he came around the house from hoeing in the garden, still carrying the hoe. Da wasn't a large man – though not small, either – but there was a kind of deathly calm certainty about him, at times when others were flapping their arms and raising their voices. Though she'd been only a little girl when they left Ireland, Seana still could remember a few times when she'd been drawn to a commotion at the edge of the campfire circle of travellers and tinkers who followed the fair: men from the town yelling against men of the caravan. When the yelling seemed about to explode into something worse, someone above her head would murmur to someone else, "Fetch Ned McCann," and not long after, Da appeared. The shouting would die down and, not long after that, the town men went away.

The Nova Scotia farmer on his plough horse pointed at Percy and said, "That's my dog."

Da said, "Is he now?"

"I come back from the fields one evening to find his broken collar at the end of his chain. He must've run away when his collar broke."

"Now why ever would your dog run away from you and not come back?"

The farmer squinted down at Da, then said, "Or maybe his collar didn't *break*." Da didn't say anything. "I'll have that dog back." Da still didn't say anything, just stood leaning on his hoe, looking levelly back at the man on the horse. But Da's loose-shouldered posture and the placid expression on his face seemed to say clearly, *"Will you now?"* After a long moment, the man turned his saddled plough horse around and went away. Percy stayed.

But that was almost ten years ago, and Percy hadn't been a puppy when he "followed Da home." Now Percy's chin was hoarfrosted with grey whiskers, and he didn't bound along the way he used to on walks through the woods. For the last few weeks he'd hardly eaten at all but would bring up green bile, and he'd lost control of his bowels. He'd gone almost as skin-and-bone as when he first came to live with them. Animals got cancers, too, or maybe his insides were just breaking down with age, same as people's. But animals couldn't tell you when they were in pain. Oh, Percy would always yelp if you stepped on his paw, and had always sometimes whimpered and squeaked in his sleep, nightmares or maybe memories of his early life. But long-term, constant pain, animals had no way to tell you – or maybe they chose not to trouble you with whining about something you couldn't do anything about.

When Seana'd dug down as far as the top of her thighs, she decided that was deep enough – given the pile of gathered rocks beside the pile of dugout earth. She perched on the lip of the trench, wiped her eyes and nose with her sleeve and reached for the flat wooden box she'd set aside, the only element of her father to come back from the war. Two years ago word had trickled north that the United States government was hiring volunteers from anywhere for its war against Mexico, especially cavalrymen. Da was born a horseman and knew how to fire a gun and the family was desperate for money.

Along with letters, Da had sent back most of his sign-up bonus and parts of his monthly pay. But after about a year the letters and bank draughts had stopped. Early this year came the news that Mexico had surrendered and the U.S.A. was now twice as big as when the war started. A while later came a package addressed to Mrs. Elsie McCann, Rawdon Township, Hants County, Nova Scotia. Inside the brown paper wrapping was this dark wooden box-case about as long as Seana's forearm, and inside the box were two letters, neither in Da's hand. One was roughly pencilled on a scrap of notepaper and said simply that Edward McCann had died fighting bravely in the St. Patrick's Battalion. The other was much more elegantly written in black ink, but in a language that wasn't English or French or Gaelic or even Church Latin, and a Dutch Village woman selling sauerkraut at the Hants County Exhibition had said it wasn't German. Mam guessed it was probably Spanish, but they didn't know of anyone in Nova Scotia who could speak Spanish, let alone read it.

Also in the wooden case was what it had been built to hold. Snugged into their hard-ribbed velvet nests were a revolver pistol, powder flask, bullet mould and tin of percussion caps. The box didn't have clasps but opened with a little key Mam usually kept in the back of a drawer. Seana took the key out of the pocket of her coarse cotton shirt but had some trouble fitting it in the keyhole – her hand was shaking and her vision was misted. She finally got it opened and hefted out the pistol, then locked the box again to keep it from spilling if it got kicked over.

The gun was already loaded. She'd taken it in to Mr. Huxley, the village blacksmith, and he'd been more than glad to do the job for free and show her how – measuring the right amount of powder into each chamber of the cylinder, tamping the bullet down on top of it and fitting a percussion cap on the nipple – since it gave him a chance to handle one of these marvellous new inventions that he'd only read about or seen in catalogues. He told her that the American war against Mexico was the first time ever that an army had bought Samuel Colt's revolvers for its soldiers, "But it won't be the last, mark my word – this here's the future."

Seana pushed the box out of the way and swivelled on the grassy ledge to face Percy on the other side of the trench. He was still just lying there with his face on his paws. Percy was looking up at her and there was something in his eyes, something from a non-human place she couldn't hope to understand, and yet... There was something in those reddy-brown eyes, clouded with age and weary pain, that she could almost read... He knew. He'd known since she'd first started digging, but he hadn't tried to get away, just lay there waiting.

A sharp-edged part of Seana told her she was just imagining it to make herself feel better. But still, the way those so-familiar chestnut eyes were looking up at her, like she was a child and he was the grownup...

A desperate thought jumped into her mind. Back in Ireland she'd heard talk of a new place in Dublin that "put pets to sleep" in a gas chamber. Maybe there was such a place in Halifax. Or maybe a neighbouring farmer wouldn't charge much to help out the widow McCann's family with this horrible necessity. No, even if they could afford it, it wouldn't be right – you take care of your own.

Seana reached out her left hand and stroked her fingertips under one soft, floppy ear. Percy's tail moved from side to side. She tried to whisper, "Oh, I loved you so," but only parts of it came out.

Seana took hold of herself by the scruff of the neck, stood up in the trench and raised the revolver. From helping her father slaughter the family pig every autumn, and doing it herself last year, she knew to draw an X with her eyes up from the corners of Percy's eyes; the place where the lines crossed was where to put the bullet. She tried to cock the gun with her right thumb the way she'd seen Mr. Huxley do, but even though her hands were long and gawky for a girl – like the rest of her – it wouldn't go. So she clasped her left hand around her right and used both thumbs. Mr. Huxley'd said that this gun was what was called a Baby Dragoon, smaller and lighter than a full-sized Dragoon Pistol, but still it took all the strength in both her thumbs to pull the hammer back to one click, and then farther to the full-cock double click. Trying to keep her hands steady, and tightening the muscles around her eyes so she could see straight, she pointed the gun barrel at the centre of the X and pulled the trigger.

Mixed with the crack of the gunshot was a high-pitched yelp that tore her heart. The pistol kicked back and up and almost flew out of Seana's hands. The air was filled with a sulphurous smoke that stung her eyes and nose. She took one hand off the gun to wave the smoke away. Percy was lying on his side now, and his legs were twitching, but Seana had seen enough animals die to know the twitching was just the fading ghost of life. As she knew that that yelp had only been a physical reaction, like a grunt when you bump against something heavy. But that didn't make her feel any less cruel.

Barely able to see or breathe for the smoke and tears, Seana threw the gun aside and climbed out of the hole. She knelt beside Percy and pushed and rolled him till he fell into his grave. Not able to look down at him, she grabbed the hoe and started pulling earth from the pile down into the hole. Soon she shifted to the shovel and then – when there was no earth left but sprinkles among the grass – to placing a layer of stones over the grave so no racoons or rats or wolves could dig him up.

When there were no more stones, Seana found where the pistol had flown to and went to put it back in its box. But her eyes were so blurry and fingers shaking so much she couldn't fit the little key into the keyhole to open the case. She decided to just put the gun and the box back in the house; maybe after washing her face and hands with cold water she could make the key work. With the revolver dangling from her right hand and its case tucked under her left arm, she went around to the front of the house – just a ramshackle cabin, really, except walled with upright planks instead of logs. But she stopped before she got to the front door.

There was a horseman trotting up the path from the road. The horse wasn't quite big enough for an Irish Hunter, only about fifteen hands high, but a fine horse nonetheless: good breadth of chest and a smooth gait. Seana recognized the horse and she knew the rider – a little, more than she cared to. The sun was behind them so she couldn't see details, just the silhouette of a blocky, broad hat on a blocky, broad man, but she knew it was Mr. MacAngus. MacAngus was a grizzled old bachelor farmer – it was said that when he'd been the age most men get married he'd been too busy turning his farm into a profitable proposition, and he certainly had, at least for this part of Nova Scotia. He did have a weary, almost wistful look about him, as though he woke up some mornings seeing he'd bartered away his best years for plenty of land and money but not much else.

As the horse and rider came toward her, Seana clutched the gun case tighter to her left breast and moved her right hand behind her leg to hide the pistol. Mr. MacAngus reined in in front of her and said, "Good afternoon, Miss Seana McCann. Is your mother about?"

"Gone into the village. Won't be back for a while."

"Have you been crying?"

"No."

"Come now, your face is all streaked with tears, and dirt."

"T'isn't. Had to dig a hole. Ground gets muddy a couple feet down."

"And you lugged away half the mud on your clothes, such as they are. Pretty girl like you shouldn't have to be wearing men's cast-offs from the Poor Box. Were I to marry your mother you'd be wearing fine dresses with lace collars."

Seana tried to keep her face blank, but some sign of her shock must have shown through, because Mr. MacAngus sort of laughed and said, "It's not such a gobsmacking notion as all that – McCann isn't much of a change to MacAngus. Oh, maybe you think I'm too old? You should pay more heed to your own old Irish fairytales. Angus Mac Og was forever young."

Seana didn't know what to say to that, and didn't want to say anything to him. She just wanted him to go away.

Mr. MacAngus leaned down from the saddle, blinking – he was always blinking, maybe his farmhands called him Blinky behind his back – fingered the collar of her shirt and clucked, "Such coarse fabric for such soft skin." Seana was glad when he let go of her collar and his knuckles stopped rubbing against her neck, but then his hand slid down across the front of her shirt, diagonally to skirt around the hardwood box pressed against her left breast. When his fingers brushed across her right breast they didn't feel like fingers but like a fistful of sausagey worms, wriggling and groping.

Seana jumped back and swung her right hand up to point the pistol at him. "You keep your hands off me! Stay away!"

Mr. MacAngus straightened in his saddle, blinking. After a moment, one corner of his blubbery lips twitched upward and he chuckled, shaking his head. "Such a big gun for such a little girl. I disbelieve you'd really shoot anybody."

"I just killed my dog, I can sure as hell kill you."

Mr. MacAngus's mouth went straight again and his blinking multiplied. He stared down at her a moment longer and she managed to keep her right arm steady, pointing up at him, though the gun was heavy. Then he turned his horse and rode away.

After Seana had washed her face and hands and drunk some cold tea left in the pot, she could indeed fit the key in the keyhole and unlock the box. She locked the pistol back in its case and put the key back in the back of Mam's drawer, then went out into the empty yard.

She was sitting on a stump out in front of the house – what they called the dooryard hereabouts – still vibrating from the events of the day, when two horses came along the road, each carrying two riders. The sunset glinted on Mam's golden hair and on Fergus and Michael's. Liam the littlest, riding with Mam, had Da's dark colouring like Seana – an even split, Da used to say. There had been a baby sister, for a few weeks, until God took her away, as Mam put it.

God seemed to be taking a lot of things lately, and without asking –
though Seana suspected that wasn't an opinion she should express to
Mam, or to Father Murray.

Fergus and Michael were riding bareback but weren't in much
danger of falling off their stocky old workhorse as it clopped along.
Mam sat stiffly in the saddle of the taller horse, always nervous of
controlling him – though Seana found Limerick a joy to ride. He'd
been supposed to be their ticket to a good life in the New World,
and would have been if only a couple of other details had fallen into
place. Da knew nothing about farming – though Mam had been raised
on a farm, and a prosperous one – but he did know horseflesh. Their
first autumn in Nova Scotia he'd spotted an odd-looking little colt at
the Hants County Exhibition. Odd-looking to everyone else, but Ned
McCann could see what he was going to grow into. Even underval-
ued, the colt had cost a good part of what money they'd brought with
them from Ireland. It was going to be worth it, though, in the long
run, and not even all that long a run. The plan had been to buy up
two or three likely-looking mares in the couple of years the colt was
growing into a stallion, and then sell the offspring that would come
every year. But the farm never made enough money to buy even one
mare that was worth breeding.

Mam handed Liam down to Seana – though he protested he
could jump down easy – then climbed down herself, seeming relieved
to get off. Seana and the older boys took the horses into the stables
– just a knocked-together shed – and gave them a dry rubdown.
When they went into the house, Mam already had a pot of turnips
and potatoes boiling over the hearthfire. Mam spared telling them for
the several hundredth time how lucky they were to have potatoes.
Whether because of Da's gypsy fortuneteller friends or just blind luck,
the family'd gotten out of Ireland just in time. Not long after they left,
all the potatoes in Ireland turned black and rotted in the fields, and
people starved to death in the streets. The Irish were pouring out of
Ireland as fast as they could get on a boat going to any other country.

As they waited for the tatties and neaps to boil softer, Mam said to Seana in a voice that sounded offhanded, "Where's Percy?" Seana knew it wasn't meant the way it sounded, because Mam knew what Seana had done. The trip to the village had just been so the boys wouldn't know. Or maybe Mam's question had also been whether Seana'd done what she was supposed to do.

Seana turned to the boys and said, "Percy's..." and then had to look down and swallow. "We all knew Percy was sick, and old. This morning he fell asleep in the sun and... didn't wake up. I buried him out back."

Liam cried; the older boys tried to be men. All three wanted to see where Percy was buried. Seana led them outside; Mam called not to be long 'cause supper was almost ready. Seana led the boys 'round back to the rock-covered grave. Michael crossed himself and said a prayer, the other two said Amen. Seana said, "We better get in to the table."

Seana didn't say much during dinner, or after, just waiting for the boys' bedtime. There was something she had to tell Mam about but couldn't until the boys had gone upstairs – such as "upstairs" was. All there was to the house was the one-room downstairs and a sleeping loft. Seana used to sleep up there, too, separated from the boys by a curtain of old flour sacks, but got moved downstairs to a cot in the corner when Da went away.

Finally the boys went up to bed. Seana waited through the distant murmur of their goodnight prayers, waited a few minutes longer, then said to Mam, "Mr. MacAngus came by today."

Mam looked up from her mending and clucked, "The one day I was away..."

"He said, 'Were I to marry your mother...'"

"Did he now?" Mam looked like Christmas. "Well, I had hopes, but to hear he's thinking on it, too..."

"Hopes?" Seana sputtered for a way to put impossible ridiculousness into words. "He's... old!"

Mam laughed, more like a girl than a mother. "Not so old as he might seem to you. People can get grey hair a lot sooner than young people think. I've got a few myself. It just doesn't show as much in fair hair."

Seana felt an eerie prickling along the backs of her arms. She said, "If he was my... stepfather, I'd have to do what he told me?"

"Of course, dear. You're still a child, and he'd be as much your father as your father was, though not a blood relation."

"Mam, he... touched me, here." She pointed at her right breast.

Mam looked confused, and doubtful. "What?"

"My shirt was dirty from digging and he leaned down off his horse and fingered my collar and told me I'd be wearing fancy dresses if he married you, and then he lowered his hand and brushed it across..."

"Oh, don't be a silly girl. 'Brushed it across,' you said. It was just his arm going loose as he leaned back up in the saddle. Just an accident."

"It wasn't."

"Really, Seana." Mam shook her head and fanned out her fingers to wave away such nonsense, dropping the needle onto the trousers she was patching to hand down from Michael to Fergus. "Girls your age, on your way to turning into women, think every man is looking at you... that way. It's obscene."

That wasn't the way Seana expected a mother to react to a daughter telling her such a thing – but then, Seana'd never had such a thing to tell before, so how would she know what to expect? She wanted to say, *I'm not a little girl anymore*, but that seemed to be what her mother was saying, only not in a good way.

Before Seana could think of a reply, her mother picked up her needle and started stitching again, saying, "Thank you for taking care of Percy. Did the revolver work the way it's supposed to?"

"Yes, worked fine," though that caught in her throat, remembering.

"Good. I talked to Mr. Huxley the blacksmith while I was in the village. He wants to buy it."

"Buy what?"

"The revolver."

"*What?* We can't! It's the only thing we have left of Da."

"We have each other. Your father left us nothing to live on. Mr. Huxley's offering to pay good money for that pistol."

"Money? Is that all there is?" All sorts of different directions seemed to be trying to push tears out of Seana's eyes. "You're trying to wipe him away, replace him."

"*Ow!* Now see what you made me do." Mam stuck her needle-pricked finger in her mouth and looked at Seana from a long way away, like someone looking down the wrong end of a telescope. Then she took her finger out of her mouth and said crisply, "All right, you're not a little girl anymore, time you stopped seeing the world through... misty peatbog fairy stories. That day I went into Halifax to the American Consulate, to ask them wasn't there some kind of pension for the widows of soldiers killed fighting in the U.S. Army, I didn't tell you what they told me."

"You did. They told you there would've been a pension if he was American, but not for foreigners."

Mam shook her head. "What they really told me was there might still've been a pension, foreigner or no, if he'd died fighting in the U.S. Army, but he didn't. The St. Patrick's Battalion was really the San Patricio Battalion, a mob of Irish American deserters who went over to the enemy side for money. The U.S. Consulate said that if one of the San Patricio Battalion chose not to send any of his Mexican gold back to his family, it's hardly the American government's problem."

The ceiling and the floor seemed to have changed places, making Seana as seasick as she'd been on the lurching ship from Ireland. Only now Da wasn't there to hold her hand and put a cold cloth on her forehead. He seemed to be slipping even farther away, as if the man she thought he was had never been there. All she could think of to say was, "That's... it's not true."

"Isn't it? That letter that came with the gun case, the fancy one we can't read – it sure to Jesus isn't in French or German, and that leaves Spanish. Why would someone write about him in Spanish if he hadn't gone over to the Mexican side for money? Money he spent on drink and Mexican whores, instead of sending it home to his family."

"But – "

"There are no buts. It's time you started looking at the world the way it is, girl, and doing what you have to do to get along in it – and help your family get along. I'm going to bed, you can stay up all night and play let's-pretend with the hearthfire sprites and be useless in the morning, if that's what you want." Mam went to the bed she used to share with Da and pulled across the curtain that had just been an old bedsheet before she painted it with Celtic curlicues – but that was in happier times.

Seana turned her eyes to the wispy ghosts of flames dancing out of the embers in the fireplace. She felt wrung out and strung up to dry in the wind. She made a grab at the possibility that Mam had just made up the story about Irish deserters and Mexican gold. But it was a devilish complicated story to make up on the spur. And why would her mother lie to her? Well, maybe to make it seem like marrying old MacAngus wouldn't be such a terrible thing. No, Mam wouldn't make up such an evil lie about Da, not for any reason. So it had to be true.

Seana pushed that aside to think on something even more evil, or at least more immediate. Or was it? Maybe Mam was right and she'd just been imagining about Mr. MacAngus – but no, there was no imagining those fat, gropey fingers and drooling piggy eyes. But there seemed to be no way to get her mother to believe it. Or maybe Mam could believe it but didn't want to – maybe it was Mam who was playing let's-pretend.

Or maybe... The possibility that began to surface was such an evil thought that Seana didn't want to look at it. But there it was. Maybe Mam knew that what Seana had said about Mr. MacAngus was plain fact, had known it all along. *"It's time you started looking at the world the way it is, girl, and doing what you have to do to get along in it – and help your family get along."* There were three little brothers to think of. Potatoes and turnips for supper today, what would there be tomorrow, or next month?

By now she was sitting with her feet up on the chair, hugging her knees. Whatever way Mam was thinking about it all, or not thinking about it, the bare fact remained the same. Looking into the flickering embers didn't show Seana any way around it. She was trapped. Chained to a post.

II
===

Sam Smith stood in the snow watching the horses – and the horse-men – get put through their paces. There hadn't been much snow yet this year, so this stretch of stubbled hayfields outside of Halifax was a workable testing ground; another week or two and it'd be like galloping through knee-high pudding. The centre of all the activity was two gentlemen in fuzzy brown top hats belled out like flower-pots, and tailored topcoats – Mr. Hiram Hyde and Mr. Daniel H. Craig. Horseshoed around them was a group of rough-looking older men in stable clothes and fussy-looking younger men with notebooks and pencils.

Mr. Craig, the older of the two gentlemen, a lanky Yankee with a billygoat beard and ice-blue eyes, took the well-chewed cigar out of his mouth and said sharply, "Who's next?"

A leathery, squinty-eyed fellow in a tweed cap pointed a thumb in Sam's general direction and said, "Him."

Sam almost looked around for who "him" was meant for, but managed to catch it and just stepped forward. *Remember, think of yourself* as "him" and "he" – not "her" or "she" or anything else. One slip-up and they'd send "Sam Smith" straight back to what "he" was trying to escape from.

A couple of weeks back, Sam had seen a possible escape hatch tacked to the notice board in the village. It seemed there was now a telegraph line from Saint John, New Brunswick, to New York City in the U.S.A. And the Cunard Steamship Lines was contracted to hotfoot a mail packet from Liverpool, England, to the closest North American port – Halifax, Nova Scotia – every two weeks, carrying the news from Europe where all important things happened. The problem was to quickly get the news across the wide gap between the dock at Halifax and the telegraph line at Saint John, across the Nova Scotia peninsula and the Bay of Fundy.

A new syndicate of American newspapers, calling themselves The Associated Press, had contracted a Halifax businessman named Hiram Hyde to put together an Express that would whip across Nova Scotia on relays of fast horses – "as fast as horse flesh can do it and live!" – to a rendezvous on the Fundy shore, where a steam launch would be waiting to speed the European news dispatches across the bay to Saint John.

Sam Smith was fairly well-acquainted with horses – or the person who'd become Sam Smith was. Not the kind of top-of-the-line thoroughbred long-distance gallopers that would get used in this Express thing, but horses were horses and two horses who looked exactly the same could have as different personalities as two horses from completely different breeds. You had to get to know them one by one. It also seemed to Sam that the kind of rider that would be wanted for this horse express would be lads who'd got almost their full growth in height but hadn't filled out yet, still sapling slender, tall enough to stand in the stirrups but still light in the saddle. Riders a lot like, say, Sam Smith.

Others seemed to've got the same idea, because about a third of the crowd who'd showed up for tryouts was about Sam's same age or not much older. The other two-thirds, though, were full-grown young men. Like Corey O'Dell, who wasn't all that tall but muscular – slim shoulders but thick chest – and had come all the way from New Brunswick to try his luck. He seemed a shoo-in, was already well-known for various horse-related escapades in his home province, and had shown up wearing high-top riding boots and carrying his own riding crop. If that was the kind of rider they were looking for, Sam Smith didn't stand much chance.

The leather-faced, tweed-capped man who'd pointed his thumb at Sam pointed his finger at a tall grey gelding standing saddled and ready, a groom holding his bridle. Sam muttered to the groom, trying to keep his voice low in his throat, "What's his name?"

The groom cocked his head like that was an odd question, then shrugged, "Wellington."

Sam reached way up to cup the big grey's ear, gently, and murmured, "Aye, Wellington, we goin' for a ride now? Eh, Wellington?" then brushed his hand down the long, furry forehead and blew softly into the big black nostrils. The groom looked impatient for Sam to get on with it. The stirrup was a bit high for Sam's foot to reach with his other foot still on the ground. He'd seen grooms give a gentleman a boost onto a high horse, but he was no gentleman and didn't want to give anyone the idea he needed any kind of help. He reached up to grip the rim of the saddle and jumped.

Sam's left foot just managed to catch in the stirrup. He settled onto the saddle and took hold of the reins. The groom pointed ahead and said, "Round that there bald tree and back again." Way off at the far end of the field was a tall tree that maybe had a few brown leaves still clinging to it, too far away to tell. And Sam knew from watching the other riders that the field was really two fields, with a ditch between, though he couldn't see the ditch from there. "Flat-out gallop all the way, if you can stay on." Sam was actually less worried about showing a good seat at a gallop than a trot – no bouncing or posting, just hold on. "Wait for the go."

Sam hunched forward in the saddle to be ready, and looked toward two leather-coated men standing nearby. One was peering at a pocketwatch, the other held a pencil poised above a notebook. Sam shifted his eyes and sighted on the tiny tree growing between Wellington's ears. Someone shouted, "Go!" and Sam dug in his heels.

Wellington didn't have to be invited twice; it seemed he'd been watching the other horses gallop and just waiting for his turn. The world disappeared, or turned onto a blur. The only concrete things were the massive body churning under Sam, the thump of galloping hooves, the wind whipping his hair back and flicking the ends of the mane against his face as he leaned forward to Wellington's neck. He saw the ditch just before they reached it – not that he had to do anything but grip his knees tighter to hold on as Wellington sailed over it and hit the ground running. As they passed the big bare tree, Sam tugged on the left rein and Wellington made a tighter turn than Sam would've guessed such a big horse had in him – so tight that Sam could feel himself sliding sideways off the saddle. The black and white blur of turned clods and snow seemed to be rushing up to meet him. He lurched his body to the left and managed to regain his seat, hoping nobody saw.

When they got back past the starting point, Sam slowed Wellington to a trot and then a walk and came back to the world after a few minutes of utter flying freedom on a horse like he'd never ridden before, couldn't've imagined a circumstance where he would ride a horse like that. As he climbed down off the saddle, still a little high, he heard the two leather-coated timekeepers muttering to each other:

"Well, the horse can run."

"And the boy can ride."

Next up was a fellow named John Thomson, whom Sam was divided about. On the one hand, this was a competition and the Express was only going to hire so many riders, so good luck for Thomson might mean bad luck for Smith. On the other, John Thomson was so much like Sam: about the same height and build, black hair, dark eyes and a suntanned look to his face even though summer was long gone – and had to try to be a horseman in worn-down lace-up ankle boots, same as Sam. Thomson got saddled with a big bay horse, literally, and Sam stood back to watch their run. It seemed to Sam that the bay, though even bigger and longer-legged than Wellington, wasn't quite as fast. No doubt, though, that this John Thomson knew something about horses, and how to ride them.

It was getting late in the day, and this late in the year the sun went down early. The gnarliest two of the stable-booted old men – looked like their swaddling clothes had been horse blankets – were arguing in front of Mr. Hyde and Mr. Craig. Well, maybe not exactly arguing, just presenting their opinions to be weighed, but presenting them with fervour. Sam sidled over closer to the group, though not close enough to be obviously eavesdropping, and pretended to be watching the current rider, the last tryout of the day. He could pick out bits and phrases of the old horsetraders' debating, depending on shifts in the breeze and other noises around him:

"... don't take a genius to calculate a horse can carry a lighter-weight rider farther faster. You don't see many great hulking jockeys..."

"... ye cannae see tha' wha' matters here is stamina? Takes a grown man wi' fully formed bones to ride hard four or five hours flat out wi'out any rest or respite, except a moment here and there changin' relays o' horses. Just as it takes a big strong horse to gallop twelve miles flat out, not some colt wi' skinny legs and..."

That was about all Sam managed to hear – though that was enough to get the gist – before Mr. Hyde cut in crisply, "We'll freeze our tongues off waggling them out here. Take it up back at the office." There was only a vague trace of Yankee in Hiram Hyde's voice – U.S.-born, it was said, but he'd lived in Nova Scotia for years. "Carstairs!"

The two timekeepers broke their huddle and came over to murmur with Mr. Craig and Mr. Hyde. After a moment, the bigger timekeeper – the one who'd held the pocketwatch, not the notebook – boomed out, "That's it for today! Line up to collect your two shillings for turning out! There'll be a list posted outside the office door tomorrow of who's hired on!"

Sam joined the line forming up in front of the two timekeepers turned into paymasters, the bigger one handing out two-shilling coins and the smaller one checking off names in his notebook. Mr. Hyde and Mr. Craig and a few others climbed onto the tryout horses to ride back into town, Mr. Hyde on Wellington. Sam noticed that Corey O'Dell was one of them, like he was already on the inside.

A couple of freight wagons had carried the would-be Express riders out of the city and were waiting to carry them back; those who'd come in from the country were climbing back onto their farm ponies to head home. This trip John Thomson ended up in the same wagon as Sam, and sat hunched forward with his hat pulled down low and his face buried in the turned-up collar of an old coat that looked too big for him. Sam almost leaned over to wish him good luck, but decided things were dicey enough if he kept all his luck for himself, much less wishing any of it away.

The wagons dropped them outside a big clapboard building that housed the Horse Express's office, near the Cunard Dock. Everybody except the drivers climbed down and went their own ways. Sam walked along Water Street to a creaky swinging sign for the Cod's Wing Tavern and stepped inside. The man behind the pockmarked bar wasn't the same one Sam had seen that morning. Fortunately not many evening customers had come in yet, and fortunately this was a place for fishermen and merchant seamen, not Royal Navy hardcases. But Sam still felt self-conscious as he walked to the bar and said, "I left my duffle here, my dufflebag, this morning. The other barman said he'd keep it in the storeroom till I came back tonight."

The barman scratched his cheek – white-bristled like a pig's hide – and said, "Didn't say nothing 'bout such a thing to me. I didn't see no bag."

Sam realized with a thud what an idiot he'd been. If he cried thief, who were the Halifax police likely to believe: a Halifax tavernkeeper who'd lived and worked in the city for years, or a nameless nobody from nowhere? And with suppertime coming on, it'd be the night police he'd be complaining to. It hadn't taken Sam long in Halifax to learn the city had two different police forces – the Day Patrol and the Night Patrol – and the night police were more inclined to whack first and ask questions later. That was understandable self-preservation in a place whose nights were filled with drunken sailors and soldiers and the kinds of scavengers they attracted, but it wasn't very reassuring for someone in a situation that would need some explaining and a bit of fudging.

Everything Sam had in the world was in that duffle. It seemed now he would've been better off to stash it under the skirts of a spruce tree on The Commons and take his chances no one would stumble across it, or take it with him to the Express office and leave it there till he got back from the tryouts – though that might've given Mr. Hyde and all the impression Sam Smith was desperate and rootless.

Sam sucked in his cheeks to moisten his throat, and tried, "Reason I left my bag here was 'cause I'd be comin' back to buy supper."

"What'll ya have?"

"Uh, bread and cheese," – that seemed safe – "and a pint of small beer." Nobody in their right mind drank city water. There was plenty of good country well water in the place Sam was supposed to call home, but there were other poisons there.

"What colour's yer bag?"

"Grey canvas. Tied up with rope." The barman went through a door behind the bar and came back with Sam's bag. It wasn't really a dufflebag, though sausage-shaped like one, just a sheet of sailcloth wrapped around Sam's worldly goods and tied together with a hank of hemp rope that also made a shoulder strap. "That'll be sixpence for yer supper."

Sam dug out the two-bob bit he'd got for showing up and riding, and put it on the counter. The barman took it and replaced it with one shilling and sixpence, then poured a pint mug from one of the barrels behind the bar. "Luly'll bring you yer supper."

Sam found a table in a corner and sat and sipped his large tankard of small beer – not as thick or strong as full-blown ale, but would do him just fine. Luly turned out to be a plump woman in a low-slung blouse, and supper turned out to be a thick slice of dark bread and a not-so-thick wedge of orange cheese. It wasn't enough to fill him up, but the beer helped. After he'd wet-fingered the last crumbs, he dragged the beer out for as long as he could, but knew he couldn't stay there all night. Eventually he had to set down his emptied mug, button his coat and clap on his cap, sling his duffle on his shoulder and go out into the cold.

A few of the streetcorners had blue gaslights and a few of the buildings' windows cast patches of yellow light. Sam walked briskly to keep warmish, uphill along George Street, skirting around the iron-fenced grounds of Province House and zig-zagging to Spring Garden Road. He crossed the road so as not to walk along beside the looming hulk of Bridewell, The House of Correction where vagrants were chained next to murderers, and The Poor House where people with no homes and no income were housed like chickens crammed in a coop until they moved on to the anonymous graveyard out back.

Past Bridewell, Sam turned left down a sidestreet of good-sized houses. On his first day in Halifax, three days ago, he'd scouted around for a house with a brick fireplace chimney on the outside and no dog. The street was quiet now and all the houses dark except for the occasional upstairs window. A couple of dogs barked at him from their fenced yards as he walked by. Frozen gravel crunched under his feet as he turned up the carriage drive of the house he wanted; he tried to set his shoes down softly.

Halfway along the side wall of the house was a bit of a niche where the brick fireplace housing stuck out from the clapboard. After spending three nights there, Sam could see it in the dark. He knelt down and untied his packsack. Wrapped around his other things – such as they were – was a thick wool blanket with the piece of canvas wrapped around it. The blanket was big enough to make a double-layered cocoon if he sat with his knees up, and the canvas a cocoon skin. The brickwork at first didn't seem any less cold than the ground, but he knew from the last few nights that after a while his back would start to feel at least a little warm.

Sam woke a few times during the night, squirmed around a bit and managed to drift off again. The fifth or sixth time, though it was still dark, he could hear the clop of delivery wagons out on the street and the rattle of servants taking out last night's ashes. He shook his head to unkink his neck and a dribble of snow fell off the bill of his cap. Sudden light from an upstairs window showed him a thin coat of snow had fallen overnight. Unless it melted before the household started moving, a bare spot would show where he'd spent the night and they'd see his footprints going down the drive. So no more nights here. Anyway, the real cold of the winter was just starting to lock in; pretty soon a night like he'd just spent would mean waking up minus some fingers and toes, or not waking up at all. As it was, he couldn't tell whether the stiffness in his joints was from sleeping cramped up or from the cold. Well, if his name was on the list at the Express of-fice today, Sam Smith wouldn't have to worry about sleeping outside. And if it wasn't... ?

With his duffle back on his shoulder, Sam wandered up and down the lower end of Spring Garden Road, waiting for the shops to open. One shop, the bakery on a corner, already had some lamps lit and probably had for some time, but its door sign still said CLOSED. Every time Sam walked by it he got a different whiff of something that was going to be fresh-baked this morning: pumpernickel bread, apple pies, cheese buns... At least the walking was working some

circulation back into his feet, tingling into some kind of warmth instead of clumping like blocks of wood.

When the bakery's door sign turned over to OPEN, Sam went in
and said to the aproned woman behind the counter – more like a girl,
actually – "Do you have any day-old buns?"

"Currant buns?"

"Just plain."

"Tuppence a dozen."

"I only want two."

"Oh. I guess that'd be a farthing."

Besides the shilling and sixpence from yesterday, Sam had a few
farthings left over from the scratchy bit of money he'd brought with
him to the city. As he felt in his pocket, the bell over the shop door
jingled again. He glanced over his shoulder and saw a large man with
muttonchop sidewhiskers and a tall top hat that made him stoop on
his way through the door. The big man tapped his walking stick on
the floor and said loudly, "You should tell the tramps to wait, and
serve the paying customers."

Sam could feel prickly heat rising in his cheeks, but the man was
a lot bigger than him and no doubt a well-respected citizen, and the
last thing Sam wanted to do was draw attention to himself. So Sam
just faced front and put his farthing on the counter. The girl behind
the counter was blushing, too, and keeping her eyes down.

As Sam's farthing clicked onto the counter, the fat man with the
fat muttonchops said, "Where'd you get that – steal it?"

Sam wanted to say, *I earned it,* but there was no winning so he
just kept his mouth shut while the shopgirl put two buns from a bin
in a small paper bag and handed it to him. On his way out, Sam had
an urge to accidentally stomp his bootheel down on patent leather
toes and grind. He was sure he could run faster than a fat man in
shiny slippery shoes. But he couldn't outrun the police who would
surely swarm to squeals of a citizen who'd been assaulted in broad
daylight, and even the Day Patrol weren't likely to ask questions

about whether an upright citizen or a ragamuffin tramp was in the wrong.

The street felt warmer and more comfortable than the inside of the shop had. The sky had brightened to a light grey and the street and sidewalks were filling up with people and horses and wheels, but Sam was almost getting used to city traffic by now, so just wove his way along munching his breakfast. Day old or not, his mouth seemed happy with the bread buns and his stomach even more so. Dry, though. A bit of snow was filtering down, not thick but fat flakes. Sam tugged off his left-hand mitt and glove and walked along with his hand held out flat, then licked his hand. The town clock chimed once, which didn't tell him anything but that it was a quarter- or half-hour – unless it was one o'clock in the morning or afternoon, and that wasn't likely.

He crossed the street to get a better angle at the clock tower on Citadel Hill: black hands on a blue face. A sky-blue clockface seemed to make sense for standing out, since the sky over Halifax seemed usually grey, at least all the time Sam had been there. Quarter to eight. So by the time he got down to Water Street the Express office should be open.

It was, sort of – the door was still closed but had the list posted on it. Eight or nine young men from yesterday were in the hallway waiting, some standing around and some sitting on the floor. As Sam came down the hallway, a couple of other young men passed by him on their way out, grumbling and mumbling – names not on the list. Sam had to force himself to keep walking at a normal pace till he got to the door, then turned a half-turn and faced the list. *Corey O'Dell... Thad. Harris... Hamilton... MacDonald... Sam Smith.*

Sam let out a deep breath he hadn't even known he'd been holding. There was a * beside his name, though, and beside three others. One of them was John Thomson. Sam looked around and spotted John Thomson hunkered down against the wall with his hands on his knees. Sam went over and crouched beside him and murmured, "What's the star mean?"

"Star?" It came out in a kind of gravelly grunt, like someone with a cold or trying to talk deep in their throat.

"Beside our names."

John Thomson just shrugged like he knew what Sam meant but didn't know what it meant. There were a few flecks of straw stuck to John Thomson's rough-cut black hair sticking out from under his cap – must've spent last night in a stable or snuck into a hayloft. Sam pointed and murmured, "You got a few bits of yer last night's bed still stuck in yer hair." The slangy words and rhythms of regular boys' speech were coming a bit more natural to Sam, but he was still sort of translating in his head. "Figured ya wouldn't wanna advertise you been sleepin' rough like me."

John Thomson grunted and nodded. The grunt might've been Thanks, maybe. He brushed his fingers through his hair, then flicked at his shoulders. Sam said, "That's got it."

The office door opened and those who'd been sitting stood up. Out came the larger of the two timekeeper/paymasters from yester-day – Carstairs had been the name Mr. Hyde had called to get the timekeepers' attention when it came time for them to turn into pay-masters. Mr. Carstairs announced, "Those of you with asterisks beside your names, go into the next door down the hall and wait."

Sam said, "Uh... asteriss... ?"

"*Asterisks* – like a porcupine star. Rest of you, come with me."

Beyond the door the asteriskers were supposed to go through was a room with a sort of pew-like bench, a few chairs, a desk with nothing on it and a side door that was closed. Sam figured he might as well sit to wait, and so did the other three: John Thomson and two others old enough to be tall but not old enough to be hefty. Sam could hear the voices of Mr. Hyde and Mr. Craig next door, pitched as though talking to a group, though he couldn't make out the words.

Given a moment to look around, Sam could see there was a film of dust on the desk and a spiderweb in one corner of the ceiling, like the kind of long-deserted back room that tramps might squat in till they got caught. Sam said, a bit nervously, "The Halifax Express don't look like it can afford to pay much rent."

"These ain't the reg'lar offices, just temp'ry" came out like "You idiot" from a slightly heftier fella than the other three – Charlie something-or-other. "Their real office's up on Hollis Street in the Halifax Exchange Reading Rooms, no place for the likes of us."

John Thomson piped up, "Halifax Express in the Halifax Exchange." And "piped up" was exactly right, as though John Thomson's usual gravelly, low-in-the-throat voice was just somebody trying to sound older. It seemed to've popped out of his mouth without thinking, because as soon as it was out he compressed his neck down further in his coat collar. If John Thomson had been a turtle, his head and hands would've disappeared.

Fortunately, before Charlie could turn his scorn on John Thomson, the door opened and Mr. Carstairs came in carrying a folder of papers and a steel-nibbed pen. Framed by the doorway – though not entirely, since the narrow doorframe couldn't quite fit in both his shoulders at once – Carstairs seemed even more barrel-bodied-big than he had outside. His long brown leather coat had paler creases at the elbows – thick, hard workingman's bull leather, not a gentleman's glove-soft calfskin. With his bushy fat mustache, short-clipped hair, bloodhound eyes and beefy fingers, Mr. Carstairs looked like he should be on the cover of the *Police Gazette*, with a handcuffed felon by the scruff of the neck – or maybe a vagrant youth.

Mr. Carstairs sat down behind the desk, cleared a dust space with one leather sleeve, took an ink bottle out of a pocket and set it beside the folder and pen, then said, "Here's the deal. Mr. Hyde and Mr. Craig couldn't quite make up their minds, surprise surprise, as to whether to go with full-grown young men as express riders, or riders who would be lighter in the saddle. So a compromise was reached, to wit: the gentlemen in the other room are being hired on as riders, you four lads will be hired on as possible substitute riders and full-time stableboys, to attend to the relay horses in their way stations and see to it they're kept fit and exercised. Once the Halifax Express has been established – to wit: once a few successful runs've been accomplished – you may well get your chance as riders. Meanwhile you'll be paid a shilling a day over your room and board and if you do get to ride, a rider's stipend for that run. If you're amenable to those terms..."

Sam certainly was, and the other three seemed to be as well.

"Good. Now before I get you to sign your names, or make your marks, I need a bit of information. Since none of you has reached the age of majority, and since you'll be working with large, spirited horses and accidents may happen... I'll need the names of your next of kin to make sure you have your parents' permission and in case of... accidents."

Sam said, "I'm an orphan."

"No next of kin?"

"None." At least none who were kin to "Sam Smith."

Two of the others told Mr. Carstairs their parents' names and addresses, then John Thomson said in his croaky voice, "I'm an orphan, too."

After they'd all signed on, Mr. Carstairs told them, "Get your gear and come with me." Sam picked up his duffle and trooped along with the others, down the stairs and around to the livery stable yard next door. In the yard were about half a dozen saddled horses and another hitched to a two-wheeled shay. Mr. Carstairs said, "Pick yourself a horse and let's get travelling." Sam made a beeline for Wellington. Mr. Carstairs heaved himself up onto a big black horse and his smaller partner climbed into the shay.

Besides the four asteriskers and Mr. Carstairs, the only other riders were Corey O'Dell and another twentyish young man. Sam wondered for an instant whether they were the only full-fledged riders hired on, but only for an instant – of course half the Express riders would stay put and be based in Halifax. The plan was for two riders per run, one from Halifax to Kentville and the other from Kentville to Granville Point on Digby Gut, where the steamboat would be waiting to carry the news packet across Fundy. But there was a lot of groundwork still to do before the Halifax Express went into business.

Mr. Carstairs led the way and they stayed at an easy trot until they got clear of the city. Then Corey O'Dell spurred his horse into a gallop and they fell into a series of short-sprint races, two or three of them galloping ahead and then slowing to wait for the others to catch up. It was a glorious day, with the sun finally breaking through the clouds, the sea air off Bedford Basin mingling with the pine scent of the woods to the left of the road, and a fine big thoroughbred prancing and dancing under Sam Smith. And he was getting paid for it.

They stopped at Fultz's Inn, or Twelve Mile House, where the road split off – west to Windsor or north to Truro. Mr. Carstairs left his horse there, with instructions that Black Maria was to be stabled and fed at the expense of the Express, and that an Express stablehand would be coming by every few days to exercise her and make sure she was getting the best care. Then Mr. Carstairs climbed into the shay and took the reins, squeezing his smaller partner to the side, and the parade carried on along the Windsor Road.

As they left Halifax County behind and entered Hants County, John Thomson pulled his cap down even lower across his face – Sam wouldn't've thought it possible – and rode with a sort of forward hunch, sticking close to the shay and not joining any races. Twelve miles or so past Fultz's Inn they came to Pentz's Inn, where they dropped off another horse and the first of the asteriskers to be left behind – the only one of the four with a family home in Halifax, so it made sense for him to get the nearest post to there. Fultz's was nearer to Halifax, but it seemed the plan was for each asterisker to take care of two posts, so he could shuttle back and forth between Pentz's and Fultz's. Pentz's and Fultz's, though, did make Sam wonder about the name of the next inn they were going to stop at. Staltz's? Buntz's?

A mile or so past Pentz's Inn, a long, low, stone wall started winding along beside the left side of the road. Beyond it, Sam could see the splendiferous lakeside mansion and coach house of the estate called Mount Uniacke. Mount Uniacke wasn't on any kind of mountain – actually in a valley between two hills – but Sam supposed that if you were that rich and powerful, a mountain was where you said it was. Past Mount Uniacke, though, the land on either side of the road was all tangled scrub forest or frozen bog.

When the Express crew crossed over Ardoise Hill the country changed, from gravelly and scrubby to tall trees and wide, rolling fields with golden stubble showing through the snow. By the time they got to Spencer's Inn the sun was setting; not only were the days still short, they weren't travelling a patch as fast as an Express rider would, come the day. Spencer's Inn turned out to be two buildings – the family home and kitchens on one side of the road and the inn on the other. Mrs. Spencer was an old Scots woman who seemed to do all the work while her husband lazed around.

It seemed the plan was to spend the night at Spencer's Inn, after a fine feed of beef stew and dumplings at the Express company's expense. Mr. Carstairs and his partner got a room to themselves while the rest all slept in a big common room. That meant changing into nightshirts and a flurry of pale male bodies, surprisingly pale given faces and hands leathered by sun and weather. A naked "Sam Smith" definitely wouldn't have fit in, even if only naked for the instant between pulling off one shirt and pulling on another. So Sam left his nightshirt in his duffle and slept in his dayshirt, which hung down almost to his knees when freed from his trousers.

Next morning when Sam was blinking himself awake and everyone else was changing back out of their nightshirts, he noticed that "everyone" wasn't exactly true. John Thomson had slept in his dayshirt, too, and looked like he hadn't slept much. There were lineups for hot water and the shaving mirrors dotted here and there around the common room. Sam didn't join any of the shaving lineups and hoped that anyone who noticed would just assume he was one of those who got whiskers later than most. John Thomson didn't line up either.

Next stop Windsor, home of the Hants County Exhibition and the biggest saltwater port on the Fundy side of Nova Scotia. There looked to be several inns in Windsor; Mr. Carstairs hove them in at one that was neither the smallest nor largest, across the road from the waterfront. While they paused to rest and refresh the horses, and themselves, Mr. Carstairs said, "Whomever I post here in Windsor will have to be responsible for three stations: here and Spencer's Inn and Hortonville down the road. So let me see, who'll it be... ?"

Sam noticed that John Thomson seemed to be trying to make himself as small and unnoticeable as possible, and Sam suspected it wasn't because of the extra responsibility. Sam half-raised his hand and said, "I'll do 'er, Mr. Carstairs."

"Same pay, mind."

"Suits me." It was still more than anybody else was offering to pay him. Since he'd ridden grey Wellington there, it was only logical that Wellington be the horse that got billeted there, and that more than suited Sam.

As the rest of the crew filed past Sam to get back on their horses, John Thomson murmured out the side of his mouth, "Thanks."

III

"THAT THERE'S THE fella you want, you can just see his head over the stall wall. Hey, lad! Hello! John Thomson!"

John Thomson's head snapped around from currycombing his horse – the Halifax Express's horse. John would've thought to've got used to it by now – being pronouned as he, him or his – shouldn't've had to think twice about it. The new rosary, repeated more times in the last three weeks than the real one in three years, was: *Your name is John Thomson, you're he, him and his.* But although "he" had heard the innkeeper speaking loudly, as usual, at the front of the stables, John had assumed that the "lad" in the conversation was the inn's stable-boy on the other side of the aisle of stalls. The fat innkeeper was standing with a tall gentleman made even taller by the kind of fuzzy brown top hat most gentlemen wore these days – and some for whom "gentleman" was a bit of a stretch. The innkeeper said, "Ya gone deef, boy?"

"Sorry, got caught up in brushing the horse." John *had* got used to keeping his voice deep in his throat, but still tried to speak as little as possible, to shorten the odds on slip-ups or the chance that some-one hearing too much of it would think it sounded as phony as it felt to him.

"This here gentleman's got business with you."

"Not you per se," said the tall man, coming down the aisle, "with the Halifax Express, but since you're the company's local representative..."

"Representative" seemed a mite fancy. John shrugged, "Sorta, I guess."

"I have an invoice here," pulling a folded sheet of paper out of an inside coat pocket, "for the printing of handbills," and held it out to John.

Instead of taking it, John held up his hands, shaking his head, "Whoa now, that ain't fer me, I just take care of the horses. Mr. Carstairs comes out every week – well, every *second* week..." A week after John and the others got put in place, Mr. Carstairs had come out from Halifax to make sure all was shipshape, then said it would be every two weeks from now on, 'to settle up on your wages and all.' John turned toward the innkeeper. "He always pays you prompt for my room and board, and Big Red's, don't he?"

"So far."

The brown-hatted man looked uncertain – unsure if maybe he was being put off or put upon. He said to John, "When's this Carson fella gonna be here next?"

"Carstairs. Next Thursday, or maybe Friday, most likely."

"Well... then you can give it to him then," and he thrust the fold-ed invoice out farther.

John didn't see much choice but to take it, and tuck it in his coat pocket – though the stable wasn't all that cold, he preferred to keep his coat on. The tall man and the innkeeper went away and John went back to grooming Big Red, getting better acquainted, getting ready for a big day tomorrow. Some people found the loamy, horsey smell of stables a bit rich for their blood, even clutching handker-chiefs to their noses; John found it homey and comforting. Though these stables had a bit more of a woody smell. Since Nova Scotia farmers tended to grow hay instead of grain, Nova Scotia stables tended to use sawmill waste for stall bedding – sawdust and wood shavings – instead of straw. Which also meant using a scoop shovel instead of a manure fork, but it would be a couple more days yet before Big Red's stall needed mucking out again.

John checked over the saddle and harness one last time before hanging them in front of Big Red's stall ready to go, then went into the Stage Coach Inn to wash up for supper. The Stage Coach Inn in Kentville was the halfway point, where the Express riders would change over – one rider from Halifax to Kentville, one from Kentville to Granville Point and the rendezvous with the steamer across the bay. John Thomson was responsible for the relay station in Kentville and the one in Aylesford eighteen miles southwest, the second rider's first change of horses. The on-paper plan for the Halifax Express was to change horses every twelve miles, but the roads and towns and inns of Nova Scotia hadn't been planned entirely for Mr. Hyde's and Mr. Craig's convenience, so a few stages got stretched out and Kentville to Aylesford was the longest stage of all. So Big Red, being the biggest and strongest of all the Express horses, got picked to be the long rider. It would be a while yet, though, before the Halifax Express was actually in business; they were still in preparation and rehearsal.

Next morning after breakfast, John walked around the innyard a while to let the eggs and sausage settle, then saddled up Big Red and climbed aboard. He walked Red out onto the road, pointed his nose south, shouted "Go!" and dug in his heels. Big Red could go, and did. John leaned forward and held on for dear life with a half a ton of horse pounding away beneath him. It was a wild ride through a countryside of white snow, grey rocks and trees and the dark green of spruce and pines, swerving around farm wagons and whipping past trotting carriages. The air rushing past John's face pushed the corners of his mouth into a grin, or maybe it went there on its own, and stayed there.

After what must've been an hour and some – though it didn't feel like that – another bend in the road showed the church spires of the town of Aylesford up ahead. John slowed Big Red to a trot and then a walk to let him breathe himself out, something that wouldn't happen on the actual Express runs – that would be left to a stable-hand while the rider jumped from galloper to galloper and kept on going. The Express horse stabled at the inn in Aylesford was a darker, browner bay than Big Red and almost a full hand shorter, which made Finbar a normal-sized, long-legged thoroughbred. After giving Red a quick rubdown, John saddled Finbar and led him out of the stable, pausing to say to the inn's ostler, "'Round this time tomorrow I'll come galloping back and wanna change over fast. So when I do, could you please walk Finbar around to cool him down and give him a good rub?"

"I don't work for you."

"Well, no, but you do work for Mr. MacDonald," the innkeeper, "and he's getting paid to board an Express horse, so he'd prob'ly 'preciate it if you took good care of that horse, if you don't mind."

On the ride back to Kentville, John let Finbar slow down for a few stints rather than do him a damage trying to match Big Red's monster heart, lungs and legs. So the ride back took longer than the ride from, though John couldn't be sure exactly how much longer, or even exactly how long Big Red's run had taken. Maybe it was time to buy a cheap pocketwatch – though not too cheap – next time Mr. Carstairs handed over two weeks' wages. At the Stage Coach Inn, John walked Finbar around for a cool-down and found his own legs were a bit stiff and more than a bit sore. Better work on that. One of the arguments for grown young men riders instead of teen-aged lads was stamina, and the whole back-and-forth between Kentville and Aylesford was less than half what an Express rider would have to do.

Next morning when John Thomson galloped into Aylesford he only hit the ground for long enough to toss Finbar's reins to the ostler, throw a saddle on Big Red and take off again. The cool-down walk this time was even more stiff and bowlegged than yesterday.

After a lunch of substantial chicken vegetable soup – almost a runny stew – and fresh-baked bread, it seemed a good idea to go up to his room and stretch out for a few minutes. But the stairway was blocked by Ella the chambermaid and the inn's all-round handyman wrestling a copper hip bath upstairs. Even after they'd got it to the top and disappeared down the hallway, clearing the stairwell, John lingered at the foot of the stairs, pondering. When they came back down, John said to the chambermaid, "Was that for one of the guests?"

"Wasn't for our recreation. And wouldn't ya know it – Mr. Glaskell's room's at the far end of the hall. Now I gotta be ferrying up kettles of hot water and a bucket of cold."

"Would it fit in my room?"

"What, way up in the gables, all them stairs? Oh, I'm just teasing. I done it before, more than once. And yeah, it'll fit, just barely. Cost ya a shilling, though."

A shilling was a whole day's wages, but that was over and above John's room and board, so... "I think I'll have a bathe, tomorrow afternoon."

Ella wrinkled her nose. "Thought you'd never ask. We do laundry, too."

That raised a good point. It'd been a while since John had done any laundering, and that included a few nights in Halifax sleeping in the clothes he was wearing. But he'd need fresh clothes to wear while these were being washed. So instead of going up to his room John went outside and turned left along the road the inn was on. Kentvillers called it Main Street or Horton Street, since it was also the road to Hortonville, and passersthrough called it the Post Road or the High Road. John Thomson called it an ankle-twisting stretch of frozen ruts at the moment.

There were three dry goods stores in Kentville, but the one with the most choices was in a big, red barn-like building appropriately named The Red Store, just a short walk down Main Street from the Stage Coach Inn. John found a pair of inexpensive wool trousers that seemed about the right size when held up against him, and a checkered wool shirt. There were rolls of cloth on cast iron rollers on the wall. John fingered a few of them, then asked one of the shopgirls to cut him a yard of a plain, lightweight flannel. At the counter, the storekeeper said, "That shirt's a size too big for you."

"I like 'em baggy."

The way back to the inn went past a cobbler's shop. In the window display was a sample pair of knee-high, black riding boots, gleaming leather that looked supple but strong. John could smell them through the glass. He thought of going in and asking how much a pair of boots like that might cost, but decided it would be better not to know specifics. Maybe a few months down the road, if the Halifax Express was still in business and John Thomson was still employed and ever got the chance to be a full-fledged Express rider. So he went back to the Stage Coach Inn and up to his room, the only place where he was safe. He never realized how much effort it was taking to pretend to be somebody else, until he got into his room and could stop pretending.

Not that it was much of a room. There was barely room to stand up beside the cornered bed, which had one side fixed to a side wall and had the knee wall of the roof slant for a headboard. But it beat sleeping in a hayloft – more like half-sleeping with one ear open in case someone came along and found you where you weren't supposed to be. Once the hook dangling from this garret inn room's doorframe was latched into the eye on the door, no one could catch "John Thomson" unawares and maybe catch some slip-up that would send John back to where he didn't want to be, and who he didn't want to be, at least not for now.

John set the new clothes aside till he had a clean body to put them on, then took out the piece of flannel and carefully cut it in half lengthwise. It was slow and tricky sawing cloth with his pocketknife, but if he'd asked Ella or someone to lend him a pair of scissors they would've asked him what for. A strip of lightweight flannel half a yard wide was perfect when folded over to half a foot wide, and now there was a spare for when this one got too rank with wear. The old one would get thrown away in the woods instead of going into the laundry with his clothes, because whoever was doing the laundry would ask questions. Questions and curiosity were John Thomson's mortal enemies.

Next morning John Thomson woke up with legs and bum feeling like they'd been stretched on a rack and worked over with a meat hammer. A normal day's riding just wasn't the same as galloping a long-distance racehorse to its limits and then jumping on another to do the same. Maybe a hot bath would help. After lunch he waited in his room for the knock on the door that announced the chambermaid and the handyman. They just managed to squeeze the hip bath in between the side of the wall-fixed bed and the other wall, with the tub's high back against the window wall and its knee-high front facing the door.

Ella said, "I'll be back in a minute to fill 'er, then you can climb in and I'll be back again with more hot water once the kettle's boilt agin."

That left John thinking he'd made a horrible mistake. If Ella was going to be bringing more hot water once John was undressed and in the bathtub, one glimpse of a naked John Thomson and it was all over. But no, Ella surely wouldn't have seen Mr. Glaskell naked yesterday, or all the other misters she poured baths for, wouldn't she? So there must be some kind of arrangement to prevent embarrassment. Mustn't there?

Ella came back lugging a big, steaming copper kettle and a dripping wooden bucket, with a rough towel slung over one shoulder and a thick flannel sheet over the other. A helluva juggling act, but she seemed used to it. Ella set down the kettle, laid the sheet and the towel on the bed, emptied the kettle into the hip bath and added dollops from the bucket till the bathwater passed her finger test. She pointed at the flannel sheet and said, "When I comes back you can pull the sheet across, for modesty-like. Don't fret, I'll knock," and she closed the door behind her.

John automatically reached to latch the door before undressing, but stopped himself – Ella couldn't very well come in with more hot water if the door was hooked, could she? Anyway, she said she'd knock. John got undressed and sat down gingerly in the hot water, knees bent over the end of the tub and feet dangling out. He brought his feet in one at a time to scrub them, then went to work on the rest of his smelly self.

The water was starting to feel cool when a knock came at the door. John pulled the sheet across and up to his neck, leaving just a space down around his knees for pouring-in, then called, "Come in."

Ella lugged in the refilled kettle, blinked at John with the sheet clutched up around his neck and said, "My, you are modest. Though not modestly endowed, I bet." John couldn't think of anything to say to that, so said nothing. Ella poured in about half the kettle, being careful not to scald, then set the kettle on the floor. "I'll leave that here so's you can add in a bit more hot when you need. When you're all done and dried off and dressed, just go down to the front desk and tell 'em and somebody'll come take this gear away."

When the door closed behind Ella, John thought of getting up to latch the door. But that would mean squirming out of the slippery tub, dripping water from the tub to the door and then squirming back in again. Anyway, Ella said she wouldn't be coming back again, at least not till he'd finished his bath, and the water was so deliciously warm and soothing on sore muscles that would probably knot up again in the cold air between the bath tub and the door. So he just furled the flannel sheet back onto the bed and went back to scrubbing and soaking.

John had just finished adding in more hot water and had leaned back to enjoy the renewed warmth when the door burst open and Sam Smith burst in, crowing, "Made it all the way from – !" Sam's voice cut off like a knife had sliced through his throat, and he goggled at the body in the bath like he'd been hit between the eyes with a fence maul. Then he turned around abruptly, closed and hooked the door in front of him and stood there stiffly with his back to the bathtub. After a moment he seemed to find his voice again, though it sounded a bit strangled. "I won't look."

Seana McCann got out of the tub quickly, quickly dried herself and pulled on her new shirt and trousers – after first tying the band of flannel around her chest to bind her breasts flat, or at least flattish. She could feel that she was flushing all over, and it wasn't just the hot bath. It wasn't just embarrassment, either. Much of it was fear. If Sam told anyone, John Thomson was finished, and then what was she going to do? She said, trying to keep her voice from shaking, "I'm dressed."

Sam Smith turned around and said like he'd been thinking out what to say, "I got troublous secrets of my own. See?" He took hold of the stomach of his shirt with both hands and tugged it up out of his pants. The skin between the waistband of his trousers and his furled-up shirtfront was just as brown as his sun- and wind-weathered face. "My name ain't Sam Smith. I'm Mi'kmaq," though the way he said it sounded more like "Migamaw" than the "Micmac" she'd always heard from the McCanns' Nova Scotia neighbours. "Well, *half* Mi'kmaq, though that makes me an Indian so far as whites is concerned. My mother married a white man, so that makes me not an Indian so far as my mother's family's concerned. Well, he was *mostly* a white man – Acadian, and mosta them's got at least a little Indian in them from way back."

Seana couldn't see how that was anywhere near as dangerous a secret as hers – Mr. Hyde and Mr. Craig didn't seem to care what colour somebody was, as long as they could ride and clean out a stable. John Thomson was proof that they would hire any fella who could do the job. The owner of the Stage Coach Inn was an Irishman, and he and his grown children who worked the inn had heard the brogue even in John Thomson's throaty, sparse-speaking voice. Which to them made him a fine broth of a boy, but to a lot of other people would mean something else entirely. In her nine years in Nova Scotia, Seana had often seen the sign in shop windows or at worksites and farm gates:

HELP WANTED

No Irish Need Apply

So if the Halifax Express didn't care if John Thomson was Irish, they likely didn't care if Sam Smith was part Mi'kmaq, or Acadian, or Zulu. So knowing Sam Smith's secret didn't seem like any reason she should trust him with hers.

Sam's face twitched into a grimace and he arched his back. He said, "I just galloped from Spencer's Inn to Kentville for practice – that's three relay stages at one go. Mind if I sit down?"

Seana warily nodded sideways at the bed, the only place in the room to sit down. Sam sat on the foot of the bed, propped his back against the wall and flexed his legs. He gave out a few little grunts and groans, then, "Ya gotta understand – whatever your story is, I'm just as screwed if I get found out. My mother and father died last year – I dunno, doctors maybe called it typhus or cholera or something, a lot of people 'round home died. My mother, after my father got taken and she knew she was goin', willed everything to the church – not that that was much, but what with the traps and furs and all, even a poor man's everything adds up to a little something when you sell it all off. The deal was the church would take care of me an' my sisters till we got to adult age.

"And there was some sense and thoughtfulness to what ma mère done, on the face of it. Ya know what happens to orphans what got no aunts or uncles or such to take 'em in?"

Seana, still standing stiffly at the foot of the copper bathtub, wasn't sure if he was telling the truth or playing some kind of cruel game. Every muscle and tendon in her body was tense and tingling with fear, telling her to grab her things and run before he could let out her secret and she could get found out and sent back. Run where? Better to play along until she knew what he was up to. She shook her head no, she didn't know what happened to homeless orphans in Nova Scotia.

"They get stood up on a auction block and auctioned off, just like a slave auction. Whoever bids the highest, ya gotta go and live in

that person's home or barn or wherever he decides to put ya, and ya
gotta work for that family till ya reach yer majority and paid off what
it cost for yer room and board and clothes – whatever *they* decide it's
worth. Might's well be a slave.

"That's what my mother was tryin' to save us from. So 'stead of
a orphan auction we got put in a church orphanage school – my sisters livin' on the nuns' side an' me on the... other side. 'Cause I got
some 'quaintanceship with horses, they put me to work in the stables,
sleepin' in a little side room in the barn. There's this... priest that a
couple months ago started every now an' then comin' out at night
to visit me, make sure I was all right out there on my lonesome, ya
know?" Sam's dark eyes grew darker and his voice grew gravelly. "A
real... *carin'* sorta priest, y'know, full of Christian charity. I managed to
put him off a few times,-but I could see that eventually... Whichever
way it went, it wasn't gonna be good. I mean, I stick a pitchfork in a
priest, who's gonna be called a devil, eh? I was trapped.

"And then I seen a handbill for the Halifax Express. I figured I'd
take a wild chance and hey, I got lucky – so far. But if they find out
I ain't Sam Smith, start askin' questions, gettin' curious... I'm church
property till I get old enough I don't need a legal guardian. Anybody
finds out – I mean anybody what ain't got a reason to keep secrets –
they'll send me back."

Seana was boggled. It'd never occurred to her that a boy could
have her same problem. She sat down on the head of the bed and
said, "Me Da – my father – got killed in a war, maybe a couple years
ago, we don't know exactly." Partway through that, she realized she
didn't have to use John Thomson's pebbly voice or his sparse and
slangy way of speaking, and slid out of it. She hadn't used her own
voice in weeks, so it sounded strange in her ears and felt strange in
her throat. "There's a rich old man wishes to marry my mother, but
I've a feeling he's just as interested in having me as a stepdaughter – having me under his roof, under his thumb, if you know what I
mean."

Sam Smith – or whatever his real name was – just nodded. Of course he knew, more than anyone else was likely to know.

"So I took the same wild chance as you. Bedamn, it feels strange not having to pretend." Sam nodded again, with a lopsided grin like they were both rowing the same leaky boat. "Not that I'm all that good at it. More'n a month since I turned m'self into John Thomson and I still need remind m'self that's my name and that 'he' might mean me."

"Yeah, I still keep gettin' tripped-up with that – or almost – still keep havin' to tell myself I'm he, not she."

Seana's spine snapped stiff, jerking her upright from leaning against the wall. What he'd just said didn't make any sense at all, not if he was just a boy pretending to be a different kind of boy. She was thrown back into wondering if he was playing nasty games with her, and his story had been just a story to trick her into telling hers, leave her open.

It seemed he picked up something of what she was thinking, because he said, "I grew up mostly talking Mi'kmaq, and Mi'kmaq's got no he and she – people and things are just what they are. And then French's got he and she for everything, so English is just..." He threw up his hands.

"Oh! Oh, I know what you mean. Even though we've been almost ten years in Nova Scotia where people speak mostly English, at least in our part of Nova Scotia, I still don't always think in English. Back home we spoke mostly Erse – Irish Gaelic – mixed with bits of the travellers' tongue."

"Travellers' tongue?"

"I guess some of it is Romany – gypsy – and some of it is the made-up words used by tinkers and other travelling folk when they don't want town people or farmers to know what they're saying." Or bailiffs and sheriffs, for that matter. "Some people call it cant, and the people that use it the canting crew. I only know bits of it, and I don't guess there's much use for it on this side of the ocean."

"Huh. Guess we're both of us kinda in foreign territory. But it ain't no guess that if we got found out we'd both be in hot water, 'stead of just one of us," and he playfully kicked the bathtub. Seana felt herself flushing again. He quickly put in, "No, I looked away soon's I saw – I mean soon's I noticed, I mean..." and he trailed off like he realized there was no graceful way out of what he'd just gone and reminded her of.

Seana looked around the room for a moment, definitely not at him, then said, "So... what's your real name?"

He said something that sounded like it started with an *m* and *g* together and then a sort of *aw* and a few other syllables with a couple of throaty sounds that were kind of a little like Erse but not really. She made a stab at it and he laughed, "Better you just think of me as Sam Smith, 'stead of gettin' easy with my Mi'kmaq name."

She hadn't even got easy with the way he said Mi'kmaq – sometimes it sounded to her like *i* and sometimes like *ee*, and then that throat-sound skip in the middle. She said, "I always heard it said 'Micmac.'"

"That's the way the English say it. I bet there's some Irish names where you just give up and let the English say like they want."

"Me Da used to say that Micmacs are obviously half Irish and half Scots – Mics and Macs."

Sam laughed, then said, "Yer Da sounds like a jolly fella." Seana shrugged and looked away. She wasn't sure what to say about her father, what to think about him, ever since her mother told her what the U.S. Consul in Halifax had told her. "I'm not gonna ask you *your* real name, prob'ly better I just know 'John Thomson' so's I can't slip up when somebody else's around."

They talked and laughed about this and that and nothing in particular until Seana realized it was almost past time the inn would be serving supper. Too late for the juicy end of the roast, and the boiled potatoes and peas had gone mushy, but Seana was too hungry to notice much and had other things on her mind. It was somehow harder to pretend to be John Thomson when she knew that the person across the table was pretending to be Sam Smith and knew she was pretending too, hard not to make dangerous jokes about cowgirls and Indians. When they came back to her room, the tub and kettle and all were gone. They jabbered and laughed a while longer before they both started yawning. Though it was a tremendous release to be able to be themselves with somebody else, Seana'd done a lot of hard riding over the last couple of days and Sam just that morning.

Underneath John Thomson's bed was a roll-out trundlebed in case the inn got overfull or someone was travelling with children. It was just a very thin mattress on a rope web in a wood frame, but Sam said he'd slept on worse beds in Halifax, and that gave them something else in common to laugh about. In the morning Sam Smith climbed stiffly back onto the horse he'd ridden there, to gallop back the three stages he'd galloped yesterday. Seana thought she might try three stages herself someday soon – from Aylesford to Kentville to Hortonville to Windsor. Sam said to send a note ahead by stagecoach to the inn he was staying at in Windsor, once she'd decided on the day, and he'd make sure the horse in Hortonville was ready. Maybe he'd even bring Wellington down from Windsor and they could race the last stage.

But before any of that could get arranged, Mr. Carstairs came through making other arrangements. There was enough snow on the roads now that he was travelling in a one-horse sleigh instead of the two-wheeled shay, though he still wore his thick old brown leather coat but now had a curly-wooled brown buffalo pelt travelling rug across his legs. Seana had seen those kinds of buffalo "robes" once or twice before, imported from the prairies of the Hudson's Bay Company's territories, as far west of Nova Scotia as Nova Scotia was from Ireland.

Once Mr. Carstairs was out of his sleigh and at a table in the Stage Coach Inn, with a hot buttered rum in front of him, he said, "Wednesday, John, we're doing a dry run of the full Express route – well, I s'pose the steamboat run across Fundy won't be dry, 'less the tide's out, but you get my drift. Any rate, the first rider leaves the

Halifax docks at six a.m. sharp, so should be here sometime twixt ten and ten-thirty – closer to ten, we pray. The incoming rider will sound a horn when Kentville hoves in sight, to give you warning. The second rider will hove in on the stage the day before, I'll make arrangements for him with the innkeeper. Any questions?"

"No, sir – I mean yessir, but not about that. And t'ain't really a question, but..." Seana dug the printer's invoice out of her coat pocket, unfolded it and handed it across the table. "Fella handed this to me a few days back..."

"And you *took* it?"

"Didn't see's I had much choice, Mr. Carstairs. Is there a problem?" She hoped not, and not just because it might make Mr. Carstairs unhappy with John Thomson. If the Halifax Express was having a problem paying its bills, it might have a problem paying its employees.

"Problem? Nothing new. Just until the Halifax Express gets in business it's all outgo and no income. Well, Hyde and Craig have the pockets for it, question is whether they have the stomach for it? Oh, fret not, young Thomson, they're in too deep to pull out now. Meanwhile I'll take care of this," rattling the invoice as he folded it up again, "but..." He raised one sausage finger. Mr. MacAngus's sausage fingers looked like pale pink pork links, Mr. Carstairs's like the gnarled and smoky kind that hung in butchers' windows. "Anybody else tries to hand you an invoice for the Halifax Express, you tell 'em to wait till they can hand it to me. And you tell 'em Old Man Carstairs told you that if you took any more paper for the Halifax Express in hand, he'd skin you." Mr. Carstairs's hounddog eyes slitted and his bushy mustache twitched inward in an appraising kind of way. "Not enough of you to make me a new coat, maybe a couple pair of gloves..."

Tuesday Seana was wheeling a barrowful of horse poop and sawdust across the innyard when she heard a distant horn note, way too early and too loud and deep for the Halifax Express and coming from the wrong direction. Stagecoach drivers' helpers riding shotgun could manage a bigger brass horn than a galloper on horse-back, though it meant setting aside for a moment the blunderbuss for scaring off road agents. The coach horn sounded again while she was upending the wheelbarrow on the manure pile out back, and by the time she got the shovel put away the stagecoach from Annapolis Royal clattered up to the Stage Coach Inn, steam rising off the horses, and the inn's handyman and stableboy were running from the stables leading four fresh horses already harnessed in pairs. The passengers climbed out to stretch their legs while the horses were being changed, all except one passenger who was staying over. Unlike the other gen-tleman passengers, he wore something like a peaked fisherman's cap instead of a top hat, though his overcoat was just as thick and long as the best of them.

Corey O'Dell went around to the back of the coach and unbuck-led the leather awning over the luggage boot without asking permis-sion. He hefted out a saddle which he handed to Seana, then a leather travelling valise, and said cheerfully, "Set that up by the horse I'm to ride, please, Johnny-lad. I'll go find my room."

Seana found a sawhorse to set by Big Red's stall, and sat the saddle on it. The saddle looked custom-made, well worn but well cared for. The plan that'd been laid out to Seana was that each relay horse had its own tack and would be standing saddled and bridled ready for the rider to jump on after jumping off the run-out horse, but it seemed Corey O'Dell had other plans. The stage coach from Annapolis Royal would've stopped at every stage along the way, so he would've had a chance to change instructions – just bridled, not saddled. If he could make his own rules he could surely make his own arrangements. Still, it seemed a bit fussy and hoity-toity of Corey O'Dell, as though the Halifax Express's saddles weren't good enough for him.

They had supper together, Corey O'Dell regaling John/Seana with funny stories of his escapades in New Brunswick and the girls in Annapolis Royal and the Sinclair Inn there, where he spent his time these days when he wasn't across the bay in Saint John. Seana didn't try to match him drink for drink, since cheery Corey was drinking a lot – though only beer, not hard liquor – sighing, "It'll be a parchy long ride between quaffs tomorrow." Partway through his second pint he said, "Which county you from?"

"Huh?" Seana McCann would've said, *Pardon me?*"

"I was born in Saint John but there was enough native Irish 'round the house I can pick up the lilt in even a laconical fella like you. But my ears ain't fine-tuned enough I can guess what county someone's from."

"Oh. We travelled around a lot, so no particular county – me Da was a horsetrader, so we followed the fairs."

"Your Da was killed in a war, I hear?"

"Yeah. Joined up the U.S. Army fightin' Mexico, 'cause we need-ed the money."

"And your Ma... ?"

"Me Mam..." Seana could feel her nose getting blocked up and her eyes starting to leak. It came at her out of nowhere, the picture of her mother and little brothers she'd abandoned, snaring her into a welter of complicated feelings. Maybe the beer didn't help.

Corey quickly shifted the subject back to where it started with, "Well, I guess you can take the boy out of Ireland, but..." One thing Seana did appreciate about being a male among males was the instant an uncontrollable emotion poked its head up, someone would change the subject to save everyone embarrassment. It also saved her coming up with explanations of how John Thomson came to be an orphan. "Here's to the green isle of Erin and all who had to sail away."

Seana clinked tankards, then quickly dabbed a knuckle at the corners of her eyes. "Musta got some bubbles up m'nose."

"It'll happen."

Ten o'clock the next morning found Seana holding Big Red sad-dled and ready on the roadside in front of the Stage Coach Inn, and Corey O'Dell pacing back and forth in his long, loose overcoat. Seana thought she heard a faint, high sound like a brass horn in the dis-tance, but the town sounds muddied everything and crows had been known to do the damnedest imitations. It seemed that Corey heard it, too, though, peering down the road towards Hortonville. Then the sound came again, clearer and closer, definitely a horn.

Seana tightened the saddle girth while Corey shucked his over-coat, disclosing a short, bum-freezer jacket and a shiny bugle slung over his shoulder. He latched his cap under his chin, handed his over-coat to Seana, tug-checked the saddle girth and nodded a thank you for doing it right, then climbed aboard Big Red and took hold of the reins. Seana heard the other horse before she saw it, pounding the frozen roadway from the east, then the sound turning wooden and hollow as the hooves hammered across the millstream bridge that marked the northeast edge of town.

As the first Express rider came into view where the High Road turned into Kentville's main street, Corey O'Dell nudged Big Red into a walk, then a trot and then a canter. The horse from Hortonville went flying past Seana, chipped chunks of road-packed grey snow spurting from its hooves, the rider holding the reins with one hand while the other lifted the strap of a leather dispatch case off his shoulder. Corey held his left arm out and back, the other rider held his right hand out and forward so as not to come up on Big Red's off side. As soon as Corey had his hand on the pouch strap and the other rider let go, Corey O'Dell spurred Big Red into a gallop and was gone down the road.

The other rider – a wiry young man named Thad Harris – slowed his horse and turned it back into the innyard. Seana took hold of the horse's bridle as Thad climbed down, stumbling around awk-wardly like a sailor on a dock still walking on sea legs. After a couple of stumbles Thad stopped and leaned forward with his hands on his knees, gasping. Seana said, "I'll take care of your horse. Maybe you'd like a drink."

"Damn... fine... idea." But he stayed where he was, hunkered for-ward and breathing himself out – looked like it'd be a few minutes yet before he was up to walking into the tavern. Maybe the stamina of a full-grown young man wasn't so far out of reach after all.

Seana expected Mr. Carstairs to tell her how the test run went when he showed up next Thursday or Friday. But Mr. Carstairs didn't show up. Instead, the next Monday Corey O'Dell rode into Kentville again, this time on a big brown horse instead of the stage-coach. He said to Seana, "There's gonna be another dry run, of a different route – north on Nova Scotia roads to Amherst, then south on New Brunswick roads to Saint John. Hyde wants me to scout out the best horses at the livery stables along the way and ride the last leg, bein' as I knows the roads into Saint John as well as anybody."

Seana sputtered, almost forgetting to keep her voice low in her throat, "But... that don't make any sense. If you wanna make time you don't go running up and down the sides of a triangle, 'stead of straight across the base." Because that was just about exactly what the Amherst route would be, all the way up the west side of the long, long bay of Fundy and then all the way down the east side.

"Right you'd be, Johnny, if'n it were just overland distance. The Amherst route is all overland, you see, but the straighter route's also got the steamer 'crost the bay, contendin' with the Fundy tides and sea ice and all and all. Hyde and Craig'd had the Amherst route half in mind from the start."

Seana remembered Mr. Carstairs saying on the day the asterisk-ers got hired on: *Mr. Hyde and Mr. Craig couldn't quite make up their minds, surprise surprise...* She said, "But what's going to happen to us?" She started to specify "the asteriskers," but that wouldn't make any sense to him.

"That ain't my business, Johnny. I just get paid to ride like hell, and that's exactly what I mean to do."

IV

When "Sam Smith" chose his phony name and then volunteered for Windsor, he hadn't realized that Smith wasn't exactly anonymous around Windsor; it was the name of one of the three oldest and most prosperous families thereabouts. There was a much-told local story about a young fella from away who'd got off the stage in Windsor looking to meet somebody but had gone and forgotten the name of the man he was supposed to meet. When he told his confusion to the post house owner, the innkeeper said, "Was it a Curry you were looking to meet?"

"No, that warn't the name."

"A Dimock, then?"

"No, no, I woulda remembered Dimock."

"Then it must've been a Smith."

"Nope, not Smith."

"Then you got off in the wrong town."

By now Sam was so used to hearing people say, "You don't look like a Smith," before they'd got it out he'd say, "Yeah yeah, I know," or "No, no – a Smith from away." But he still wished to hell, for the sake of not sticking out, that he'd had the sense to name himself Jones or Brown or Abercrombie.

Sam was chipping away at the ice sealing Wellington's stall window hatch when Carstairs came gingerly around the corner of the stable barn, slipping and sliding on the glittering mess the ice storm had left behind. With his wrinkled brown leather coat and fat, droopy mustache, Carstairs looked like a walrus flopping about on dry land, minus the tusks. Sam decided not to say so. Carstairs beckoned Sam to follow him into the inn and solid footing. Settled at a table in the public room, Carstairs ordered a pint of bitter and Sam just a half pint of small beer – best not to give the bosses the idea that the shilling-a-day above his room and meals was enough to live high. After a sip of bitter to moisten his throat, leaving a bit of foam on his mustache – like snow-dabs on a walrus – Carstairs said, "About a week from now our first mail packet will steam into Halifax, no more test runs."

"So yer gonna use this route 'stead'n of Amherst?"

"Pfft." Carstairs waved his hand like brushing away a fly. "The Amherst route took nineteen hours and forty-two minutes – give or take for timepiece variations. This route clocked in at sixteen hours, thirty-eight minutes – and that was even with wading out across the tidal mud flats to get the packet to the steamer, and dodging ice floes on the bay. Any rate, the difference was sufficient to convince even *the gentlemen* to make a decision. Barring some monumental cock-up, there'll be no more talk of running the Express through Amherst.

"*But*, given the condition of the roads – this ain't likely to all melt off by next week – there'll be no one riding this route this run."

"Howzzat? Sir? Didn't you just say – ?"

"More stability travelling in a one-horse sleigh like mine, 'cept lighter weight for speed. The horses may not prefer it, but they're accustomed – we made damn sure all our horses were broke to harness as well as saddle and bridle, just in case of such a case. There's sacks of harness in the back of my sleigh, three sets for you, two for the other lads. Come the day, the Express horse at each station will be in harness and waiting – just a question of unbuckling the arrived horse from the shafts and buckling the new horse in."

Sam thought, *Easy for you to say, won't be your cold fingers tryin' to deal with froze-stiff leather and steel*, but didn't say it.

As Sam was helping Carstairs rummage out the right sack of harness – wasn't too hard to guess which sack held three sets of harness instead of two – Carstairs said, "Come the day, you'll have no warning 'cept the rider's horn. The steamer left Liverpool noon sharp Saturday – leastwise that was the schedule, so we presume... The crossing takes eleven or twelve days, depending, damn sight better'n any windjammer. But as to when the steamer actually reaches Halifax – nothing and no one can bring you advance warning ahead of the Express rider. Was there a way for news to travel across the province faster'n the Halifax Express, we wouldn't be in business, would we?"

Carstairs laughed at that, so Sam put on a bit of a chuckle and put in, "Guess not, sir."

"So as of Wednesday noon, consider yourself on active duty till the sleigh gets here and leaves again. The wait might be a few hours, might be twenty-four or more. If you have to catch a catnap, make damn sure there's somebody alert to shake you awake if they hear the horn."

"Yes, sir."

"No more rehearsals, Sam lad, it's up to you and everybody else along the line to do your jobs smart and efficient. If the gentlemen of The Associated Press don't see the Halifax Express can get the news to the Saint John telegraph enough faster'n a steamer to the Boston telegraph, our first run'll be our last."

"I'll do my damnedest, sir." Sam didn't add that not even Misters Hyde and Craig had more reason to want the Halifax Express to stay in business, excepting maybe John Thomson.

"Good lad. And good luck."

"Oh, sir, just occurred to me – the bridge outta Windsor's a toll bridge. Ya wouldn't want the rider – I mean the driver – stoppin' to rummage out pennies... ?"

"Don't you worry about that." Carstairs continued settling himself into the sleigh and pulling the buffalo robe over his lap. "Arrangements have been made. Ask not for whom the bridge tolls," and he popped his buggy whip over the horse's head and trotted away. Strange bird, for a walrus.

The three sets of harness in the sack were, of course, all tangled together. Sam took them into the stables to thaw out and eventually managed to get them separated, then fitted one set onto Wellington, adjusting the buckles and straps so it could just be slipped on like it was tailor made. Next morning he rode Wellington to Spencer's Inn – carefully on the icy road – to do the same thing with the Express horse billeted there. Turned out that big ol' Carstairs had already made arrangements there for somebody to be on stable duty from noon Wednesday till the Express came through, same in Hortonville.

Late Wednesday morning Sam buckled the sleigh harness onto Wellington and walked him around the innyard to get him comfort-able in what he was going to have to be wearing till he'd galloped the sleigh to Hortonville – maybe hours, maybe days. After an early-ish lunch, gobbled so he could be on active duty by noon sharp, Sam stood out in front of the inn leaning against a hitching post, putting most of his attention into his ears.

When his feet started going numb he wandered up and down Water Street – not so far he wouldn't be able to hear a horn from the High Road – looking out over Windsor harbour. It was low tide, so a couple of ships were sitting on ice-crystalled red mud with the crossbars of their masts about level with the wharf; another four or five hours and they'd be riding high again. The cribwork legs that held up the long, covered bridge over the Avon River were exposed all the way down to muddy pools around their feet. A muffled sound of malleting came from the big boatbuilding sheds between Water Street and the high tide line; another two or three months and it'd be a lot louder, when they went to work on the half-built ships in the out-door cribs.

Even muffled, though, the hammering was loud enough to maybe mask the sound of a distant horn, so Sam went back across the road to the Shipyard Inn. He slipped into the dining room and snagged a chair, set it outside by a front corner of the inn and sat and watched the world go by: fancy cutters and tall thoroughbreds carrying the gentry of the town, ox carts bringing farm goods in to market, freight wagons sifting out puffs of plaster of Paris from the gypsum mines. After a while he went inside and brought out the quilt from his bed. So what if he looked like an old granny wrapped up in her invalid chair, at least he was warm. Ish.

He wondered what John Thomson was doing to pass the time but stay alert in Kentville. Maybe reading – there'd been a couple of old magazines in her room, the kind with several stories in them, and a dog-eared book from the Stage Coach Inn's library for guests. She had a remarkable ability to disappear into a book or newspaper story like stepping into another world – at least it seemed remarkable to Sam. He could read well enough, but not get absorbed into the pages like that, like in a dream.

He'd noticed, though, that she did have a hard time stepping back out of that other world again, took her a minute or three of blinking at the light. So maybe instead of reading she was right now, like him, just sitting watching the world go by. Not that landlocked Kentville had near as much traffic as the biggest seaport on the Nova Scotia side of Fundy, but maybe that made what traffic there was more interesting.

Every now and then Sam got up and wandered around the yard to keep his arms and legs alive. At suppertime he ducked inside for long enough to ask the waitress to bring him out a bowl of soup. Unfortunately, a bellyful of warm chicken broth and chunks and noo-dles and savoury things made him dozy. Not much traffic on the road now, and not much light except from a few windows and outdoor lanterns. The inn's handyman kindly slung some lanterns on the pole that hung out over the front door, something usually only done when they were expecting a dark-of-night stagecoach. Thoughtful of him, or maybe that was just one more thing the old walrus had arranged ahead of time. If the Halifax Express's first run did turn out to be a night ride, fortunately Wellington and the other horses had been galloped from station to station enough times to know the road – or at least all the horses who were in his and John Thomson's care.

Sam started slipping into the inn from time to time to peek at the clock over the front desk. 7:35... 8:02... 8:47... 9:13... Maybe next time he should poke his nose in the kitchen and ask them to refill the teapot? But before next time came, he thought he heard something. He got up out of his chair and his quilt cloak and stepped out onto Water Street, peering down the dark road as though that would help him hear better. It came again, piercing through the bedtime murmur of the town and the lapping of the tide coming in. This time it was definitely the clear, high peel of a hunting horn.

Sam ran to the stables and led Wellington out of his nice warm stall into the cold and onto the road. Now he could hear the sound of galloping hooves but he couldn't tell which street it was on: when the Post Road came into Windsor it split into Gerrish Street or King Street, either two blocks or three from the Shipyard Inn. The all-night lantern in front of the Post Office showed him a horse and sleigh swerving and skidding onto Water Street, so it had come down King Street, a bit longer around but not as tight a turn. They were flying, literally – half the time the sleigh was airborne bouncing over ice ruts in the road.

Thad Harris reined the steaming horse to a halt in front of Sam and jumped out to stamp some circulation back into his legs and hold Wellington while Sam unfastened the horse who lived at Spencer's Inn. Fortunately, the shaft harness buckles were warm from the heat off the horse, or at least not burn-your-fingers frozen, but Sam's fingers were clumsy with trying to get it done too fast – he forced them to slow down and do one thing at a time. He got Brown Bess clear of the sleigh shafts and Thad took charge of her while Sam took hold of Wellington's bridle.

Wellington balked at being backed between the shafts – never liked walking backwards – but they didn't have enough hands to pull the sleigh forward to him and still hold both horses. But after a moment of coaxing and pushing, Wellington got the message and a moment later the sleigh was gone in a clatter and hiss of iron horseshoes and steel runners on icy road.

All that was left for Sam to do was put Brown Bess in Wellington's stall, strip off her harness and give her a rubdown and a feed of hay and he'd done his bit. All the rest of the run was out of his hands, which didn't make him too happy since what was out of his hands was going to decide whether there still was an Express to give him an income and a place to hide out.

A few days later another one-horse sleigh hove in from Halifax, but this one was driven by a walrus with buffalo fur over its legs. Carstairs seemed unhappy, or at least preoccupied; even his mustache looked weighed down. Once they were sat down in the tavern, Sam said, "Did the run go good?"

"Hm? Oh, could've been better. What with the slippy roads and dragging a sleigh, the horses didn't make near as good time as they should. And then Digby Basin was so unusually excessively lumbered with sea ice it took the *Commodore* near twelve hours to wriggle out to clear water. All in all it ended up taking the Halifax Express almost twenty-seven hours to get the news to Saint John. Only saving grace was it took the Cunard steamer forty-seven hours to get from Halifax to Boston."

"Well... guess we'll do better next time, eh?"

"Guess we bloody better. Next run's exactly two weeks after the first – or at least R.M.S. *America*'s due to leave Liverpool exactly noon Saturday, so whenever it gets to Halifax... But after that, Cunard's Royal Mail Ships steam out of Liverpool *every* Saturday, so the Halifax Express runs once a week." Carstairs took another quaff of bitter, wiped the light brown foam off his dark brown mustache, and his

eyes flicked around the room, seeming to shift from customer to customer at every table. "You notice any odd folk nosing around lately?"

"Uh... don't think so, not to notice. Should I be lookin' out?"

Carstairs's bloodhound eyes shifted directly to Sam. "You know
what Wall Street is, lad?"

"Uh... not sure I do, sir."

"It's the street in New York City where the Stock Exchange is.
That's where all the stocks and bonds and commodities futures shares
get traded. Some might call it flat-out gambling, betting on whether
the price of copper or hogs or coal is going to go up or down. But it's
betting on a grand scale. A trader can make or lose tens of thousands
of dollars – even millions – depending on whether a given company's
shares are worth two dollars apiece or a dollar eighty-seven.

"If you knew an hour in advance how a horse race was going to
turn out – even five minutes in advance – knew who was going to
win, place or show, do you think you might be able to pick up a bit
of money?"

"Dependin' on the race, I might could make a *lot* of money."

"Now, say the mail packet from London included the news
there's agitation in Egypt against the British pasha who whispers in
Ali Pasha's ear – "

"British pasha?"

Carstairs waggled one meaty hand like *Don't quibble details*, and
went on, "That's going to up the price of cotton."

"It is?"

"Supply and demand, lad. If the supply of Egyptian cotton gets
questionable, the value of American cotton from the southern planta-
tions is bound to go up, and up and up."

Sam was willing to take Carstairs's word for it. He was still trying to get his head around the notion of a British pasha, since "pasha"
conjured up a picture of a dark-skinned fella in a big silk turban.

"So say you are a Wall Street stocks 'n bonds man and you manage to get the news about the agitation in Egypt a half an hour before The Associated Press, which means *more* than half an hour before

it's printed in the newspapers where other stocks 'n bonds men are gonna see it. And say that stock in some big American cotton con-sort-eeum is currentwise going at a dollar thirty-seven a share. You quick-like buy up ten thousand shares. Next morning the news is out and American cotton goes up to two dollars a share, then three, then five... By the end of the week those shares are trading at *ten* dollars and thirty-seven cents. And you've just made ninety thousand dollars. Now say it's not just you but you've got a few friends to club in on the deal, and together you bought a *hundred* thousand shares before the price started going up... Get the picture?"

Sam nodded, though the numbers and dollars were so immense he couldn't really picture it.

"So, rumour has it that an anonymous group of Wall Street ty-coons have hired a Nova Scotia businessman name of Barnaby to set up a horse express from Cunard's Royal Mail dock in Halifax to Granville Point on Digby Gut, whence a fast steamboat will whisk the news across to the telegraph at Saint John. Sound familiar?"

"Just a bit, sir."

"Except the news in their dispatches will be a little different than ours, only news what might be useful to stock exchange trad-ers. And their telegram from Saint John won't go to The Associated Press but to a Wall Street telegraph office. But other than those little details... Well, imitation is the sincerest form of flattery they say, but I don't think Mr. Hyde and Mr. Craig feel particular flattered. So, have you noticed any odd and curious strangers nosing about the inn or the stables?"

Sam tried to think back over the last week or so, but had to ad-mit, "No, sir, but I aren't really been lookin'. I'll try and keep an eye out in future."

"Good lad. There's no law says the Royal Mail ship can't carry two foreign news dispatches for two couriers waiting on the dock, more's the pity. We don't yet know where they plan to set all their relay stations, though I do know their first changeover's at Ten Mile House instead of Fultz's Inn Twelve Mile House. Any rate, Mr.

Barnaby's at a bit of a disadvantage, since we already bought up most of the finest horseflesh in the colony – at least most of what anybody's willing to sell. Nova Scotia ain't exactly crawling with high-grade horses.

"Mr. Barnaby well knows, and I don't doubt he's passed it on to his minions, that if he can't beat our time he's no use to the money men on Wall Street. So Barnaby and his people will be looking for any kind of advantage they can get, and I don't think they'll be too partic'lar about how they get it. So if there's somebody lurking about the stables, ask 'em what their business is. And if something doubtful strange pops up on your horizon, send me a note via the stagecoach."

"Will do, sir."

A few days after that, a passenger got off the stagecoach from Halifax that Sam wasn't expecting to see in Windsor, or at least not see climbing out of a stagecoach instead of down off an Express horse. And it seemed Thad Harris was only getting out for a rest stop while the coach horses were changed, and meant to keep on to some stop further down the line. He seemed to see the surprise on Sam's face, and maybe a bit of suspicion – Barnaby couldn't get his hands on the Halifax Express's horses, but maybe he could hire away the riders – because Thad said, "Corey O'Dell's got business in Saint John that's going to keep him there a while, so this run I'll be riding the leg from Kentville to Digby. Burt Hamilton'll be riding this leg. Not my choice, I was just getting comfy with this half the run, and your horses."

"Oh, I'm sure you'll find John Thomson takes as good care of his horses as I do mine. Maybe better."

Come the Wednesday when the mail ship might be expected, Sam paced back and forth in front of the inn or sat in his quilted chair as before – except that this time he placed the chair so he could see the stable doors as well as the road, and kept glancing in that direction in case somebody he didn't recognize tried to sneak in. This time the town of Windsor went to sleep with still no sign of an Express rider. Sam stayed up, sipping strong tea to stay awake.

A bright full moon came up, with not many clouds to slide across it, so at least the roads would be well lit. But that would be as much a blessing for Barnaby's rider as Burt Hamilton. As the night hours ticked away, though, Sam began to think that the first run had just been first time lucky – for him – and Cunard's Royal Mail ships were more likely to reach Halifax Thursday mornings than Wednesday evenings. The sky went pink with dawn and still no sign of a galloper, not from Hyde's Express or Barnaby's.

When the sky turned blue and the town was rustling awake, Sam yawned his way into the stables and gave Wellington some oats and loosened his saddle girth a little more. It seemed that the sensible thing to do, once the Shipyard Inn's ostler came on duty, was take a catnap in the hay and ask the ostler to wake him if he heard a horn.

But the next person to come into the stables wasn't the ostler, it was the innkeeper's third son, about twelve years old. The boy said, "There's a lady come lookin' for a Sam Smith. Said she didn't wanna come out in the stables in her long skirts."

"Can't be me – Windsor's crawlin' with Smiths."

"She said a Smith from away."

A wash of fear jerked Sam alert faster than a dose of smelling salts. He couldn't think how the church orphanage could've found him, or how they could know he'd taken the name Sam Smith, but he couldn't think who else might come looking for him. But if it was a nun asking for him, the innkeeper's son surely wouldn't've just said "a lady." Would he?

As that was passing though Sam's mind, his legs were carrying him to the back door of the inn and down the hall. The lady waiting in the lobby was wearing a dark green cloak over a light green hoop-skirt, and a flowered bonnet over straw-blonde hair that looked a bit brittle and brassy. Friends of the Church, though, and of the charitable orphanage, came in all shapes and sizes. Sam cocked his head at her and said cautiously, "You lookin' for Sam Smith? Ma'am?"

The lady looked at him dubiously. "You are he?"

Sam couldn't very well deny it, not with the desk clerk looking on. "Yes'm."

"Samuel Smith from Truro?"

"Uh, no, ma'am. I been there once or twice, 'round the outskirts, but I ain't from there."

"You're not Sam Smith son of Obadiah Smith of Truro, Nova Scotia?"

"No, ma'am."

"Strange, I heard there was a Sam Smith here who wasn't a Windsor Smith and I was so hoping it might be... You're sure your grandfather wasn't the Ezekial Smith who was captain of the *Mary Claire* out of Parrsboro?"

"Certain sure, ma'am. Now if ya don't mind, I got things I gotta take care of – "

"Oh, sorry to trouble you, here's a penny for your trouble..." She started digging in her purse. "I know I have one in here somewhere..."

"No need, ma'am," and he gave her a little wave as he turned and started back down the hall.

She called after him, "You're sure you're not from Truro?"

He tossed over his shoulder, "Sorry, wrong Sam Smith, ma'am," as he hurried for the back door. On his way across to the stable barn, he heard a distant high horn note – not all that distant, might not be the first. He ran into the stables, dragged Wellington away from his half-eaten oats, tightened his saddle girth and led him at a jog-trot out to the roadside.

Just as they got there, Brown Bess from Spencer's Inn exploded into view with Burt Hamilton clinging to her back. Burt Hamilton was a couple years younger than Thad Harris and Corey O'Dell, half-way between their age and Sam's and John Thomson's, which gave Sam hope the Express might someday give the asteriskers a chance. Though younger, Burt was a bit heavier built than Thad Harris, but he seemed to have a good seat on a horse.

As Burt reined Bess to a dirt-spraying halt, Sam reached out to take hold of her bridle. Burt jumped down, dispatch bag flapping under his elbow, walked briskly twice around Sam and the horses, shaking his knees and ankles, then jumped up onto Wellington and was gone again.

Sam watched him go until he disappeared into the covered bridge across the Avon River to Falmouth. It was a bit of a wistful watching, thinking, *That coulda bin me*, but maybe it would be on some Express run in the not-too-distant. Sam was just starting to walk Brown Bess up and down the road to cool her down when he heard a stricken shout and neigh from across the river, then a bunch of yelling voices drifting over the wide water. The only words he could manage to pick out were "Express" and "down." He clambered onto Brown Bess and kicked her back into a gallop. The bright sky disappeared as they charged into the wooden tunnel of the bridge, Brown Bess's pummelling hooves echoing like the inside of a drum.

It was a lo-o-ong bridge – an engineering marvel, they said – but at the moment all Sam cared about was getting to the other end of it without ramming into something. The only light was from the occasional glassless window between patches of gloom. Bess swerved around a freight wagon he didn't see till they were half past it. There was a carriage coming toward them and an ox cart in front of them. Sam slowed Bess to a walk, wondering if he wouldn't've been better off leaving Brown Bess at the inn and running, so he could dodge around things. As soon as the carriage was past he dug in his heels and twitched the reins to gallop past the farm cart and out into the open.

Wellington was standing empty-saddled, looking down at Burt Hamilton who was flat on his back on the ground. A grey-haired man was kneeling beside Burt, propping his head up, and other people were starting to gather around, including a lady in a black silk dress who was probably from the fancy carriage stopped by the side of the road. Sam jumped down and dropped Brown Bess's reins to the ground to let her know to stay there – she was probably too tired to wander off anyway. As Sam scuttled over to Burt Hamilton, he noticed something shiny on the sooty snow near Wellington, something with a brown tail: a stirrup with a broken strap.

The lady in black took a little silver cylinder from her handbag and handed it to the grey-haired man, who uncapped it and waved it under Burt's nose. Even from a few feet away, Sam's nose wrinkled from the stab of ammonia and some sort of perfume. Ladies' smelling salts worked just as good on gentlemen. Burt's head jerked back, his eyes popped open and his chest heaved up and down with short, quick breaths. The grey-haired man started to help Burt up to his feet, Sam stepped forward to help and they walked Burt around with their shoulders under his arms. Burt seemed to be coming back to himself but his left leg seemed lamed.

Sam got a tingle of joy as it occurred to him that if Burt couldn't ride the last two legs to Kentville, he would have to. But it didn't seem all that joyful that he'd get his first chance at Burt Hamilton's expense, and anyway he wasn't dressed for long-distance riding and he'd been up all night.

As that passed through Sam's mind, a sound of hollow thunder came rolling toward them. He and everybody else looked toward the sound just as a rider on a beige horse spat out of the mouth of the covered bridge and pelted full tilt down the road through Falmouth. Burt Hamilton muttered thickly, "That'll be Barnaby's express." He shook his arms free of Sam's and the older man's shoulders and walked a circle on his own steam. "I'll catch him."

Sam said, "You can't ride with one stirrup."

"I can, so long's I know it's not there. Give me a hand up."

Sam crouched forward beside Wellington and made a stirrup with his hands. Burt Hamilton raised his boot onto Sam's hands and Sam gave him a boost onto the saddle. Wellington took off like he thought they'd never stop standing around going nowhere.

As the big grey horse and blue-coated rider disappeared down the snowy road, Sam picked up the broken stirrup. He was sure he'd checked it all over carefully before saddling and bridling Wellington.

But the strap on this stirrup only ran about a hand's length before ending in a jagged, slanting tear. Looking closer, though, one part of the tear wasn't ragged and jagged and didn't look like a tear. The strap was made of two strips of leather stitched together along both sides. One side ended in a neat, straight line across the seam, like it'd been cut with a razor or a very sharp knife. Cute – open one seam and the rest of the strap would gradually give way as the rider leaned his weight on the stirrup. The bloody damn lady in the willow-green dress must've had a friend. And bloody damn stupid polite Sam Smith had fallen for it.

A few days later a little one-horse sleigh carried big Carstairs and his big mustache into Windsor. Sam was more than a bit nervous about something he was going to have to say to Carstairs, didn't want to get to it directly. When they were sat down at an inn table with their pint of bitter and half pint of small beer, Sam said, "How'd we do? The run?"

"Well, all in all our speed from Halifax to Digby Gut averaged out to almost seventeen miles an hour." Sam just whistled. He'd heard or read somewhere – most likely John Thomson had read somewhere and mentioned to him – that scientists had calculated the fastest speed a human body could possibly stand travelling was twenty miles an hour. Any faster and your insides would start to jangle and rattle together like shaking a clock. An average of seventeen miles an hour meant that some of the riders must've come damn close to going as fast as any human person could go. Mr. Hyde had said in that old handbill "as fast as horse flesh can do it and live!" but it seemed he could've added "human flesh" as well. "But even with that, Barnaby's express beat us to the Fundy shore by two and one-half minutes."

Sam shrugged, a bit guiltily, "Well – two and a half minutes..."

"Doesn't sound like much, but if their steamer *Commodore* – previously our steamer *Commodore* till Barnaby hired it away – ran a shade faster than our *Conqueror*, that lead might become five minutes by the time they got across the bay to Saint John. And then, the telegraph is first-come-first-served, so if Barnaby's telegram took longer than five minutes to send, ours would be that much longer behind. And the same applies all down the line – the electric telegraph, like horses, can only gallop so many miles at one go, for the telegraph it's about a hundred and fifty miles maximal, so there's four or five relay stations between Saint John and New York, so by the time our separate telegrams reach New York City, that five minutes could become twenty minutes.

"You can make a fortune on Wall Street in twenty minutes, with the right inside information. And that twenty minutes would get longer once the telegrams reach New York City – you can bet that Barnaby's employers have a runner waiting in the Wall Street telegraph office to sprint the news across the street to the Stock Exchange, while even if The Associated Press *does* send pertinent bulletins over to Wall Street, it's bound to take longer." Carstairs nodded gravely and took another sip of his bitter.

Then his tone of voice changed. "But, as it turned out, when Barnaby's rider reached Granville Point, the steamer *Commodore* was nowhere to be seen – hadn't made it across the bay yet – while our *Conqueror* was sitting there huffing and puffing and all steamed up ready to go. So their two and a half minutes went for naught."

He winked and clinked his pewter tankard against Sam's and maybe even smiled, though with his mustache covering his mouth it was difficult to tell.

They both drank to that, then Carstairs said, "Even with losing twenty minutes here, and almost losing Mr. Hamilton, we beat them hands down."

"Uh..." That seemed to be Sam's cue, though he didn't want to take it. He took the stirrup and its ribbon of strap out of his coat pocket and handed it across the table. Carstairs looked it over, bushy eyebrows frowning, but didn't seem to quite see. "Look at the seam on one side, sir. That don't look to be wear and tear."

"Ah. I see."

Sam told him about the lady in the green dress, though not about why he couldn't have just brushed off a message that someone had come looking for him. "I know you told me to keep an eye out, sir, and I did, but I wasn't expectin'..."

"Hm. I think it's probably safe to assume that no one in Windsor had seen that woman before, or since, so we can't prove anything. But I think it's also safe to assume," waggling the ragged end of the stirrup strap, "what we're assuming. Hm, I wonder... It could be, too, that a reason Barnaby's people chose to sabotage in Windsor – besides the fact that right near the start of the run might've seemed too obvious – was to undermine our faith in you instead of the stablehands at Spencer's Inn or Hortonville or Aylesford or what-all."

"In me, sir?"

"You and the other three lads looking after our horses and way stations. Sometimes a fella don't know all his advantages till he sees what the competition's trying to cut away from him. Must mention that to Messers Hyde and Craig." He looked down thoughtfully at the stirrup and strap-end in his hands and gave the strap a tug, other hand tugging the stirrup. He murmured, maybe to himself, "Wonder maybe a lighter rider and it wouldn't've..." Then he looked up directly at Sam. "Well, you know what they say, lad – Fool you once, shame on them; Fool you twice..."

"Shame on me. It won't happen again, sir."

The hounddog eyes said quite clearly, *It better not. We got lucky this time.*

Once Carstairs went on his merry way, Sam went into the stables to give Wellington a bit of exercise and incidentally test out the new stirrup strap. After a galloping stint when they slowed to a walk, Sam let his mind drift while his body rocked gently from side to side with the swaying of the horse's broad back. Where Sam's thoughts drifted was to the picture of whatever-her-name-was in that copper bathtub, half-reclined, in her room at the Stage Coach Inn. It had only been an instant's glimpse, but still the image was etched on his memory's eye as indelibly as a daguerreotype on a copper plate: long thighs and naked breasts, not barmaid breasts but definitely there... What boggled Sam was trying to fit that picture with the image of John Thomson in his raggedy baggedy old coat and his corduroy cap pulled down low over his eyes. He tried to fit them together whenever the bathtub picture came to mind – which was just about whenever he didn't have something immediately in front of him he had to deal with – but they just wouldn't go.

V

JOHN THOMSON STOOD on the front step of the Stage Coach Inn as Mr. Carstairs's sleigh pulled away. Seana's natural impulse for the circumstances was to stretch up her arm and wave it over her head, but she intercepted it and just semi-raised her right arm from the elbow, first two fingers half-unfurled. Mr. Carstairs sort of nodded as he went past. Male protocol was such a convoluted and constricted road, she was constantly having to pull on her own reins.

Mr. Carstairs had been deflective about the "accident" with the broken stirrup, about whether it'd truly been just an accident or someone was sneaking dirty tricks. Seana McCann might've been able to tease or cajole it out of him, but John Thomson couldn't play those kinds of cards, and certainly couldn't press one of his bosses for a straight answer if that boss didn't feel like giving it to him. Either way, accident or nasty trick, Seana wondered if Sam Smith was feeling guilty or down about it, since it'd happened on his watch – she certainly would've. Probably feeling even more down and guilty if it was just an accident; saddlery accidents shouldn't happen if the saddler's paying attention.

There were still a few days left before the next Express run, plenty of time to try a three-stage practice run: from Aylesford to Kentville to Hortonville to Windsor. The stagecoach from Annapolis Royal to Windsor ran three times a week, so next time it came through she handed a note up to the driver for Sam Smith, and next day when the stage came back the other way she rode it to Aylesford and slept in the stable in her clothes – John Thomson's clothes. Next morning, after two bowls of porridge and a bit of a walk around to let them settle, she saddled up Finbar and galloped to Kentville. Well, not entirely galloped, Finbar wasn't Big Red and needed a few slow-down breathers for the eighteen miles between Aylesford and Kentville. In Kentville she had to pause to saddle Big Red. She expected to have to do the same with the Express horse in Hortonville – and by the time she got there was actually looking forward to getting her feet on the ground and hobbling around the stable – but he was already standing saddled and bridled in front of Fowler's Inn, as was grey Wellington, and Sam Smith was sitting on a bench beside them with his feet propped on a crusty snowbank.

Sam Smith stood up as Seana creaked her way down off Big Red, and he said, "Not feeling *horny* today?"

"Pardon me?" Damn, should've grunted, *What?* or *Huh?* – too late now.

A stablehand laughed at Sam's boys'-room joke. Sam became a bit stammery, like he'd forgot for an instant they weren't all boys here but still had to pretend they were. "I thought you might blow yer horn, to give me warning-like."

"I aren't got a horn to blow. No sense buying one till they give us a chance at riding the Express for real." Better, that sounded more like John Thomson. "Anyways, I didn't know you was gonna be here."

"I warned ya I might bring Wellington to Hortonville and make it a race."

"If you figure yer up to it."

"We'll see. Jake here'll take care of Big Red."

Seana handed the reins to Jake the stablehand and hiked herself onto the Hortonville horse. He was about Wellington's size, skewbald white-on-brown, and seemed to smell a race in the offing. She remembered a fragment of a song her Da used to sing, about a famous race on the plains of Kildare between a grey thoroughbred and a scruffy skewbald horse whose name got misheard, for five hundred gold guineas and side-bets in the crowd:

> Stewball was a good horse, and I wish he was mine,
> He never drank water, he always drank wine...

When Seana was on board, Sam said to Jake, "You say go."

"Well, I would for a race. Ain't no race without stakes."

Sam said to Seana, "Loser buys the beer?"

Seana nodded. Jake raised his arm and called out with great seriousness, "Ready, steady – Go!"

Seana dug in her heels but that turned out unnecessary; the skewbald horse jumped to it like he'd been waiting to show Wellington what's what since January. They barrelled down Hortonville's main street knee to knee, not leaving much room for any other traffic and slim chance of swerving if anything darted out in front of them. Fortunately, the inn was near the edge of town and there wasn't much town to begin with, so in a minute they were on the open road. Seana didn't know this road as well as Sam and Wellington – a twisty, hilly road sometimes pinched narrow – but hoped her horse might from Sam's practice runs. The skewbald certainly showed no signs of uncertainty, just charged full tilt around corners and up inclines. Seana held tight and leaned forward with her eyes slitted against the coarse mane hairs whipping back at her, stretching her right arm back to ply Da's old riding crop against the skewbald's rump for encouragement, still neck and neck and nose to nose with the grey.

They passed through the outskirts of Lower Horton, fortunately even smaller than Upper Horton so there wasn't much outskirts to skirt. The road flattened out and Seana could see the blue-grey blur of the Minas Basin close on her left. Wellington began to fall back, or Seana's horse surge ahead, enough that she couldn't see Sam's horse without craning her head around. Sam hollered from behind her: "Stop!" Fat chance of her falling for that when she'd finally started to break out in front. He shouted again, so loud it must be cracking his lungs and his throat, "Look ahead!"

Seana straightened her back to see farther in front of her than twenty feet of road. Up ahead was the Gaspereau River – hardly a river like the Shannon or the Boyne, but wide enough to have a swing bridge across it. At the moment the bridge was swung open to let a sailboat pass by. The boat didn't have a sail set, was just rowing along through the breaking-up ice to get to the open water of the Minas Basin, but its mast was still too high to pass under the bridge.

Seana and Sam slowed their horses to a halt on the riverbank. Standing in the stirrups to see down past the skewbald's nose, Seana saw a steep drop down to the river and getting steeper with the tide going out. Sam said, in between panting from the hard ride, "I been up and down this road enough to know to look ahead for the bridge."

"Glad you did."

The swivel base for the swing bridge was on the west side of the river, Seana and Sam's side. One of the men from the sailboat scrambled up the other bank to haul on the rope that swung the bridge back into place. Once there was a bridge to cross, Seana and Sam trotted across it side by side and then kicked into a gallop again.

The road grew up and down again and had a lot of twists and turns but not a lot of traffic, so there was always room to swerve around. Except once, when a two-horse freight wagon lumbering west and another one plodding east happened to coincide. Seana and Sam took to the ditches, Seana the right-hand one with trailing branch-ends whipping at her and the skewbald horse.

She and Sam got back out of the ditches at the same time and
continued pounding down the roadway neck and neck, more or less:
sometimes Wellington's nose was level with Seana's knee, sometimes Seana's skewbald horse was near far enough back to sniff
Wellington's tail. At one point when Seana and Sam were exactly
side by side, they took to whacking at each other with their riding
crops and laughing, giddy with speed and horsepower. The rumble of
the horses was so loud in Seana's ears she couldn't hear Sam laughing,
had to see it on his face.

A sharp bend in the road stopped her laughter and focused her
attention on staying on the careening horse. Refocusing brought Seana
to notice, once the road straightened out again, that the inside of her
right thigh was getting rubbed raw from the saddle rim – an unfamil-
iar saddle and one whole stage longer than she'd ever galloped before.
It probably wouldn't've been a problem if she'd had proper riding
breeches with a leather insert, but there was no sense putting out
that kind of expense until she knew for sure she was going to get a
chance at being a full-fledged Express rider with the kind of wages
paid to Thad Harris or Corey O'Dell. The pain got forgotten quickly, though, as she began to pull ahead again – so far ahead that she
couldn't hear the hammering of Wellington's hooves anymore, only
her own horse's.

Seana straightened up in the saddle for just long enough to catch
a glimpse ahead. She could see the pointed crown of the blockhouse
of Fort Edward on the hill above Windsor. Not much farther and
she'd be able to see the church spires. Another verse of the old song
about that other skewbald's race on the plains of Kildare came back
to her:

> I bet on the grey mare, I bet on the grey,
> If I'd bet on old Stewball I'd be a rich man today.

Well, grey Wellington wasn't a mare, and free beer wasn't five
hundred guineas, but bet beer tasted better than bought beer and she
could already taste it in her parched mouth and throat, parched from

a very long morning's ride with only a couple of sips of water while changing horses in Kentville.

But then she began to hear Wellington's hooves again, and getting louder. She looked back over her shoulder. Wellington's head and whole body were ploughing forward like a mad thing. Sam wasn't even plying his riding crop, just hunkering down and hanging on. Seana slapped her horse's rump with her riding crop and shouted, "Come on, Stewball!" even though that likely wasn't the Hortonville horse's name. It was no use, though. Wellington caught up and passed them, spraying them with specks of frozen road kicked up by his hooves until they got out of range.

When Seana walked the skewbald horse into the stable, Sam was stripping off Wellington's saddle and reaching down the dandy brush and dry rags – there was just about nothing worse for a horse than being rode hard and put up wet. Sam said, "'Fraid I played you a bit of a trick – let him fall back till he got mad. Wellington don't like the look of another horse's ass."

"You must have to sneak up on him."

Sam laughed. Seana figured she was maybe getting the hang of this male/male humour thing. It had something to do with the notion that if you said something disparaging to somebody's face, you wouldn't say it behind his back. And maybe it wasn't such a bad idea to say nasty things you didn't mean instead of nice things you didn't mean. But you had to be careful about who you said them to.

In the pub of the Shipyard Inn, Seana paid for their half pints of small beer and the two of them stretched out their legs and arched their backs in their chairs. After a bit of dissecting the race they'd just run, and the road they'd run it on, Seana said, "You've got a Bank of Nova Scotia here, all I've got in Kentville is a piddling little local bank." And all she had in it was a piddling little one pound, eight shillings and sixpence saved from what the Express paid above her basic room and board, but it was a start. "Maybe I'll move my savings account here."

"Why?"

"Me Mam and Da had a bit of money in a little local bank back home in Ireland. The bank went bankrupt and their money was gone," she snapped her fingers and waved bye-bye, "just like that."

"Well, I don't have to worry 'bout that."

"Where do you keep your money?"

Sam's dark eyes slitted like that was a questionable question. Then he just shrugged, "It's safe, 'less some squirrel or racoon gets a taste for metal."

"I hope it's safe. We all of us only got till autumn to salt away what money we can."

"Why d'ya say that?"

"As soon's the ground thaws enough to dig postholes, Mr. Hiram Hyde and Mr. Daniel H. Craig are gonna start building a telegraph line from Halifax to Amherst, same time as a New Brunswick company's building a line from Saint John to Amherst. Oh, I don't mean Mr. Hyde and Mr. Craig will be putting up any poles themselves, or stringing wire with their own hands, but hiring workmen to do it. Plan is they should be done by September."

Sam cocked his head and looked at her sideways. "Who told you that?"

"Newspapers. Seems like most of what they print is just to throw dirt at the government – or at the opposition, depending what side they're on – but the information's still there, if you look for it. Once there's a telegraph from Halifax to Saint John, ain't much use for a horse express. Kinda funny, eh? The same people we're working for are working to put us out of business."

"Ha ha. Well, even if that's how it pans out, I can still get a pretty good stake salted away by September."

"Be a lot bigger if they gave us a chance at express riding for real, pay us like they pay Thad and Corey and Burt."

"How much *do* they get paid?"

"Don't know, but it's a lot more'n a shilling a day. Thad told me, one of the times he was staying over in Kentville, that they only get paid for the run they ride – paid a good whack – and the rest of the time they all got other things to do."

"A *lot* of other things Corey do. Owns a cab carriage in Saint John and I don't know what all else he gets up to. Hah – maybe he's one of the Saint John fellas in on buildin' the telegraph line to Amherst."

Seana took another sip of her beer – getting near the bottom – and looked around. The Shipyard Inn's public room was starting to fill up with a lunchtime crowd, though their corner table still felt a little private. Her eyes drifted back to Sam Smith and she suddenly wondered if when he looked at John Thomson he could see her bath-naked. She could feel herself starting to blush, and not just for the obvious reason – the wondering also brought on a kind of naughty tingle that wasn't entirely unpleasant but certainly wasn't proper. Maybe the beer was making her silly – only small beer but she was only a small person, at least compared to the hefty workmen downing pints at other tables. Or compared to the blouse-bursting barmaid approaching their table. The waitress said, "Are you in for dinner, Sam? Today's mutton stew."

"Yes please, Kate. And two more of these," raising his half-pint mug. "She'll pay for the beer."

"*She?*" burst out of the barmaid; Seana was frozen with fear and shock, followed an instant later by an urge to stick a fork in Sam Smith's eye, if she'd had a fork.

Sam, without a flicker of hesitation, pointed across the table and crowed, "He's a girly-boy what me an' Wellington left in our dust this morning. Shoulda rode sidesaddle."

Seana stuck her hand down into her tankard – glad for a change that her fingers were long and gawky for a girl – then flicked a fan of droplets at Sam's face. "*You're* the girly-boy."

Kate the waitress rolled her eyes, muttered, "*Boys*," and took their empty mugs away. Sam pursed his mouth and rolled his eyes at Seana, but in a different way, more like, *Sorry, I'm an idiot.*

By the time Kate came back with their refilled tankards, Seana's heart had stopped battering at her front ribs. As Kate plunked down the beers, Sam pointed across the table again, saying, "Like I said, he's buyin'."

"I already bought you a beer!"

Sam shook his head and waggled a finger. "Bet was to buy the beer, not *a* beer."

Seana grumbled, but it was mostly for show, and dug in her pocket for some coins. The thought of impending dinner made her wonder if that was another reason the beer was making her silly, it'd been a long morning's hard riding since breakfast.

After their plates had been cleaned and cleared away, and their beer mugs re-emptied, Sam sighed and said, "Good hot grub after a long gallop always makes me yawny."

"Me too."

"There's a trundlebed in my room. We could both have a bit of a nap."

But once they got up to Sam's narrow little room, Seana didn't feel sleepy. She felt like she'd been walking around wearing a head-to-toe suit of heavy armour, and all the iron plates had fallen away as soon as Sam closed the door behind them. Sam seemed to feel somewhat the same. He started with, "Sorry, sorry, sorry. I'm such a fool-mouthed... fool. *She's* buyin'."

"Well, you covered it up right smartly."

"So did you. Anyway, ya see how it's a good idea I don't know your real name? I'd be blurtin' it out all over the place..."

Instead of pulling out the trundlebed and getting afternoon naps, they sat on either end of Sam's bed and babbled away at each other like they were travellers in a foreign country who'd finally bumped into someone who spoke their same language. They talked of their families and strangers and horses and rivers and funny things they'd overheard, about whether the winter was almost over and about being Catholic in mostly Protestant Nova Scotia, "talked from Bantry to Antrim and back again," as Seana's Da used to say.

At one point it seemed to Seana that Sam wasn't really listening to her, though he was looking directly at her. She trailed off. He blinked at her, then said, "Oh, sorry. Guess I was listenin' to yer voice, not to what it was sayin'. You got a soft voice, when yer not bein' John Thomson. Not whispery, just... soft. Guess maybe it's the Irish."

"Oh, Irish voices can be harsh, believe me. You've got a soft voice, too, when you're not playing Sam Smith. I guess it's the... Meegamaw."

"Huh. You aren't heard my granny yellin' at the dogs."

They talked until suppertime, then went back down into the public room for fresh flounder and not-so-fresh potatoes and onions. They also went back into being John Thomson and Sam Smith, which Seana found much harder after a few hours of being herself. She figured it was probably harder for Sam, too, though he didn't have quite as far to pretend. Then again, maybe pretending not to be Mi'kmaq was as complicated as pretending not to be female, how would she know?

After supper they went back up to Sam's room, Sam letting her go first – and carry the candle – up the narrow stairway to the cubbyhole garret rooms. Once his door was closed behind them, he said, "Yer walkin' funny. I mean, kinda limpy, yer right leg."

"Oh, I chafed it a bit on the saddle, the last part of the race."

"Lemme see."

"You're a doctor now?"

"Not hardly, but if yer thinkin' of puttin' that leg acrost a saddle tomorrow, better see what it looks like tonight."

He had a point. She unbuttoned her trousers and stepped out of them, then sat on his bed and furled her front shirttail up between the top of her thighs, so he could see the chafe and nothing else. It wasn't quite a welt, just a pinky-red feather across the inside of her thigh, blurred around the edges. Though it wasn't oozing blood, the centre red line looked like it would if it was rubbed much rawer – blood or pus.

Sam peered at it a moment, then said, "Huh. There's somethin' I noticed out behind the stables, before the snow got too deep..." He rummaged in his canvas bundle of things by the foot of his bed and came out with a long, wide, wooden-handled sheath knife. "My mother didn't auction all my father's things."

Seana said, "Amputating is not in the cards."

"Aw, you never let me have any fun." He stepped to the door. "I'll be just a few minutes. Don't go anywhere."

"Do I look like I'm going anywhere?"

When she was alone, Seana sat with her hands trellised in her lap, looking around at the rough-plastered .walls. She looked to the gable window, but all she could see in the glass were her own bob-haired reflection and candlelit patches of the room. She moved the candle down onto the floor behind the foot of the bed, and the window turned into a window again. Beyond the shipyard shed roofs across the road, the lanterns of anchored ships and fishing boats bobbed in the harbour. High above were thousands of colder lights that didn't sway with the waves. Seana picked out the two bright eyes and the hoof and wingtip of the constellation Pegasus. One clear and moonless night in Ireland, Da had pointed out those stars to her and told her of the winged horse that could carry its rider to freedom – freedom from all the cares and chains and worries of the world.

Now, though, the story and the memory tasted sour to her. For all she knew, that clump of stars was just a nameless clump of stars and Da had made the story up, like he'd made up the story he was going to join the U.S. Army for family's sake and send his money home. She pushed the memory away and tried to think of something real and now. Something did come to mind, but it didn't make her feel much better. Right now, less than a day's ride from where she was sitting, Liam and Michael and Fergus were looking up at the same stars she was, if they were still awake.

The door jarred open and Sam Smith came in, one hand holding his big sheath knife and the other something wrapped in a rag. He set them on the floor and unfurled the rag. Inside was a sickly-white cluster of root tendrils, like sprouted potato eyes tangled together. Out of his coat pocket he took a chunk of icicle and set it on the rag, saying, "It's meltin' pretty fast, good. I gotta mash this stuff up and wet it into a paste."

"I could just chew it up and spit it onto the cloth, like me Mam does for a poultice."

"Oh no." Sam shook his head. "You don't go chewin' this stuff, less'n ya wanna take a trip to the moon and not come back. I gotta sluice my fingers off good with what's lefta the icicle when I'm done."

"And you want to put that stuff on my *leg*?"

"It's different on skin, 'specially broken skin or rubbed raw, ya just don't wanna be puttin' any in yer mouth." By then he'd chopped and mashed the rootlets with the blade and spine of his knife, and mixed the bits with melted icicle. "Oh damn."

"What?"

"I hadn't thunk of... This bit of rag's big enough for a poultice, but not big enough to tie around yer leg. Maybe my bootlaces..."

"No, I've got something better. Turn your back." He did. Seana reached both hands up under her shirt, taking its hem up with them, and tugged down the flannel band that bound her breasts. Once it was loose around her waist, she tugged it till the knot was in front, wrestled the knot open and held out the strip of flannel with one hand while the other furled down her shirttails. "You can look now. Better too long than not long enough, hm?"

"If you say so." He got her to hold the improvised poultice against the sore on her thigh while he tied the flannel band around it, leaving two long trailing tails. "There, if that stays on all night it should help."

"Should?"

He shrugged. "I'm just rememberin' what my granny used to do – hope I'm rememberin' right."

They sat and talked some more about other things, but after a while Seana's head started to droop. Talking and listening so intently all afternoon and evening took a different kind of energy from riding a galloping horse, but it was still tiring, and that was on top of a long morning's gallop. This time it was Seana's turn to sleep on the trundlebed. They both slept in their dayshirts.

In the morning Seana peeled off the poultice and found that what had been a red, almost-oozing sore was now healthy-looking skin with just the barest trace of pink. She said to Sam, "That's amazing! How did you know to do that?"

"I dunno, maybe not so amazin'. Maybe it just needed to be left alone overnight to heal itself."

"I don't think so – not that fast."

"Well, I was just rememberin' what I saw my granny do, hopin' I remembered right. Just natural stuff around here. No big secrets."

"But my family's been living in Nova Scotia for nine years and wouldn't know that. Neither would any of our neighbours."

"Most people in Nova Scotia lives in towns or farms, not in the woods."

Seana looked at the length of flannel that'd held the poultice. "Now I'll have to fit this damn thing 'round my chest again. You might as well go on down to breakfast, I'll follow in a few minutes – or however long it takes."

"Or I could give you a hand... I mean, I turn my back and you get it in place, in front, and then you turn your back and I tie the ends together."

That did make sense. Though when Seana started thinking in terms of sense and nonsense, the whole binding business seemed like a silly rigmarole over a couple of sticky-out lumps of flesh on her chest – and not hugely sticky-outy in her case – but that was the way of the world and the world wasn't interested in Seana McCann's opinion. "Okay."

Sam turned his back. Seana pulled on her trousers without tucking in her shirttails, then laid the length of flannel on the bed and folded it in three lengthwise. She lifted the middle part up under her shirt, held it in place with both hands and said over her shoulder, "Okay." She could feel Sam's hands taking hold of the trailing ends, then his knuckles against her bare back. "Not tight enough. *Uh!* Too tight. There, that's about right. Just a reef knot's fine – you know, a square knot?"

"Yeah, like the one I tied the bandage with last night."

"Oh, yeah, like that."

Once she was bound up again, baggy shirt tucked in and coat on for further camouflage, they headed down to the Public Room. It was only logical that after breakfast Seana would ride the skewbald horse back to Hortonville and then Big Red back to Kentville. Once Stewball was saddled and ready, Seana turned to Sam, unsure what the protocol was. There were a few other people in and around the stables, not exactly watching but bound to notice anything odd. Sam said, "See ya," and punched her on the shoulder – more of a tap than a punch; an awkward, bent-elbow sort of move.

Seana mimicked the move back at him, "Not if I see you first," then climbed aboard, feeling like she was almost second-nature with this boy stuff now. As she trotted out of the innyard she raised her right hand just high enough to be seen over her shoulder, in an off-handed kind of non-wave wave, then kicked the skewbald horse into a gallop.

The next few runs of the Halifax Express went off without complications, or not many. One time a first-time rider – square-shouldered young man with a blond mustache – rubber-legged off the saddle in Kentville swearing his first run was going to be his last, even if they doubled the pay. And once or twice Barnaby's express beat Hyde's, but since it only took about ten minutes to send the stockbrokers' message and about three hours to send the three thousand words of European news for The Associated Press, coming second was less of a shin-kick to Hyde's express than Barnaby's. Funny thing – or at least Mr. Carstairs seemed to find it funny when he told John Thomson – while the newspapers in Nova Scotia called it Hiram Hyde's Express, it was known in New Brunswick and the U.S.A. as Daniel Craig's Express. Seana didn't find it as much funny as worrisome. If Mr. Hyde and Mr. Craig weren't cozy partners, maybe the Halifax Express wouldn't even last until September.

As March wore on, the snow wore away, though there were still white patches at the edge of the woods and in shadowed ditches. The ground began to thaw and soften, heading for mud. Mr. Carstairs was back in his two-wheeled shay instead of a sleigh. The Cornwallis River on the westerly edge of Kentville grew high and turbulent with runoff. On a sunny Sunday morning Seana went for a walk to see if the river was flooding. She ambled past the big fancy houses on the other side of Main Street from the Stage Coach Inn and turned right up the angle of Cornwallis Street, past the school and the growing piles of building materials for the new courthouse and jail. But of course nobody was in school or working on a Sunday, so the street was pretty much deserted.

The river was still within its banks, barely, snaking along through hayfields on the edge of town. Kentville was as far inland as tidal waters came up the river from the Bay of Fundy, miles and miles away, so freight boats could ride the tide in carrying dry goods for the Red Store or wet goods for the bar at the Stage Coach Inn. No boats to watch today, though, so Seana wandered back down Cornwallis Street until it forked and took the right-hand fork called Church Street. The bell spire of Kentville's only church – St. James Anglican – was ringing the end of Sunday service. Seana wouldn't have known what to do in an Anglican church, and certainly couldn't take Communion. She'd heard talk among the Kentville Irish of some-day building a Catholic church on the other side of the Cornwallis River – since the river was the town boundary, the good Protestants of Kentville wouldn't be able to complain about a Papist church in their town. But so far it was only talk.

Anyway, even if there was a Catholic church, she could hardly go to confession. She didn't know the official name for the sin com-mitted by a girl pretending to be a boy, but she was quite sure it was a big one, and she wouldn't be able to tell the Father Confessor she would go and sin no more.

Out the doors of St. James Church came a parade of families in their Sunday best: women in silk-flowered bonnets, men in brushed-shiny top hats. A little dark-haired, dark-eyed boy a lot like Liam, except dressed in a costly blue velvet suit, came out holding the hand of his big sister. Seana tasted tears in the back of her nose, and her throat constricted. Boys didn't walk around weepy. She clenched her lips and squinted to shut the tear ducts. There was a leftover snow-bank between two storefronts. She stripped off one ratty woolen glove and stuck her hand in as she went by, then rubbed her hand down across her face and wiped the drip off with her gloved hand. Better, a bit. Big Red needed a good brush and combing now that his winter coat was moulting off. Keeping busy in the here and now was the best prescription. Besides, if that little black-haired boy coming out of church had been Liam and she the sister holding his hand, who would've been holding her other hand? Gropey-fingered Mr. MacAngus?

One muddy afternoon Mr. Carstairs rolled into Kentville with his brown leather coat spattered with splatters of different browns. Once he and Seana were sat down with beer mugs in front of them, he said, "I guess you and the other three lads have been champing at the bit – Ha! apt – to get a chance at being Express riders instead of just stablehands and grooms."

"Yes, sir!" Seana sat up straighter in her chair. The dank Public Room suddenly seemed brighter, its colours clearer and outlines sharper, and the Stage Coach Inn's small beer had more of a taste to it.

"Week after next, not the next-coming run but the next-next, Thad Harris and Burt Hamilton both have prior commitments. Mr. Hyde was thinking of putting out an advertisement, but I reminded him we already have several potential riders in reserve. Mr. Hyde being an affable gentleman was glad to be reminded. Any rate, you and Sam Smith have distinguished yourselves by taking practice runs – breaking yourselves in and building yourselves up – while the other two lads've been content to just exercise their horses to a minimum and otherwise loll around waiting for me to call on them. So, week after next, the Express rider who'll hand off to Corey O'Dell here will be Sam Smith."

The beer turned to acid in Seana's stomach. It seemed pointlessly cruel that Mr. Carstairs would build up her hopes just to knock them out from under her, unless that was how he got his fun. And Sam Smith was supposed to be a friend of hers. The only friend she had, since everybody else only knew John Thomson.

"Sam told me it should be you, since you're the better rider – in his opinion. He may even be right in that, I don't know. But as I told Sam, Corey O'Dell will only ride the second leg – unless we add a bonus to the extravagant rate we're already paying him – since all his other interests are in Saint John or Annapolis Royal. Sam's got himself well-acquainted with the road and horses on the first leg – at least from Spencer's Inn to here – just as O'Dell knows the second leg. So, there it stands. If Sam Smith can show that a young lad can match the time of a young man – maybe even better it – that a younger, lighter rider can have the stamina to gallop seventy-some miles at one go... Well, maybe you'll both get a chance."

Seana forced herself to swallow her disappointment, though she had a feeling it would come back on her. When Corey O'Dell came in on the stage a few days later, he didn't seem his normal jolly self, didn't bubble out his usual fount of funny stories – at least not to John Thomson. As he took the dispatch pouch from Thad Harris and charged off on the second leg of the Halifax Express, Seana realized that was one thing she and Sam hadn't practised – the full-gallop handoff. Maybe in the next few days she should take a ride over to Windsor and they should give it a few tryouts on the road outside of town. It grated a bit to think of helping him do well in the opening that should've been hers, or at least could've. Then again, if he didn't do well on his first chance, she probably wouldn't get one.

Thad Harris didn't seem his normal jolly self, either. Thad was never the winking blarneyer that Corey was, but he was usually cheerfully exhaustedly relieved after a safe and successful run, making jokes about saddle-pummelled portions of his anatomy that he wouldn't've made to John Thomson if he'd known she wasn't a he. This time, though, Thad Harris seemed politely distant, same as Corey O'Dell.

Seana finally figured it out while eating her supper alone in the Public Room of the Stage Coach Inn, watching Thad Harris drinking and laughing with a tableful of Kentville young men. Quite likely the Halifax Express was planning to pay the asteriskers less per run than they paid the full-grown riders. Not exactly child labour, but something in between. So to Corey O'Dell and Thad Harris, Sam Smith and John Thomson might be undercutting them out of a job.

VI

THE OSTLER AT the Shipyard Inn was from the Black Loyalist settle-
ment of Three Mile Plains, a couple miles west of the outskirts of
Windsor, and though he was definitely decades older than Sam it was
impossible to guess how many. Sam's mother used to say, "The darker the skin the stronger, and the slower it wrinkles – we age better'n
white folks, but black folks ages best of all." Sam asked Clifford about
seeing to Wellington and the incoming horse on the day Sam made
his run, but Clifford said Carstairs had already slipped him a little
money to do Express duty, and Clifford had already slipped a little of
it to the stableboy to stay awake and alert for the sound of a distant
horn if Clifford needed to take catnaps.

So all that left for Sam to do was climb on the stage to Halifax
when the time came. Since the Halifax/Windsor line ran daily, he
could wait until the day before the Liverpool steamer's earliest possible arrival, instead of kicking around Halifax with nothing to do.
All he took with him was a canvas sack containing his new riding
boots and breeches made by a Windsor cobbler and tailor, who were

well set up for such gear thanks to the Windsor Turf Club of rich
hobby horse racers. The boots and breeches had cost Sam more than
Carstairs was paying him for the run, but should last for years and
Sam wasn't planning his first run to be his last. Sam was quite sure
the Express was paying him less than it paid Corey and Thad and
Burt – hadn't seemed polite to ask, and he probably wouldn't've got
a straight answer anyway. But then, the Express was already paying
him a shilling a day plus full-time room and board, which it wasn't
paying to its regular riders. Room and board for Corey O'Dell probably would've cost the Express more'n all four asteriskers combined,
given the style to which he seemed to be accustomed.

There were only three other passengers on the stagecoach, so
Sam had no problem getting a window seat, though it meant travelling backwards. More like sideways once they got east of Spencer's
Inn and Sam could study the thirty-some miles of road he wasn't all
that familiar with but would have to gallop back over soon, maybe in the dark. Luckily it wasn't a stormy day or the other passengers would've groused him to roll down the leather curtain furled
above the window. The picture through the window was jouncing
and bouncing as the stagecoach sometimes threatened to throw him
off its padded leather seat. The rounded bottom of the coach body sat
cradled on two thick leather straps slung between the axles, so any
rut or bump in the road transmitted itself up or sideways or every
which way. The design seemed more concerned with the long life of
the coach than the passengers.

Trying to focus through the window while travelling up and
down and backwards made Sam a bit seasick, but he kept his eyes
on the passing picture. Along the streams the pussy willows were just
starting to show fuzzy silver buds, and when the road snaked into
the tall woods the maples were sprinkled with red and orange dots of
the big trees' tiny flowers.

A couple miles east of Spencer's Inn the road took a sharp, steep jog to the right – Sam reminded himself to watch for that on the way back. After a longish rise – would be a longish drop on the way back – the road levelled out, sort of, clinging to the side of a ridge that must be the south wall of a valley. Seemed a damn silly way to build a road when the floor of the valley was surely fairly flat and carried on at the same level and same direction as the road had been going before the road had suddenly veered off to the right and started to rise. Seemed even sillier when they reached the east end of the valley and the road had to veer left and drop down again. But then again, maybe the floor of the valley was veined with streams that would need bridges that took time and money to build and could wash out with spring floods. Sam could hear the ghost of his father saying, *Don't think yourself so smart and other folks so stupid till you think a minute.* Sam told himself to stop thinking about what the road should've done and pay attention to what it did.

"The dandelions are awful early this year."

Sam peered at the passing ditches for dandelions that shouldn't be there – way too early – and didn't see any. There were a lot of low-lying yellow flowers that looked a little bit like dandelions, but not much. The dandelion remark had come from the only female in the coach, a youngish woman with brown ringlets poking out of a pink-ribboned bonnet. Since hoopskirts took up too much room in a coach, she was dressed in what was called travelling costume, which included a modestly long skirt but with no hoops in it. Ladies in travelling costume who wanted a bit of a walkabout while the horses were being changed tended to just walk back and forth behind the Shipyard Inn, since walking by the roadside in an unhooped skirt might show the contours of their lower limbs – as proper folks' proper language had it – to passing eyes.

Sam said, raising his voice to be heard above the rumbling and rattling of the coach, "Them's coltsfoot, ma'am, t'ain't dandelions." He just barely stopped himself from saying there wasn't a Mi'kmaq name for them, so they must've come with the white man, but the Mi'kmaq knew they made good cough medicine or, if you rolled the leaves up into little balls and burned them, the ashes made good salt.

"Properly called Son-before-the-Father," said the young man sitting across from the lady, in an English accent he maybe wasn't born to, "because the flowers come before the leaves."

"How interesting," said Lady Ringlets – to the man across from her, not to Sam. Her comment about dandelions had been to the *gentleman*. Sam became sharply aware of what a ragged little stableboy he was, with the sack at his feet holding his ridiculous fancy boots and breeches and ridiculous hopes to be a rider for the Halifax Express. Who did he think he was fooling? He turned his head and leaned his face closer to the window, not quite out but away from the people who were swaying to the rocking of the same coach as him but living in a different world. There was a split in the roadside where the freeze-thaw and runoff had maybe washed a little gully right across the road, better remember that for the ride back...

The gaps of woods between the farms grew narrower and then the houses grew closer together and then they were in the city. Last stop for the stagecoach was naturally the waterfront; in Halifax everything flowed down to the harbour. Ol' Walrus Carstairs was waiting at the terminal stop – maybe for efficiency's sake, maybe to head off raggedy-ass stableboys heading up to the Exchange Reading Rooms to ask for instructions. Carstairs walked Sam through the livery stable and got him sorted out: come tomorrow the Halifax-Fultz's Inn horse would be stabled in a shed near the Cunard wharves; when the Royal Mail ship blew its steam horn – this run R.M.S. *Caledonia* – Sam should just have time to tighten the saddle girth and get out on the dock; a stableboy would keep watch on the dock if the wait was so long Sam needed to catch catnaps. Meals would be brought over from a tavern on Upper Water Street. "Just sandwiches and beer, but the Express is paying, so gift horses..."

Sam doubted he'd need any napping, no matter how long the wait – or doubted he'd be *able* to, he was so primed-up. In the morning he changed into his new, tight breeches and high-topped boots and left his old pants and ankle boots in the livery stable office to pick up when he brought the horse back. Turned out he needn't've got tricked out so early. The sun went down over Citadel Hill with still no sign of R.M.S. *Caledonia*. He waited through the night and into the next day and was actually asleep in a pile of hay beside the stall when the stableboy shouted through the doorway, "Sam! She's comin' in!"

Sam shook himself awake, brushing hay out of his hair. "What time is it?"

"Suppertime – 'bout six o'clock. Hurry!"

Six p.m. meant about half the run – or half Sam's half of it – would be night riding. Sam tightened the saddle girth, climbed aboard and trotted out onto the dock. The Cunard dock was a milling racket of stevedores, import agents and passenger-awaiters, just the kind of thing to send a horse into a panic – needn't've worried, this horse had done this a half a dozen times before and wove her way through the crowd like they were trees or lampposts. R.M.S. *Caledonia* was coming in fast, belled-out sails on the three masts and bowsprit, smoke-stack powering the twin paddlewheels kicking up white water at her sides. An ant-swarm of sailors furled her sails and the chug-clang of her steam engine slowed as she glided into shore.

There was another horseman on the dock, sitting tall in the saddle, a young man with thick muttonchop sidewhiskers and a broad felt hat with the front brim cocked up. Sam preferred to ride without a hat, figuring the galloping wind would keep the hair out of his eyes. When the other rider's eyes lit on Sam, the hat gave a little jerk and one side of the sidewhiskers lifted in a half-smile. It wasn't a friendly smile, more like *This should be easy*, and the head-jerk was more of a snort than a nod. Sam remembered Carstairs pointing out that Barnaby's riders wouldn't long have a job if they couldn't beat the Halifax Express's time, and remembered that Burt Hamilton's cut stirrup strap could've banged him up a lot more serious than it did.

The ship was close enough now for Sam to hear a bellowed, "Reverse engines!" and the paddlewheels churning backwards as *Caledonia* cozied up to the wharf. Two men were leaning out from the bow holding out leather shoulderbags and shouting. One was yelling, "Barnaby!" and the other, "Halifax Express!" Sam reached up but just as he got his hand on the Express pouch, Barnaby's rider jostled his horse against Sam's so the bag almost fell into the water. Sam managed to grab it, slung it over his shoulder and headed his horse off the dock as fast as he could without trampling anybody.

Clattering up and down brick and cobblestone streets – everything was up or down in Halifax – it wasn't possible to work up to more than a trot, not much room to manoeuver around the home-for-supper traffic. There were a couple of routes out of Halifax to the High Road, but Barnaby's rider took the same one the Halifax Express always took: up Cornwallis Street and turn right along Gottingen Street. The street soon turned into a dirt road and as the buildings and the traffic thinned out, Sam kicked his horse into a gallop and Barnaby's rider did the same. They ran neck and neck, just like Sam and not-John Thomson on much of the race from Hortonville to Windsor. But not exactly just like – Sam had a feeling that if he started trading riding crop whacks with the muttonchop-whiskered rider nobody'd be laughing.

Sam gained a bit of a lead at Ten Mile House, where Barnaby's rider changed horses. Five or six minutes further on, about half a mile before Fultz's Inn/Twelve Mile House, Sam swung up his dented old brass hunting horn – slung from the opposite shoulder as the dispatch case – and blew a blast. It was a kind of shrunk-down coach horn he'd found in a pawnshop in Halifax's Water Street. Windsor had a Water Street, too, but not quite the selection of pawn shops.

One thing Sam hadn't thought of, though, when he'd tried the horn out out behind the livery stable, was it was a bit trickier on a galloping horse, tricky to clap the metal mouthpiece to his lips without knocking his teeth out. He managed it – would prob'ly be easier next time – and blew out a two-note blast, changing the burring of

his lips and strength of breath to change the pitch the way he'd practised. A moment later he blew again, in case the first one was too far
off, and then again.

The Fultz's Inn horse was saddled and waiting. Sam jumped off
and jumped on without pausing to shake out his knees and ankles,
and was back on the road before Barnaby's rider rounded the bend
behind him. Sam kept generally running ahead – such a lighter rider
his horse might's well be running free. If he could get into Kentville
before Barnaby's rider, it would prove the lads could do as well as
the young men, maybe even better. They were riding straight into the
sunset now, the road ahead just an orange blaze with vague shadows,
but soon they'd be on forty miles of road Sam could ride with a bag
over his head.

But it seemed the horse the Halifax Express kept at Spencer's
Inn wasn't quite as fast as the horse Barnaby's rider changed to. By
the time they got to Windsor they were neck and neck again. After
they'd changed horses there – Barnaby's rider at an inn just down the
road from the Shipyard Inn, Sam gasping out, "Thanks, Clifford," as
he bounced onto Wellington – they quick-trotted knee to knee across
the covered bridge and then broke into a gallop again. The sun was
too low now to burn out anybody's eyes, but still cast a trace of daylight. Instead of trying to keep pace with Barnaby's rider, Sam hauled
back on the reins and held Wellington in until Wellington had had
a good long look – getting longer – of another horse's tail in front of
him, then let him go. Sam couldn't be absolutely certain, but it did
seem a lot like Wellington flicked his tail in the other horse's face as
they blew past.

After the swing bridge at Lower Horton, the road turned southerly and would stay that way all the way to Granville Point at Digby
Gut, but most of that would be Corey O'Dell's lookout. But only a
couple of hundred yards past the bridge, Wellington lurched sideways
like one of his hooves had skittered on a slick patch. Instead of falling
over, though, and likely rolling over Sam, Wellington found his footing and carried on full-gallop without a hitch.

The close call made Sam wonder if maybe there was another reason him and John Thomson had been favoured as possible Express riders over the other two asteriskers, besides that they'd been practise-galloping while the other two were sitting on their duffs. Carstairs hadn't said anything about this other possible reason, but then he wouldn't, would he? Fact was, Sam Smith and John Thomson had identified themselves as orphans, no next-of-kin no liability in case of accidents. Sam wondered whether he should mention that to John next time he saw her. He didn't wonder long, though. Mostly he was wondering how much longer he could cling to a galloping horse with muscles and bones and sinews that just wanted to lie down now, please.

In Upper Horton Sam was sore tempted to walk around for a bit before climbing onto the skewbald horse, but told himself there was only one more leg to go, though he felt like he had only one leg left himself. He did have to ask Jake the stablehand to give him a hand up. As he galloped out of Hortonville he tried to tell himself that that was no shame, since there'd been a few times he'd had to give a Halifax Express rider a boost onto the saddle in Windsor, and that was only *four* stages out of Halifax.

The sun was down now and the moon not yet up, but on this road Sam only needed vague shadings to know where he was and what was coming up next. He couldn't hear any sound of other hoofbeats behind him, but the other rider would've had to be awful close behind to hear through the barrel-roll of the skewbald's hooves. He began to feel a misty drizzly rain patting his face – maybe should've worn a hat after all, but not far to go now. So not far, in fact, he should start blowing his horn.

Sam was just lowering his horn from his first "incoming" to Kentville, when the skewbald horse neighed and shied and reared, almost throwing him out of the saddle – would've been a long drop onto rocky ground. The skewbald settled back onto all four feet but just stood there stiffly, showing no inclination to proceed. Sam's nose and a flash of white in the darkness told him why: a skunk was ambling across the road like he owned it. Sam waited a few long-seeming seconds, then clucked the skewbald into walking ahead gingerly. In the relative silence, Sam could hear a galloping horse – still a fair ways behind him, but closing the gap now. The skewbald consented to be nudged into a trot, then into a gallop again.

The horn was on its way back up to Sam's mouth – just round this bend and then blow another blast – when he saw light ahead. Shouldn't be – Kentville was still three-quarters of a mile away, or a half-mile at least, and the town couldn't throw light that far. Two tall torches were burning on either side of the road, and between them a man with a lantern. There were a few other men as well, some holding pitchforks or long cudgels and one holding a shotgun. Sam halted the skewbald before he smashed into them, the sudden stop almost throwing Sam out of the saddle and over the horse's head. The tall torches were at either end of a poplar trunk slung across the road on makeshift trestles. The right side of the road was crammed against the house-size boulder that it bent around, the left side was a steep drop into a ravine. Good place for a roadblock.

The grizzle-bearded man with the shotgun shouted, "Stand and deliver!" like he'd read it in a book, or more likely heard it in a barroom ballad. Before Sam could think of what to say to that, Barnaby's rider came careening around the bend and then frantically hauled back the reins to a rearing halt. When the Wall Street express's horse got all four hooves back on the ground, its nose was about half a length back from the skewbald's, and its rider held it there. The double-barrelled shotgun swivelled back and forth between the two riders, as if to show it had a barrel for each of them. The grizzle-bearded man behind it shouted again, "Stand and deliver!"

Sam looked to Barnaby's rider. Mr. Muttonchops, though older and larger, seemed content to hang back and let Sam deal with it, since he was there first.

"I *said*, Stand and deliver!"

"Deliver what?" Sam asked logically.

"The gold!"

"Uh... what gold?"

"The gold you got in them satchels! Who'dya think yer foolin'?"

"Can't fool us," came from one of the younger men, holding a torch in one hand and a pitchfork in the other. Even in the flickering light of the torches and lantern, the young men all bore some kind of resemblance to the one with the scraggly beard and the shotgun, like they were his sons or maybe his nephews.

Among other things, Sam was aware that it wasn't a good idea to let the skewbald stand too long hot and sweaty in the drizzly night and then make him gallop again. He said, "I don't think we're foolin' anybody, sir. We got no gold."

"Horseshit! You ain't goin' to all this trouble gallopin' back and forth just to deliver newspapers. Yer carryin' gold!"

"Aye," put in the one with the torch and pitchfork, "from the banks in England to American bankers."

Sam had to bite down on his teeth to keep from laughing, it was all so ridiculous. But the long cudgels were obviously meant to knock him off his horse, and if that didn't work then the pitchforks, and if not them then the shotgun.

The sound of a galloping horse cut in on them, coming from the direction of Kentville. Some of the amateur highwaymen turned nervously in that direction. Scragglebeard gave a half-glance over his shoulder but mostly kept his attention on the two horsemen in front of his shotgun. Then the galloping horse sound stopped, like it'd turned off on a side trail through the woods.

Scragglebeard shouted, "I ain't waiting all night! Hand over yer satchels!" and jerked his shotgun up and down to make his point. One of the younger men holding a long-handled cudgel cocked it over his shoulder, like it was time to stop waltzing around. Sam thought of maybe opening his shoulderbag to let them see there was nothing in it but paper, and not paper money. But what if they started tossing the papers out looking for gold, tossing them into the wind and rain?

A gunshot cracked the night – not from the shotgun but from the other side of the barrier. Sam saw the muzzle flash in the gloom beyond the torchlight, a flare of fire and sparks shooting straight up into the black sky, but the would-be road agents had been turned the wrong way to see it. They sure turned that way now. John Thomson's throaty voice called out of the darkness, "Back off and let the Express rider pass." Sam could now see the dim shape of a horseman on the far edge of the torchlight, right arm raised and above it the glint of a pistol barrel.

"Or *what*?" Scragglebeard called back, still holding the shotgun on Sam. "You already fired off yer pistol, what the hell ya gonna do now?"

Another gunshot and the pistol spat fire and smoke into the sky again. John Thomson's voice, loud but not shrill, came out of the dark, "You hearda *revolvers*? We all carry one. Where's yours, Sam?"

Sam thought just barely quick enough to say, "It's in my bag."

"Well, haul it out. Between the two of us we can blow this lot to hell in about three seconds. Be a self-defence turkey shoot."

Sam started rummaging in his dispatch case as though looking for his revolver, wondering how long he could pretend before they started wondering just how small his revolver was and how much damage it could do them. Needn't've worried – after hesitating about two seconds, the mastermind with the shotgun ran to the drop-off side of the road and jumped off feet first. The others followed. For a moment there was a rustling and crackling of the bold highwaymen scurrying away through the bush, then just the sound of a dropped torch sputtering in the mud and the ones at the ends of the barrier hissing in the drizzling rain.

John Thomson shouted, "Get going, Sam – Corey's waiting."

Sam looked at the poplar trunk barrier – about four feet high. He didn't know if the skewbald was a jumper, but for sure a game horse. He dug in his heels and shouted, "Hyah!" Just enough of a running start for the skewbald to sail over the fence. The other, heavier rider seemed to hesitate, but Sam didn't look back. As he neared the edge of Kentville he raised his horn and blew a warning, then went to get the dispatch case unlimbered for the handoff. Damn, he'd gone and slung the horn on over the shoulderbag, criss-crossing the straps. Getting them unscrambled while still holding the reins and keeping his seat was dicey, but he managed just in time to reach out the bag in his right hand to meet Corey O'Dell's left hand reaching back from Big Red picking up speed.

As Big Red galloped away, Sam slowed the skewbald to a walk and turned his head back toward the Stage Coach Inn's stables. Sam slumped in the saddle, now that it was over, but then straightened up again as his chest literally swelled with a big deep natural breath that seemed to breathe itself, and then another. He'd done it. Actually factually done it. All the way from Halifax to Kentville, and got there before Barnaby's express. Every muscle and bone from the top of his neck to the balls of his feet was sore, but he'd done it. With a little help – a *lot* of help.

Which got him to wondering why Corey O'Dell hadn't come to help John Thomson help him. Well, it did make some sense that if Corey O'Dell and Big Red were going to gallop full-out to Aylesford – and Corey all the way to Digby Gut – they wouldn't want to wear themselves down with a sidetrip beforehand. But then maybe too, Corey wouldn't be too sad if the first of the young lads to try a run didn't make very good time.

As Sam was wiping the sweat, foam and rain off the skewbald, John Thomson came trotting into the stable on one of the Stage Coach Inn's horses for hire. Sam wasn't exactly doing an A-1 job with the brush and rag, feeling a bit slack-armed and bowlegged, but he figured he should give it a try, given why the Halifax Express's regular Kentville stablehand hadn't been there to take charge of his horse. As John Thomson climbed down off the saddle, Sam said, "I dunno, uh, how to thank you for – "

"You can buy the beer."

As she stripped down and rubbed down the Kentville Inn's horse, and he continued with the skewbald, Sam said, "How did you, ya know... ?"

"I had this horse saddled and ready, just in case. In case of what, I don't know, case yer horse pulled up lame or something. If your first chance at riding express got screwed up, we'd never get another chance. I heared yer first horn-toot, then nothing, and the minutes passed, so..."

"But how the hell – *where* the hell – did ya ever get a revolver?"

John looked around warily. Sam looked around, too, and couldn't see anybody. Nonetheless, she said under her breath, "Tell you later."

Sam wrung out the wipe-rag, took a couple more weary swipes at the skewbald, then slumped back against the stall wall. "I oughta should get out the hoof pick and see if there's any pebbles or grit..."

"I can do that tomorrow morning before you head back – or you can. Come on, you got beers to buy."

The Public Room of the Stage Coach Inn was still part-full but winding down. Along one wall was a line of narrow wooden booths with fixed tables, like shortened-off church pews without the curlicues; the one at the far corner was empty. Once they got sat down, John Thomson pulled something out of his/her waistband – hidden by the table rim and coatflap – and clunked it down between her thigh and the wall, then said in a low voice, "It's perfect-safe unless you cock it, and that's damn hard to do even when ya want to."

After paying for the first round of ale – no small beer tonight – Sam took a sip and then a substantial quaff, then said, "Funny, Kentville beer tastes different nor Windsor beer. Nothin' wrong with it, just different. Tastes kinda like... chestnuts, or maybe walnuts..."

"*You're* nuts."

"Nuts" reminded Sam of food, he'd been sorta preoccupied the last four or five hours. Though it was well past suppertime, John managed to convince the barmaid to cobble together a thick beef and cheese sandwich with horseradish. Didn't take all that much convincing, the staff at the Stage Coach Inn seemed to regard John Thomson as family. If the Kentville Inn was anything like the Shipyard Inn, most of the staff *was* family.

Sam tore into his sandwich while John nibbled at the bits that fell off. In between chewing, they talked of how each horse had done on the run, about whether the roads were just about done with melt-off mud, about everything except what Sam wanted to hear about. But John had said, "Tell ya later" so it was up to her/him to say when later was.

After they'd finished their sandwich and ale, they went up to John's room and she dropped John Thomson's guttural voice. Must be hard on her throat. She took a flat wooden box out of her dufflebag, opened it with a little key and proceeded to carefully clean and reload the two chambers of the cylinder she'd fired off. In between concentrating on tricky bits, she said, "A few years ago, the United States army was hiring on foreign volunteers to fight in the Mexican war. We were desperate poor for money so me Da went down and signed up. For the first six months or so, he sent us letters with half his pay in them. Then the letters stopped coming."

Sam found he had to concentrate too, to take in what she was saying. He kept being distracted and baffled by the notion that the pink, slightly rounded lips the words were coming out of were actually a female mouth, despite the blunt-chopped hair and coarse, baggy workshirt.

"Then last year out of nowhere we got a parcel in the post. Inside was this box with his army revolver in it, and two letters. Well, one was hardly a letter, just a scrawly pencil note saying Da was... killed fighting bravely in the St. Patrick's Battalion."

Sam mumbled, "Sorry."

"The other one's more of a real letter, but we cannot read it and don't know of anyone who can – it isn't in English or French or Gaelic, we think probably Spanish." She paused to fit percussion caps onto the cylinders' steel nipples – Sam guessed they'd probably explode if pushed too hard. "Me Mam went to the U.S. consulate in Halifax to see might there be a widow's pension for foreign soldiers fighting in the U.S. army. They told her that the San Patricio Battalion was Irish Americans who turned their coats for Mexican gold. They said that if one of those turncoats chose not to send any of his traitor-money to his family, it was naught to the U.S. Government." John's voice had got a bit harder there, as if hardening herself to say it.

"So," she shrugged like shrugging that off, or pretending to, "when I decided to run off and try to join the Halifax Express, I took the revolver and all with me – the letters were still in the box. Mam was just going to sell the pistol anyway, even though it's about the only thing we had left of Da."

"Well, I'm damn glad you did, though I guess there's five sharp-as-hammers bandits who ain't." So they talked and laughed about that a while, about how scared they'd both been and how screwed they would've been if the roadblockers had called their bluff. In not very long, though, the long day and long ride caught up with Sam and his eyelids began to droop.

John said, "Though it's my room this time, I'll sleep on the trundlebed. I think your battered bones are better suited to a feather mattress than a straw tick."

They stripped to their dayshirts, climbed into their beds and Sam blew out the candle – might be her room, but the nightstand the candle was standing on was handier to him. Lying in her bed, between the sheets she slept between, Sam dozily pondered on what she'd told him of how she came to have a revolver. It did seem a bit strange that she seemed sorta closed-in defensive about the fact her old man had changed sides mid-war. Why should she care one way or t'other about Mexico or the U.S. of A? Oh, of course – if her father'd gone over to the Mexican side for big money but hadn't wrote home to say so or sent any of the money, he hadn't just turned his coat away from the U.S. Army but away from his family.

Sam could see how that might twist somebody's guts up. His parents hadn't betrayed him, just died from something nobody could control. There'd been times he'd thought his mother'd sold him down the river, but she'd only done what she believed was best for her children; there was no way she could've guessed what kinds of things might go on inside that orphanage school. Neither of his parents had turned their back on him, like John Thomson's father had on her and her mother and brothers.

But maybe the story the U.S. Consulate had told her mother wasn't all there was to it. Maybe that long letter in a foreign language told a different story. Thing was, Sam knew of someone in a place not far away who could read that letter for her – if it was in Spanish. It wasn't someone Sam liked to think about, or a place he liked to dwell on – or in – but there was probably the key to open John Thomson's letter. Question was, did she really want to know what was in it?

As Sam was picking at his breakfast and John wolfing down hers, she said between mouthfuls, "Not very talkative this morning."

"No, uh, just... tryin' to decide should I tell you something or not."

"Tell me what?"

Well, that'd gone and made the decision for him. "There's a place about a day's ride from here, *long* day's ride – not quite so long a day by stagecoach, coach-horse relays mean yer goin' at a brisk trot or gallop all the way, couldn't do that on one saddlehorse and you couldn't very well use the Express relays for private business..."

The expression on John Thomson's face said she could likely have figured all that out for herself, what new did he have to tell her?

"The Church moves priests around a lot, all over the world – *some* priests. There's a Father Gomez, he can translate that letter for you, if it's in Spanish and not Portuguese. I can't go there, but you could – or John Thomson could. How's yer French?"

"Huh? Ain't got none, or just about none."

"Well, you can get by there in English with most of the priests and some of the nuns. Won't be much Erfe spoke there."

"*Erse.*"

"You'll have to say you heard about Father Gomez from yer parish priest or some such..."

When Sam creaked up onto the skewbald to ride him back to Hortonville, his body told him that practice-riding three stages wasn't the same as galloping six stages for real. *Well, you asked for it, didn't ya?* The second half of an Express rider's job was to ride all six horses back to their billets, though nowhere near the same pace as he'd rode them out, and then take the stagecoach back to his. As Sam cantered out of Kentville, he had to wonder if he'd just done Miss John Thomson any favours.

VII

SEANA WAS ACQUAINTED with most of the stagecoach drivers from their relay stops at the Stage Coach Inn. This one, Orland, said when Seana told him where she wanted to go, "We don't usually stop there, Johnny-lad, just at the post house in the nearest town. But I think today I could maybe have a little harness trouble right around there," winking, "and tell the other drivers to watch for you flagging 'em down on your way back."

With the winter ice and spring mud finally gone, more people were travelling. The coach seats were full, so Seana and a couple of other passengers had to ride on top. It made for a lovely view, but you had to keep a good grip on the low railing that ran around the roof of the coach, and be careful not to grab onto one of the four lanterns at the corners for night-running – not that they were lit and hot in daylight, but if a rough bounce broke one off in your hand it would cost you more than your fare.

It was a long, rattley ride but still early afternoon when the coach stopped in what seemed the middle of nowhere. Seana picked up her dufflebag – only part-full, she'd left most of her things at the Stage Coach Inn – and climbed down uncertainly. Orland, apparently fussing with a harness buckle, pointed to a gap in the forest wall where a narrow road fingered off the High Road. Instead of calling out her thanks and drawing the other passengers' attention, Seana threw Orland a furtive half-wave half-salute and headed where he pointed.

The offshoot road was just a couple of ruts with weeds growing between, arched over with tree arms sporting new-green leaves. After a longish walk, the forest opened up to a collection of wood and stone buildings, some of them quite large, surrounded by lawns and fields. Sheep were grazing on the lawns, boys and girls of various sizes were hoeing in the red-brown furrows, and here and there were black-cassocked priests and black and white nuns. Seana's first thought was it seemed an odd place to build an orphanage; her second thought was that it made perfect sense: way off here in the depths of the forest, it would be daunting for a child to run away. Though for a Mi'kmaq boy raised in the woods...

Seana decided her best bet was to head for the biggest building and ask inside. Before she got there, a nun stepped in front of her and said something in French with a question mark at the end. In her John Thomson voice Seana said, slow and loud in case this nun didn't speak English, "I am looking for Father Gomez."

"Father Gomez? Mais oui, venez," beckoning to follow and moving toward the big building Seana'd already had in mind, but to a side door, not the main door Seana had been heading for. Inside was a corridor with closed doors too close together to be classrooms. The nun knocked on one of the doors and a deep voice inside called, "Entrez."

The Sister opened the door and gestured Seana inside, saying something to the room in French. There was a desk with a large, badger-haired priest behind it, writing something in a ledger. The priest stood up, saying something in French at Seana.

Seana said, "You're Father Gomez?"

"Ah – yes, I am." He nodded at the nun, who closed the door as she departed, then he gestured at a chair in front of the desk. "What is your name, my son?" His *Ses* had a kind of gap-toothed sound to them, though his front teeth showed no space between them, and *your* sounded more like *jor*.

Seana sat down – more like perched uncertainly – saying, "John O'Neill, Father." O'Neill was her mother's maiden name, shouldn't be too hard to keep straight.

Father Gomez sat back down and set down his pen. His big square hands, garden dirt embedded in the fingernails, seemed more suited for a straight-handled spade than a straight pen. He reminded Seana of one of those Irish country priests with coarse, patched and mended cassocks, who could as likely be found rebuilding a fieldstone wall as in the pulpit. "So, John O'Neill, were you sent to come here?"

"Not exactly, Father, not the way ya mean. I got told there was a priest what speaks Spanish at the orphanage – "

"We are not just an orphanage, my son, but a boarding school. Many of our pupils do have families at home, but home it is an isolated fishing village or farm that has no Catholic school nearby. So, John O'Leary – "

"O'Neill, sir."

"Ah, John *O'Neill*, you were sent here but not exactly... ?"

"Yes, Father. You see, this here letter," pulling it out of her inside coat pocket, "come from far away last year, but it ain't in English nor French. We thunk maybe it's Spanish." Hoped it was, or she'd just come a long way for nothing.

Seana handed the letter across the desk. Father Gomez unfolded it, flicked his slate-blue eyes back and forth across the first page, then said, "Yes, it is Spanish, and a very elegant Spanish it is." He flipped over to the second page. "It is from a brother of the Dominican order, somewhere nearby Mexico City." Back to the first page. "It is address to a Señora McCann... ?"

"My aunt, widow of my Uncle Ned." That caught in Seana's throat – maybe it was the "widow" or maybe the oddness of saying Da's Christian name out loud, or maybe just from saying too many sentences in John Thomson's guttural voice.

"Brother Matteo speaks very tender and respectful to your aunt, and regretful. He tells her that Eduardo McCann was kill-ed fighting heroically in the last battle in front of Mexico City." Now it was Father Gomez's throat that something seemed to get caught in. He pursed his mouth, sighed through his nose and blinked his eyes. Maybe it was the desperation suggested in "the last battle" or maybe it was that it had been fought in front of Mexico City – maybe he was Mexican. The blink-slicked slatey-blue eyes went back to moving side to side across the page. "Ah yes, then Brother Matteo explain-ess to your aunt about the San Patricio Battalion.

"Brother Matteo writes that many Irish inmigrantes did enlist with the United States Army to fight in a war to defend American settlers in New Mexico. But when the U.S. Army cross-ed the Rio Grande and kept on conquering southward, it became plain that this was not a war to defend but a war to *take* – take mucho land away from Mexico. This was not right, was not just, and so these Irish inmigrantes did cross over to the other side and so the San Patricio Battalion. It seems they fought a lost cause, because the ending of the war was that all of New Mexico and the California Territories are now part of the United States of America. But who knows, maybe the San Patricio Battalion stopped the U.S.A. from taking all of Mexico?"

Father Gomez lowered the letter a moment to speak for himself. "Batallón de San Patricios are unknown in the gringo world – pardon me, the English world – but I have hear many stories. They were not just Irish Americans but German Americans, American Americans, Frenchmen, runaway slaves... But the mostest group was Irishmen, so they were all St. Patrick's and their flag was green with a golden harp – The Minstrel Boys. Their last battle, last bastion before Mexico City, was at Churubusco, wall-ed convent mission – like The Alamo, except this time it is the American army outside. And, like

The Alamo, no matter how brave the fight, the army outside was too many, the men inside too few.

"As the battle grew hopeless, three times the Mexican soldiers fighting beside the San Patricios run up the white flag, and twice the San Patricios pull it down, because for them there is no safety in sur-render. But the third time they leave it up and take down the green flag, for the sake of their Mexican comrades who would be prisoners of war." Father Gomez looked at the letter again. "Ah, Brother Matteo says that luckily Eduardo McCann was kill-ed before the surrender."

"Luckily?"

"Yes, my child. To die in battle was a far less brutal fate than be a captured deserter traitor. Ah..." Father Gomez got teary again, blink-ing at the letter. "These Irish men of the San Patricio Battalion were faithful sons of the Church. When they realized they had been help-ing a Protestant country take land and people from a Catholic coun-try, they felt they must change sides."

Seana doubted that, at least as far as her father was concerned. Mam used to say that if church attendance were up to their father, her children would all be little pagans. But Da felt as strong about some things as some people felt about their religion. When the news came from Ireland to Nova Scotia that Daniel "The Liberator" O'Connell had been arrested and put in chains by the English over-lords, Mam had said to Da, "And how many others got scooped up that didn't make the newspapers? Men with smaller names but just as big mouths." Like many things Mam said to Da, she'd said it with a mixture of exasperation and affection.

Father Gomez suddenly let out a laugh – just a chuckle, actually, but he coughed it away as maybe unseemly. "Brother Matteo writes that at Churubusco there were many more American officers kill-ed than is usual. Usually it is many more plain soldiers than officers who are casualties. The San Patricios, you see, recognize their old officers, and made sure to shoot them first.

"Ahem. Lastly Brother Matteo writes that Eduardo McCann spoke often of his wife and children, his lovely daughter and three sons, and agonized that he could not so easy send letters home from blockaded Mexico as he could from the U.S. Army. But then Eduardo would say that since he was no longer in the U.S. Army he had no pay to send home anyway. Huh. Your Uncle Ned sounds like the kind of man who could make jokes while the bullets are flying."

"Yes." Seana had never seen Da when bullets were actually flying, but she'd seen him in other grim situations. "Yeah, he was."

"You were very close to your Uncle Ned..."

"Yeah, guess I was."

"Brother Matteo closes with his blessings and tells your aunt that her Eduardo is surely now in Heaven along with all the other brave martyrs who gave their lives defending Holy Mother Church." Father Gomez refolded the letter and handed it back across the desk, then took out a big, polka-dotted handkerchief and dabbed at his eyes and nose. The slate in his eyes was shining, tear-moistened and then polished with blinking the wetness away. "Your Uncle Ned sounds like a man you can be proud of."

Seana just nodded.

"You must be hungry, coming all this way."

"No, I ate at – " Seana cut herself off from saying the last Post House, the stagecoach dinner stop. Something told her not to be too specific about how she'd got there and which direction she'd come from. " – along the way."

Now that the letter had been dealt with, Seana had room to wonder about Father Gomez – wonder if this was the one, the priest that made Sam Smith run away and become Sam Smith. Looking sideways at Father Gomez, so as not to be obviously staring, she doubted it. He looked so blunt and weathered and straightforward, the kind of priest who'd lend a hand – and strong shoulders – at a barn-raising.

Father Gomez said, "Well, suppertime will be in another hour or so, and you do not wish to be travelling at night. There is no room in the dormitories, but you can bed down in the barn and be on your way in the morning."

There was something in the way he'd said that, and the flicker of hunger in his eyes – their brightness wasn't all from the blink-polished tearfulness of the letter – that reminded Seana of Mr. MacAngus leaning down from his horse and fingering her collar. A voice in her head said, *Yeah, that's the one – unless there's more than one.* A mischievous imp whispered she should take him up on his offer, just for the look on his face when he came out to the barn and she pulled up her shirt and pushed down her trousers. But then, maybe he was the kind who liked girls as well as boys. This wasn't a situation to play around with.

She said, "Thanks, Father, but I gotta be going. Got a ride partway with a farmer going to town, he said he'd be passing by your road again on his way back 'round sundown." She stood up and picked up her bag. "But thanks for helping out with the letter. It means a lot to me, and to my aunt."

"That is what the church is here for, my son, to help you through this life. If you are ever passing by this way again..."

"Thanks, Father, you bet. Bye now."

When Seana opened the door to leave, she found her way blocked by a boy standing at the threshold, a boy not quite as tall or dark as Sam. The chocolate brown eyes met hers for just an instant, then he looked down and stepped aside. Father Gomez called out something in French. The boy slunk inside and closed the door behind him. Seana got out of there.

The days had grown long enough that the sky was still blue when Seana got to the end of the school road. She sat on a mossy rock and watched the evening traffic rumble by – either home from market or into town from business in the country. A farm wagon slowed beside her and the driver called, "Need a lift, lad?"

"No, thankee sir, I'm waiting for someone." No point getting a ride a little ways down the road when this was the place the stagecoach drivers would be looking out for John Thomson – if Orland remembered to spread the word. The next stage wouldn't come till morning, but that would still get her back to Kentville faster than depending on kindly farmers to carry her a few miles at a time.

The friendly farmer did make her consider, though, that sitting by the side of the High Road she might be taken for a runaway from the orphanage. So she moved back into the woods, near enough to see the road but still be hidden by the undergrowth. One of the blankets out of her duffle, folded into a pad, made for a comfy place to sit and plant her back against a tree. For supper she had a couple of sardine sandwiches wrapped in butcher paper and a jar of beer; she left just enough for a nibble and sips in the morning. The vesper sparrows began to live up to their name, singing evensong, so Seana figured she better scout out a place to sleep before night came down. Clouds were gathering, maybe rain, so she found a wide pine tree with room to crawl under its skirts. It took some feeling around to find enough space between gnarly roots for her to curl up on. A doubled blanket gave enough padding for a prickly bed of fallen needles.

As the sun went down, the air turned cold, but not near as cold as the nights she'd slept rough in Halifax. And there was a warmth inside her that couldn't be entirely accounted for by the sandwiches and beer. She had her father back, thanks to Brother Matteo and horrible Father Gomez. The natural sounds of the forest grew eerie as it grew dark, but she was quite sure bears or wolves wouldn't venture so close to a road of human traffic when they had thousands of miles of wilderness still to themselves. Quite sure.

That wouldn't have been enough to keep her imagination from building bear claws out of two twigs scraping together, except that now it had another place to go: memories of perching in front of Da on a trotting horse – or behind him when she got bigger, clutching onto the back of his jacket; of Da grinning from the other end of a bucksaw as she "helped him" clear the tangle of trees in front of their Nova Scotia home; of Da winking down at her at an Irish horse fair when some horsetrader stretched the truth a little... There'd been kind of a veil between her and those pictures ever since Da's letters stopped coming, grown into a wall since Mam told her what the

American consulate had told her. But now they were free and clear again.

Mid-afternoon the next day found Seana back at the Stage Coach Inn. Fortunately, there was no miffed message, or unmiffed, from Mr. Carstairs waiting for her. She'd been worried he might pass through while she was gone, and wonder why the Halifax Express was paying John Thomson a shilling a day to maintain the Kentville and Aylesford stations when he was neither in Kentville nor Aylesford. There were three newspapers waiting for her, though. Megan the barmaid had been saving newspapers left in the Public Room ever since she found out "young Johnny" was interested in newspapers, which was ever since Seana had decided that someone whose living depended on what went into newspapers should have some idea what came out in them.

Today's haul, a two-day haul, was a copy of *The Nova Scotian* from the day before yesterday, yesterday's *British Colonist* and this week's *Acadian Recorder*. All three had articles and editorials about something bizarre that had happened in Canada. A mob of rioting Canadians had burned down their own Parliament Buildings, including the Parliamentary Library – out of 12,000 books in the library, only 200 had been saved. Seana had been half-thinking of going west to Canada when the Halifax Express was done, make herself a new life in a not-too-foreign place where there was no chance someone passing on the street might recognize her. But now – did she really want to try and make a life among people who were that crazy?

There were plenty of other, different things to read about: advertisements for someone to explain your dreams; for ointments and salves and pills and tonics; for barrels and crates and bales of cargo from the latest ship to sail into Halifax harbour; for farms and houses to sell or let; for The British Woollen Hall and The China Emporium. Amazing how much the Nova Scotia newspapers could cram onto four pages – actually just one page printed on both sides and folded over. There was usually a poem and a short story, though it was sometimes hard to tell the difference between the stories and the ads for pills and tonics and the news stories.

Sitting in the Public Room of the Stage Coach Inn with her newspapers, Seana could travel to other North American colonies, far-flung corners of the British Empire and to foreign countries. Ireland seemed to fall somewhere in between – besides the columns for Empire News and Foreign News there was sometimes one titled Ireland News. This one was headlined: Tragedy In Doolough. Doolough seemed like a name she should remember, but Ireland was so distant and she'd been so young. The news story said that hundreds of starving people had staggered to a place where they were to be given three pounds of grain apiece, if the officers judged they were starving enough. But the officers decided instead to go to a place twelve miles away, and left a message that anyone who wasn't at the new place by seven the next morning would be struck off the list. Hundreds of "walking skeletons" – as the newspaper put it – stumbled through the hills in a night of fierce winds and sleet. Some died in the ditches and were found with grass in their mouths from desperately trying to get some kind of sustenance to keep them going toward those three pounds of grain.

Then Seana remembered why she knew Doolough. Every August her family would travel through County Mayo to the horse races on the long beach of Doolough Strand. She remembered sitting on Da's shoulders to see a race go by, the muffled drumming of hooves on sand, and the salt air mingling with the smell of whole sheep roasting over fires behind the beach. And she remembered Mam and Da arguing there over whether they should leave Ireland for the New World. She couldn't remember who was on which side, but it had to be a few years before anyone dreamed there could be such a thing as the Great Irish Famine. Some of those who died in the ditches with grass in their mouths may have been ones who patted her head as she built sandcastles on Doolough Beach. She turned over the page.

In a corner of the next page was **RANAWAY**
from his employer, on the 12th this month WILLIAM BIGLOW, an
Indentured Apprentice, 17 years of age, dark complexion, round
shouldered. I hereby caution any person from harbouring him, as
they will be dealt with as the law directs.

James Hall
Onslow, Colchester County

Seana's throat went dry. That could be Sam. Not that he was
round-shouldered, or anybody's official apprentice, but he was still
the property of his guardians, the church. *Any person harbouring him will*
be dealt with as the law directs. As far as she knew they hadn't troubled
to put notices in the newspapers – they did have his parents' money,
after all, whether he was there or not. If he got found out, the Halifax
Express could be guilty of harbouring him. So if they suspected anything at all, they'd get rid of him immediately. And the same thing for
her.

Her eyes went adrift and unfocused and wandered across the
double open page. They caught on something even more alarming:

TELEGRAPH BEGINNINGS

What jolted her was it looked like it was going to say the Nova
Scotia telegraph line was beginning to be in business, which would
mean the Halifax Express was going out of business, a lot sooner than
she'd expected. But no, it turned out to be just one of those history
tidbits the newspapers kept around in case they needed something
to fill up a page. As she read it, she started to laugh, and wished she
could tell Sam about it now, instead of having to wait till the next
time she saw him.

The article said that one of the experiments that made the telegraph possible was a hundred years ago in France. Abbé Jean Antoine
Nollet had an idea that electrical impulses travelled instantaneously,
or at least so fast they might as well be instant. So he got two hundred monks to stand in a circle a mile round, each holding the end of
a wire in each hand, another monk holding the other end. Once they
were all in place clutching their wires, the Abbé Nollet hooked the

ends of the whole chain to a battery of "Leyden jars." Seana laughed out loud picturing Sam laughing at the picture of two hundred Father Gomezes with their hair standing on end and their eyes bugged out, maybe spurting words that weren't in the liturgy. Her laugh was so out loud that other people in the Public Room turned to look at her. She held her breath to hold the laugh in and lowered her head to seem like she was studying the newspaper intently.

She *had* been studying newspapers for the last few months, thinking about how those printed words didn't just appear magically. They were the product of dozens of people: reporters and editors and printers and telegraph operators and, yes, express riders who went galloping through the dark to carry the news from the Old World to the New. *More* than dozens for the New York newspapers, which Seana guessed must be bigger than these folded-over one-sheets. All those people had a part to play so that someone could sit at a chair in a tavern or kitchen and travel around the world or down the street or into the houses of parliament.

But then she asked herself who she thought she was fooling, besides herself. She was no more a part of it than the people who swept the floors and carried out the slops. Except that she was sweeping stables and wheeling out horse manure. She wasn't a rider for the Halifax Express and likely never would be.

VIII

WHEN SEANA NEXT sat down across a table from Mr. Carstairs, passing through on his more or less bi-weekly rounds, he said, "Luck shines upon you, Johnny-lad – or maybe doom. Not this coming run but the one after – next-next run – it's going to be young laddybucks all the way, Sam from Halifax to Kentville and you from Kentville to Granville Point."

That didn't leave Seana much time to get riding boots and riding breeches made – they didn't standard-size things that had to fit that well. She called herself several unpleasant names for not going ahead and getting that done as soon as Sam got his first chance at an Express run. But then, what if she'd gone ahead and spent the money and it turned out Sam's first chance was the asteriskers' last chance?

Though she'd been eyeing the sample riding boots in the Kentville cobblers' window, the fact was she could get boots *and* breeches in Windsor. And probably better made boots, since the Windsor Saddlery did more trade in that line so had more experience, thanks to the Windsor Turf Club. Seana was a bit nervous about coming anywhere near the circle of the Windsor Turf Club. Da used to spend some time there – where they'd be glad to listen to his opinions and advice but would never hire him on or pay him – and sometimes he would take Seana along. But the last time had been three years ago at least. She'd grown a lot taller since then, and she'd been playing John Thomson for long enough now that nobody would guess she was a girl. She hoped.

The morning after Mr. Carstairs's visit, Seana gave Big Red a gallop to Hortonville – a Sunday stroll to him – and the skewbald on to Windsor. Sam was in the Shipyard Inn's stable rubbing nose-stinging horse liniment into Wellington's offside fore hock. Sam seemed a bit surprised to see her, but didn't say so. As she stripped down and rubbed down the skewbald, she told Sam she'd been to the orphanage.

"Father Gomez still there?"

Glancing across the mottled brown and white back at Sam, Seana saw his eyes had gone slitty and his face hard. She said, "Yeah. Something creepy 'bout him. But he did translate the letter and I do believe he did it true…" She told him more or less what Father Gomez had told her. Sam seemed genuinely happy for her, like he understood, though oddly a bit relieved too, like he'd had his doubts things would turn out so well.

When she got to the part about some of the San Patricio Battalion being runaway slaves, he said, "Huh – acourse, that's why Clifford's here."

"Huh?"

"Clifford's pa was a slave in New York or Pennsylvania, one of them northern states, and in the old war of 1812 the deal was if an American slave took up and helped the British fight the war he could come north across the border and be a free man. So, a war with Mexico, makes sense a slave in Texas or whatever – one of them southern states – would wanna skip south across the border and fight for Mexico."

"Except it didn't turn out that well for the runaway slaves in the San Patricios."

Sam shrugged. "Guess they was all runaway slaves, one way or 'nother."

"My father was no slave!" By that time they were up in Sam's room and didn't have to pretend, though Seana did have to keep her girl voice from penetrating out into the hall or through the thin walls between garret rooms. From the look on Sam's face, she'd just got dangerously loud. She hissed, "Sorry, but you can't say – "

"Hell, we're all slaves, ain't we? Tuggin' our forelocks and sayin' yessir, no-sir, if-you-please-sir." That mollified her a little, though it did seem a bit childish of him to stretch that into meaning slavery. Everybody in the world had to say yes-sir no-sir to somebody. But the clanging of the noon bell in the shipyard across the road reminded Seana's stomach that there were more important things in life than arguing over words.

After lunch they walked down Water Street to Gerrish Street and uphill to Windsor Saddlery Ltd. Seana was glad to have Sam along, since he'd done this before. Inside, the sprawling rough-timbered shop smelled of saddle soap and leather and brass polish. Sam led her over to a back corner and called through a curtained doorway, "Hello?" Out came a balding, waistcoated gentleman with fuzzy white sidewhiskers joined to a mustache. An ivory-coloured tape measure hung from his shoulders like it had grown there. "This here frienda mine needs ridin' boots and britches. He's a Express rider, too." Sam turned to Seana. "Same kind as mine all right by you?"

Seana flicked back through memory-pictures of Sam in his riding gear at the Stage Coach Inn: cream-coloured doeskin riding breeches and black basic riding boots. It wasn't a very detailed picture. She said, "I guess..."

"Full seat?" asked the breeches/bootmaker.

That baffled her, picturing a pair of riding breeches with only half a seat in them, like long johns with the flap down. Sam said, "He means do you want a leather piece sewn on?" His finger drew a line up from one knee to his crotch and down to the other knee. "Supple leather but grippy," though his supple sounded more like soople. "Worth a few extra shillin's to wear-and-tear pigskin, not yers."

Seana rasped in her John Thomson voice, "No skin off my arse." Sam elbowed her and she elbowed him back. The snow-whiskered tailor seemed unperturbed by the shenanigans of young gentlemen, seen it all before and more. Seana nodded at him, then added, "Yep, full seat." Even though she hated to part with a few more shillings of her savings, she remembered the welt on her leg that Sam had soothed with a poultice. And that was from only three stages of a practice run, not the five she'd have to ride for real.

"If the young gentleman would take a seat and take off his... shoes."

Seana sat in the wooden armchair indicated and unlaced her battered ankle boots. The measuring man perched on a sort of elongated footstool and lifted Seana's right foot onto its slanted wooden nose. He plied his measuring tape back and forth and side to side on Seana's feet, pencilling in a notebook, then remarked, "Small feet for a lad this height. Perhaps the young gentleman has some Welsh in his background?"

Seana shrugged and grunted, "Could be," though her parents would be appalled.

"If the young gentleman would please stand up, feet apart..."

As Seana was rising out of her chair, the shop bell tinkled and a portly gentleman came in and headed for their corner. Seana recognized him. He and Da had had a difference of opinion as to whether a certain mare was pregnant or just a late heat. Da had turned out right. The measurer called, "Oh, Mr. DeWolfe, I shan't be but a moment..."

"No hurry, Abner, I'm just loiterin' away the day," and Mr. DeWolfe ambled off – not far enough off for Seana's liking – perusing the various saddles mounted on trestles. All it would take was for Mr. DeWolfe to remark, "That lad looks a lot like the McCann girl,

the runaway," and she'd be grabbed and bundled back to her family –
quite likely Mr. MacAngus's family now.

Abner bent forward to measure Seana's waist and hips, hands
and tape wrapping around her in a way they surely wouldn't if he
knew she was a girl. She found it difficult to stand and be measured
when what she really wanted to do was get out the door and away
from where Mr. DeWolfe's eyes might linger on her and jog his memory. Abner frowned at his notes, measured her hips and waist again,
then shrugged without correcting and knelt in front of her. Holding
one end of the tape measure against the top of her ankle, he ran it up
the inside of her leg to within a fingernail of rude and jotted down
the result. "On which side does the young gentleman dress?"

"Uh..." She wondered if maybe that meant which pant leg the
young gentleman put on first, and what possible difference that could
make.

Sam coughed and said, "He means which side ya tend to hang
yer tackle, so's he can tailor in a bit of slack. Me, I dress right."

"Oh. Me too."

"Dress right," Abner murmured to his moving pencil. "And would
the young gentleman also care to purchase a pair of spurs to go with
his order? We have a various selection of choices," gesturing at a distant wooden rack with sunlight twinkling on steel.

Seana hadn't considered that question. When she was little she'd
heard big people saying to each other that spurs were just for very
experienced riders or inexperienced horses, but maybe things were
different in Nova Scotia. The three horses she'd been practising on,
though, didn't seem to have any trouble reading her foot signals without spurs. And when she thought back to Sam's first run in his new
gear, when he'd handed off the dispatch pouch to Corey O'Dell and
then climbed down at the Stage Coach Inn, he hadn't been wearing
spurs. So if he had bought spurs with his outfit they'd been a waste
of money. "No thankee, won't need spurs. Not with the horses I'll be
riding." She hoped that was true of the three horses she'd be riding
after Finbar's leg.

"Very good. I believe I have all the measurements needed. Your boots and breeches should be ready for you in three or four weeks, depending."

"But I need them in nine days – in Kentville!" Seana only remembered halfway through to drop her voice into her throat and make it more slangy. Maybe Abner would think the young gentleman's voice was still changing.

Sam said to Abner, "You done mine in a week."

"That was then. Summer's coming on and all our patrons are getting primed for outdoor activity."

Seana clutched a straw. "Ya know, people gather on the streets to gawk at the Express riders galloping by – be even more so now as summer's coming on. Last run Sam rode, I had a couple people ask me if I knowed where he got them fancy boots and breeches."

"Hm... Maybe I *could* bump another order aside and have yours done within the week..."

Riding the skewbald and Big Red back after they'd already had a hard gallop today would not be a good idea – twelve miles might be easy for Big Red, but twenty-four wouldn't be – so Seana stayed over in Windsor. At one point when they were talking in Sam's room – talking softly so no one passing by the door would hear a girl's voice – she happened to notice how the candle amber-highlighted the contours of the left side of his face: straight nose, lips with an almost feminine curve, the beginnings of laugh lines – or sad lines – at the corners of his eyes, lines that shouldn't be there in somebody so young. Though his nose was straight from straight-on, from the side it stuck out proudly and had a hawklike hook to it, not a pitiful little snub like hers. In the morning after breakfast she happened to notice the lithe and springy curve of his back when he bent to check the skewbald's saddle girth. She was quite sure those were things John Thomson wouldn't be noticing, or shouldn't.

John Thomson's new riding boots and riding breeches arrived on the stage from Windsor on Monday of the week he was scheduled to ride. By that time Seana had several times over worked through every panicked possibility of what to do if her new gear didn't show up in time – from making the run in her clumsy farmer boots to trying to fit into Sam's riding boots and breeches, and doing it quickly when the changeover wasn't supposed to take any longer than the changeover of riders passing on the mail pouch like relay racers handing on the baton. Especially panicked since there'd been a couple of times already that the Royal Mail ship from Liverpool had crossed the ocean lickety-split and the rider from Halifax had galloped into Kentville half-past Tuesday – the first time had been one hell of a surprise and a scramble.

As soon as she got the Windsor Saddlery parcel in her hands, Seana ran up to her room and changed. Fit like they were made for her, so to speak. Abner and his elves had done their job well – bloody should, given what she'd she'd paid for the gear. The thighs of the breeches weren't quite skintight, had just a little bit of flex room in them. Riding breeches weren't cut tight and precise for looks – any creases or wrinkles between you and the horse could be worse than uncomfortable, especially when riding seventy miles at one go. These ones opened on the side, with a bit of drawstring lace-up snuggery on one hip, same at the bottom of each leg where they fit into the boots.

The boots didn't even need breaking in, were already supple in the places where they should be. But she would've felt silly stomping around the inn in them when she didn't need to, so she changed back into her regular clothes until after noon on Tuesday, the very earliest possible time the Express might get to Kentville. Tuesday afternoon and evening passed in a strange amalgam of sharpness and dullness, pacing the same stretch of stableyard or fidgeting in the same chair, trying to keep her edge without wearing it down with nervous energy, eating enough supper to get her through the night but not so much she'd have a leaden lump in her stomach if Sam came galloping in before she'd had time to digest. He didn't.

A while after midnight, Seana curled up on a horse blanket on the hay pile in a corner of the stable. She didn't really expect to sleep, just lay there vibrating, but next thing she knew the stableboy she'd given sixpence to stay up and keep watch was shaking her shoulder shouting, "I heared a horn!" She was on her feet before she was awake, fumblefingering to tighten Big Red's bridle buckles and saddle girth. As she jogged out of the stables holding Big Red's reins she asked Leonard the stableboy what time it was. "'Bout four – was three-thirty last time I ducked in to have a look."

So more than an hour before sunrise. Luckily a lot of the miles she'd be riding in the dark was road she was familiar with – she'd even galloped the leg from Aylesford to Middleton a couple of times. As that was passing through her mind she was lining Big Red up on the road and making a jump for the stirrup – missed, got it the second time and swung on board. She heard the ta-ra of Sam's horn – most riders were satisfied with a one-note blast, but Sam always blew two notes rising, rousing – close-in now, then thumping hoofbeats growing out of the stillness.

The big skewbald and its puny rider came into the light of one of the lanterns at the ends of Mill Bridge, disappearing into the shadows between them and reappearing larger. Seana nudged Big Red with the heels of her new boots and he clopped into a trot and then a canter. She reached back her left arm for the handoff like she and Sam had practised, hoping it would come off for real. Needn't've worried – Big Red and the skewbald had done this for real a dozen times before with half a dozen different riders. As she closed her fist around the dispatch pouch's shoulder strap, Sam shouted, "Got a few minutes!"

She only half-heard him. She yelled, "Hyah!" and Big Red steamed up to a gallop. She waited till he'd hit his stride and she stopped bouncing before shifting the mail satchel's strap over her head and onto her shoulder. Thinking back and deciphering what Sam had shouted, she had a few minutes' lead on Barnaby's rider. Given what she'd seen of the horse Barnaby's riders used on this leg, and what she knew of Big Red, time to open up that lead.

One thing about riding in the small dark hours of the morning, there was no other traffic to worry about, and any odd souls who might be on the road would hear a galloping horse coming miles away. They galloped straight on through villages where in daylight they might have to slow to a trot to weave around farm wagons and pedestrians. In the darkness, she was mostly sound and feeling: the swell and ebbing of the immense lungs between her knees, the surge and thunder of their forward motion...

The ostler at Aylesford grumbled about having to stay up all night; Seana didn't pause to listen, just jumped up onto Finbar and back on the road. The sky started to lighten as she left Middleton on a horse she wasn't well-acquainted with, onto roads she knew even less.

The black sky became dark blue and the bouncing stars began to fade out. Off to her left, the first hint of red crept over the South Mountain. Way off to her right, the black scarp of the North Mountain separated itself from the sky. Actually, the North and South Mountain weren't really mountains but the long ridges that formed the walls of the Annapolis Valley, and they were as much east and west of each other as north and south. Factually, Seana didn't even see the sense in calling it the Annapolis Valley. Kentville was officially in the Annapolis Valley, but it was on the Cornwallis River flowing northeasterly; the Annapolis River flowing southwesterly didn't even appear till around Aylesford...

Seana shook her head to clear it of such saddle-punchy wanderings and focus on the here and now. Unfortunately, what that made her notice was that the saddle on the Middleton horse was rubbing her the wrong way, even through the leather overlay on her riding breeches. Corey O'Dell's insistence on bringing his own saddle and shifting it from horse to horse didn't seem so hoity-toity now. Well, she didn't have her own saddle anyway, and she'd be off this one in just a few more miles to the next change – try to ignore it and just keep your mind on the horse and your eyes on what's in front of you.

The sky turned pinkish-grey, then blue and white; the North and South Mountains turned green, mottled shades of evergreens and summer leaves. Likely the morning birds were singing, but Seana couldn't hear them through the booming of hooves, the creaking of the saddle and the horse's straining breathing and her own. It was full light by the time the road wound up a hill whose tall trees had been logged for timber; back behind her was a stretch of flatlands with only a few trees in the red-brown fields. So a look to her left gave a clear view of the couple of miles of road behind her. A tiny ox cart and a slightly less tiny hay wagon were gradually moving toward each other. Between them was a smaller dot moving much faster – had to be Barnaby's rider. Maybe a one-and-a-half-mile lead: six or seven minutes, more or less – would've been less if the horse behind had been Wellington.

In farm fields or villages, people stopped what they were doing to wave their hats as the Halifax Express passed by. Sometimes Seana could even hear cheers, but there really was no sound left in the world but the staccato earth-drum *Fa-da-lump* that'd been thudding in her ears and through her body since the dawn of time. None of the villages, though, seemed big enough to be Bridgetown, the next relay station. It was supposed to be about thirteen miles past Middleton. She was sure she'd gone that far already, though just guessing by the seat of her pants – literally – and by how hard the horse was labouring, with flecks of foam flying off his sides.

For a long time now the road had been snaking through a forest looming so thick and dark and tall she felt like a mouse skittering along the floor of a crowded cathedral. She began to think she must've gone and passed through Bridgetown without knowing, but then a break in the trees and a bend in the road showed her a river on her left – had to be the Annapolis. And since it was still on her left, she couldn't've passed through Bridgetown yet: she'd been told Bridgetown got its name because that was where the High Road crossed over the Annapolis River. So the feeling that she must've gone farther than Middleton to Bridgetown was just because she was tireder than when she rode from Aylesford to Middleton.

The forest faded to farm fields and the needles of church steeples appeared up ahead. More than one church, had to be a town not a village. She brought her horn up to her mouth and blew a blast, then another a moment later, but she had to put the horn down and slow down as the road became a street. She'd been told there were three inns in Bridgetown, but one being The Temperance Hotel left only two of any interest to the Halifax Express. Those two were straight across the street from each other and the one Seana wanted was Quirk's Golden Ball Inn, the other was the relay station for Barnaby's Express. But Seana suddenly couldn't remember which was supposed to be on the right side of the road and which on the left. Up ahead on her left she saw a red-shirted man leading a saddled black horse out onto the road and stopping there. It was a big, glossy horse, no farm cart plodder or dainty lady's trotter, and the man in the red shirt made no move to mount him, just held his bridle and waved toward Seana.

But what if the left side of the road was Barnaby's side? What if Barnaby's people had heard that this leg of this run of the Halifax Express was going to be ridden by a first-timer and decided to try a trick? The black horse looked big and strong, but there was no way to tell whether its wind was broken or it had a weak leg that would pull up lame after a mile. Then something glinted in the tree the big black horse was standing beside. The tree was a tall Lombard poplar, pointing all its feathery fingers to the sky, and hanging from it was a gold-painted ball. Quirk's Golden Ball Inn.

Seana reined in and jumped down and almost fell down, her legs had gone so alien – rubbery and stiff at the same time. The red-shirted stableman didn't seem surprised, just stooped forward and trellised his hands to give her a boost up onto the black horse's saddle. It would've been embarrassing except that Sam had told her that some of the full-grown riders needed a boost up after three or four stages. She wouldn't have known if Sam hadn't told her, since in Kentville the riders didn't have to mount up again.

As he boosted her up, Red Shirt said, "Aren't seen ye before. First time, lad?"

"Yeah," was as much an intake of breath as a vocalization.

"Ye just stay straight on this road, don't take the turnoff to the bridge." Seana just nodded, took hold of the reins, dug in her tired heels and held on to the fresh horse and fresh saddle. As the town petered out, there was a faded wooden sign: Granville Road. Logically the road to Granville Point. Granville Road turned out narrower than the High Road, and Seana hoped had less traffic as well. She was finding it increasingly difficult to breathe – her breastband seemed to be getting tighter and was itchy as hell. Her stomach was reminding her she hadn't eaten for nine or ten hours and had taken a pounding since then. She hadn't slept more than one hour in the last thirty. Her eyes were dry and prickly from peering ahead into the wind. Wouldn't hurt to close them for just a moment, could it? The horse surely knew this road.

The velvety black in front of her eyes looked so soft she fell into it. No, she *was* falling – she opened her eyes with a yelp and saw green ditch weeds rushing by straight below; she was slumping and sliding off the saddle. She grabbed hold of the saddle rim and righted herself and held on tighter than before. That burst of fear was enough to keep her alert and focused for another couple of miles, but then the pains and weariness began to creep back. She told herself there was only one more change of horses to go. But maybe that was one too many. After all, by the time she got to the last changeover she would've already galloped as far as Sam Smith and half the other Express riders – the second half of the run was actually some miles longer than the first, since Kentville and the Stage Coach Inn hadn't had the thoughtfulness to build themselves at the exact halfway point between the Halifax waterfront and Granville Point. And after all she was just a girl – even if only Sam Smith knew that – couldn't be expected to match up to the likes of Corey O'Dell.

What difference would it make if she told the ostler at Granville Ferry – the last relay station – that he could have twenty percent of John Thomson's pay for this run if he rode the last leg? Maybe the stableman wouldn't full-out gallop the whole way and maybe Barnaby's rider would catch up and pass him, but so what? The

Halifax Express had come in a few minutes behind Barnaby's a couple of times before and it'd been no great disaster. John Thomson could just go back to being a stableboy at a shilling a day plus board and room. Or could he? If all the Halifax Express wanted the asteriskers for was to take care of the horses, Mr. Carstairs could've just paid all the inn's ostlers a little something and check up on them every couple of weeks. And what had all those practice runs been for, and the new riding breeches and boots? And all that big talk and high opinions of herself, being able to make her own way in the world?

The road wound along the river flats now. Up ahead she saw a tall flagpole flying a flag that wasn't a Union Jack, and remembered someone saying something about Hall's flag at Hall's Entertainment House, the last changeover of horses. In Ireland an Entertainment House would've meant at least some music or maybe a play, here it just meant a place that entertained you to a meal and a bed for the night. While that pebble was rolling through Seana's battered brain, she was raising the horn to her lips and blowing a feeble blast. Then she had to pay attention to what was on the road in front of her – Granville Ferry was the name of a town, not just the ferry.

Nearby the flagpole, a baldheaded man was holding a big brown horse already saddled and bridled. A boy was quickly running the flag down the flagpole and had a folded red flag tucked under one arm. As Seana slid down off the black horse, she still hadn't made up her mind whether to quit and make an offer to the ostler or the stableboy. But the baldheaded ostler was already bending forward with his hands cupped together. Her aching left leg automatically raised itself to put its boot sole in his hands. Next thing she knew she was up on a new saddle and reaching for the reins. The ostler said loudly, like he expected her to be a little dull of hearing by now, "Easy directions from here: just stay on this road, if yer horse starts swimmn' ye've gone too far. Just fifteen miles and yer race is run."

Fifteen miles? didn't quite jump out of Seana's mouth, the brown horse was already jumping into a gallop. Nobody had warned her that the last stage of this leg was twenty-five percent longer than a regular relay stage, just when a rider was just about done in. Well, the brown horse must be used to it, so all the rider could do was hold on. As Seana left the town behind her, she heard a one-syllable bark of thunder from way off on her left. She remembered reading there was a British army fort at Annapolis Royal, across the river from Granville Ferry. She guessed the red flag was a signal to the fort to fire a signal gun to warn the steamboat waiting at Granville Point. The long arm of the Halifax Express sure pulled a lot of levers.

The air turned soft and salty as she galloped south from Granville Ferry, with the tide-washed Annapolis River Basin on her left and the Bay of Fundy just the other side of the escarpment on her right. The countryside galloped by in a blur of brown and green and grey, time had become a blur as well. Her back felt like someone'd been hammering her spine for a fencepost. When – if – she ever finished this ride she hoped she wouldn't have to sit down on anything for a week.

The one constant and clear-focused spot in her field of vision was a place on the road about a hundred yards in front of her, always moving forward but always just far enough ahead that she could bring the horse to a stop without a tumble that could break its legs or hers. But after a blurry while something peripheral caused her eyes to flick upward for an instant. Somewhere off ahead and to her left, a column of grey-black smoke was rising into the sky. It was too thick for someone burning off a brushpile, not wide enough for a forest fire. She lowered her eyes again and kept them on the road.

The treed wall of the North Mountain began to press in on her right, threatening to squeeze the road into the water. Then the road left the flat pastures behind and climbed into the woods, winding along the face of the escarpment. Through gaps in the trees on her left, Seana could see steel-grey water a long fall below, sunlight glinting on the waves. The sea smell grew stronger as the road broke out of the woods and took a steep drop down towards a long wooden wharf with a stone breakwater beyond, and beyond that the wide Annapolis Basin narrowed abruptly, choked into a tight channel by green and black cliffs sloping in from either side. That pinched-in channel would be Digby Gut, the bottleneck the fearsome Fundy tides squeezed through, and beyond it open water all the way to Saint John on the New Brunswick shore.

Seana wasn't as aware of the tides as folks who lived near the shore, but she guessed the tide must be almost all in or just starting out, since the pilings of the wharf were darkened damp for about six feet above the water. There was a steamboat moored on either side of the wharf and their decks were about even with the dock, instead of riding far below as they would've been at low tide. The column of dark smoke – she could see sparks in it now – came from the two smokestacks, widening and joining as they got higher. Seana didn't know much about steam engines, but she guessed the signal gun from Annapolis Royal was so they'd have time to build up the fire and enough steam pressure to get under way the minute the news packet got on board.

Both ships had hove in backwards, tied to the wharf with their bows pointing toward open water. In the stern of one boat stood a man with a spyglass, scanning the road; in the stern of the other stood two men smoking cigars: Mr. Daniel H. Craig and Corey O'Dell. Seana slowed her horse to a trot, then to a walk along the maybe-slippery wharf. As she got closer, tuft-bearded Mr. Craig remarked, "What – Hyde's hiring children now?"

Corey O'Dell tossed the stump of his cigar in the water, saying, "Well, he got here, didn't he? And ahead of Barnaby."

Mr. Craig didn't reply to that, just snatched the dispatch case from Seana's outstretched arm, turned and shouted, "Cast off!"

Another voice – Seana assumed it was the captain – bellowed, "You heard the man, cast off!"

As a couple of sailors scrambled to unfasten the lines and get back on board, Corey O'Dell jumped off onto the wharf. Seana slid down off her horse onto wobbly legs, unsure what to do next. There was no inn in sight where she could stable the Granville Ferry horse and collapse. Corey O'Dell came toward her saying, "Damn lucky for you the tide's not out or you'd've had to pull your ride up short and climb down thirty feet of wharf ladder to hand off your satchel." Seana didn't know what to say to that, so just shrugged. "Though I bet you've had enough riding for one day – or one month. Kinda dizzy-making, eh?"

"Yeah."

"But a helluva ride."

Seana grinned. "Yeah."

"Well, you don't have to climb back on a saddle today. I got a carriage coming, out of Granville Ferry – deal was he was supposed to harness up and start for here as soon as the Halifax Express passed by. You can hitch your horse to the back of the carriage and hitch a ride with me."

"Grand. Thanks. But... where to?"

"The Sinclair Inn and Posthouse in Annapolis Royal. That's the regular bivouac for Halifax Express riders once they've done their run. Didn't Carstairs tell you?"

"Maybe I forgot."

"Doubt that. He probably figured Craig would tell you. Foolish fancy – these all-fired Yankee businessmen got no time for niceties when there's money to be made. For Hiram Hyde the Halifax Express is an adventure, for Craig it's just a business venture. Ach, I shouldn't give you the notion Craig's just a cold sorta fish. He must've been a boy once – he started his career raising pigeons."

"Pigeons?"

"Natural progression. Newspapers' been using homing pigeons since the dawn of newspapers, to fly messages back to headquarters from roving reporters. Then Craig moved up to horses – ran a horse express afore this one, down south, galloping news and mail to Washington from the Mexican war." That circle-twisted Seana's already dazed and dizzied mind. Maybe Daniel Craig's horse express had carried some of her father's letters in its mailbags, and here she was riding for Daniel Craig's Halifax Express.

Corey O'Dell brought her back to the present with, "So Craig knew how to run a horse express and Hyde knew Nova Scotia, so here we are. Speakin' of which, we'd best be gettin' off this wharf 'fore we get trampled by Barnaby's galloper. Though I've got half a mind to stand your horse sideways and block him – but we've enough of a lead now to get to the telegraph office first and foremost."

Off the wharf, the Granville Ferry horse bent her head to nibble at juicy spring grass. Seana kept half an eye on her so she wouldn't eat too much before cooling down. Corey O'Dell took a silver cheroot case out of an inside coat pocket, stuck one in his mouth and proffered the case to John Thomson. Seana said, "No thanks, they turn me green."

"And too late for St. Paddy's Day. But wise lad, they stunt yer growth, and I should know." Standing so close, in her new boots without rundown heels, Seana realized she was nearly as tall as Corey O'Dell, though he had more heft to him. From a distance it was hard to gauge how tall or not-tall he might be, because his head was a size too big for his shoulders – big head but not big-headed.

In between puffs on his cheroot, Corey told her a story about Hiram Hyde, not exactly a disrespectful story but not forelock-tugging respectful either. Seemed Mr. Hyde was as fond of a drink as the next man, and didn't take his money as seriously as serious businessmen were supposed to. Seana felt a bit privileged to be privy to the kind of inside information Corey O'Dell was floating her way. Well, John Thomson was a member of the club now, a full-fledged Express rider, even if an exhausted Express rider.

The Granville Ferry horse raised her head and nickered, hearing another horse on the road before Seana did. A horseman came galloping past them and onto the wharf. After handing off his shoulder bag to the waiting steamer, the rider looked around uncertainly – like he was expecting a place to put up his horse and put up his feet – then turned and trotted grimly back up the road he'd galloped down. Although he was a rival rider, Seana felt for him at the bottom of her aching bottom. Especially since he was kind-hearted enough to let his galloped-out horse pace an easy trot that bounced him up and down on the saddle. Then again, posting with the trot did mean his bum was in the air for every second bouncy horse step.

Not long after Barnaby's rider bounced out of sight, an open carriage came down the road. They hitched the brown mare to the back of it and climbed aboard. Seana was pleased to discover that straightening her legs out and angling her back rested a different angle of her butt on the button-leather upholstery than would've sat on the saddle, felt hardly painful at all, almost comfortable. As they trotted along in style, she said in her John Thomson voice, "I should pay yez half the carriage-hire."

"No fear, it's on the Halifax Express. Provided tight-arse Craig don't squint too close at the accounts. Ach, there I go again soundin' disparagin' of Mr. Daniel H. Craig. He's usually pleasant enough company, but just now in a bit of a twist over Fog Smith."

"Fog Smith?"

"Mr. F.O.J. Smith, known as Fog with good reason. Old crank owns the only telegraph line 'tween Portland and Boston. Foggy's taken it in mind to refuse to transmit messages from any entity what's connected with Daniel Craig. It may be that our Danny Boy done him some insult or injury in the past, or maybe the Wall Streeters are bribing him, but either way he won't budge. So The Associated Press is trying to inveigle another telegraph company to run a new line, but in the meanwhile Craig's had to hire an express railway train to run the dispatch from Portland to Boston every run. That takes a bite out of the profits. I'm guessin' the A.P. pays the Halifax Express about a thousand U.S. per run, but Craig and Hyde would like to keep as much of that in their pockets as possible."

Seana's mind boggled at such a gigantic figure as one thousand American dollars. But then, once you took out the expenses of buying and boarding all those fine horses, and the riders' fees, and the steamer across the bay, and the asteriskers and Mr. Carstairs...

Nonetheless, she was still boggling when they trotted into Granville Ferry. The ostler at Hall's Entertainment House took charge of the brown mare as well as the carriage horse and carriage, leaving Seana and Corey free to ride the ferry across the river to Annapolis Royal. The Sinclair Inn turned out to be a big pink building with double doors in front and only a short walk from the quay, which was lucky since Seana didn't know how far she could walk. Everything seemed numb and cottony to her, everything but the aches and pains to remind her various parts of her body were still there.

In the Public Room of the Sinclair Inn, the barmaid bugled, "Corey! I thought you weren't riding this run."

"Didn't, came over with the steamer. Me mate Johnny Thomson here did the ridin', and he's probably even hungrier nor I am. I know we're past breakfast and 'fore dinner, but..."

"Clam chowder's on the simmer."

"Sounds lovely, Maisy darlin'. And a couple pints of ale."

The clam chowder and butter-slathered soda bread slid down easily, as did the ale. With a couple of different kinds of warmth glowing in her stomach, Seana stretched out and grew comfortable. So comfortable and incautious that she said to Corey O'Dell, barely remembering to keep to her John Thomson voice, "I thought you'd be kinda sour on us asteris – us young lads, being as how we're sorta... stealing from you, doing your job for less'n the Express'd pay you."

"Did piss me off at first, but then I thought maybe gettin' a few cut-rate rides out of you lads lets the Express stay in business and pay us what we're worth – and I've got other interests besides the Halifax Express." He angled his size-too-large head sideways and squinted at her. "You look about all in, and I know the feeling. Maybe mid-morning by other people's clocks, but the middle of the night to you. Come on, I'll show you your kip. T'ain't much more'n a cubbyhole the Express rents for its riders, but all you want is a bed."

It *was* a cubbyhole – barely room to stand beside the skinny bed. Seana drowsy-mouth murmured to Corey O'Dell standing in the doorway, "But where'll you stay?"

"Don't you worry 'bout me, I got more palatial digs when I'm lodgin' on me own stick. Just flop down and sink away – you've earned it."

After Corey was gone, Seana noticed that the cubbyhole did have a brass bootjack screwed to the floor, which saved her calling him back to manhandle her riding boots off. She just took off her boots and breeches and jacket and flopped down on her back, but as soon as the back of her body hit the bed she let out a yelp and rolled over. She thought of knocking on Corey O'Dell's door and asking him if there were actual bruises on her ass, then decided that wouldn't be such a good idea. The thought did prove to her, though, that she'd definitely gone giddy, and not just from weariness and ale. Saying and thinking she could ride an Express run was one thing, doing it was another. Now she'd done it. And if she'd done it once she could do it again. She sank into sleep with a smile.

Not quite done it, though. Come next morning she had to ride four of yesterday's five horses back to their home billets. The Granville Ferry horse was already where it should be, but that still left a lot of riding. She thought of offering to buy one of the embroidered throw-cushions on the sofa in the Sinclair Inn's parlour, but decided it wouldn't be practical. Not much galloping on the way back, just an easy canter or trot – easy on the horses.

The asterisker at Middleton, though, didn't make things easy. His name was Charlie something, he was only a bit taller than Seana but bigger-boned and wider, and she guessed he must do his stabling and saddling jobs all right or Mr. Carstairs wouldn't have kept him on. What Charlie hadn't done, she'd heard, was go beyond the bare bones of his job and take it upon himself to practise galloping back and forth between his stations. So it was his own damn fault Mr. Carstairs hadn't given him a chance to ride an Express run for real. Charlie didn't seem to see it that way.

As Seana was creaking down off the saddle, Charlie said, "If you was a real Express rider I'd saddle up Finbar for you, but bein' as yer just another stablesweeper what sucked up enough to get a try at ridin' one run, you can saddle yer own damn horse."

Seana didn't say anything, just went into Finbar's stall and saddled and bridled him. As she was leading Finbar out toward the light, something hit her on the back of the shoulder and bounced off. A dried horse turd – well, mostly dry.

What a boy should probably do was turn around and punch Charlie on the nose and they would scrap it out. Problem was, she wasn't a boy. She'd wrestled with her brothers plenty and could still handle Michael even though he was about her same size now – or had been last time she saw him. But she didn't think wrestling was what Charlie had in mind, and even if it was, clutching and grabbing and rolling on the ground would quickly show Charlie the secret she very much did not want him to know, him or anybody else except Sam Smith. John Thomson probably would've had a couple dozen schoolyard and backyard fist fights behind him by now, and have some idea how to handle himself, but she wasn't John Thomson. She thought of telling Charlie – and it would be true – that Mr. Carstairs wouldn't be pleased that one cog in the Halifax Express machine was grinding its teeth against another. But that sounded a bit too much like: *I'm gonna tell on you!* So she just climbed onto Finbar and trotted away, with Charlie calling names after her.

She was on Big Red, partway between Aylesford and Kentville, when the road skirted a small lake, more like just a widening of the river. On any of the other Express horses she might not've been able to see over the spring green shoreline brush, but Big Red was like sitting on a tower. On the opposite shore stood a birchbark wigwam with smoke coming out of it. Two birchbark canoes were pulled up on shore and several near-naked children were running around them. A woman in one of those colourful, odd-shaped Mi'kmaq hats – more like a hood with a curl on top – sat smoking a pipe, the smoke from her pipe making a little sister to the column of smoke from the wigwam. The woman and her children and their movable home looked as much a part of the landscape as the river and the trees and the blue jays flitting in the branches.

Seana wondered if that could've been a picture of Sam Smith's family before his parents got sick and died. But no, Sam had said the Mi'kmaqs hadn't accepted his family as Mi'kmaq. But then again, that wigwam on the lakeshore was just one family, not a tribe. They reminded Seana of her own family in the Irish summers, and their caravan wandering wherever the roads would take them, just like those canoes could wander wherever the rivers would take them.

By the time Seana reached Kentville Sam was of course gone, relaying the horses back to their regular billets. It took three or four days before Seana could climb out of bed in the morning without grunting and groaning like an old woman. And another couple of days before she bounded out of bed feeling like herself again. She'd proven she could ride an Express run as well as any full-grown man. Maybe even better, maybe Barnaby would've come in first this time if Hyde and Craig's horses hadn't been carrying such light riders.

Seana's bright mood only lasted through her first few bites of breakfast. The weekly newspapers had come out yesterday and Meg the barmaid had saved a left-behind one for her – or for young Johnny the Express Lad. Seana sat spooning up raisined oatmeal with her right hand and holding the newspaper in her left. The front page had a long editorial headlined:

ASTOR PLACE RIOTS NOT WHAT THEY SEEM

The appallingly barbaric events in New York City the night of May 10 – mobs running riot – are claimed to be a clash between supporters of the great English tragedian Macready, appearing in Macbeth at the Astor Place Opera House, and those of his American rival Edwin Forrest, appearing in the same play at the Broadway Theatre. But not even our volatile cousins to the south could, for such a trivial cause, erupt in riot that left 23 dead and countless numbers grievously injured...

Seana shook her head to clear it and peered at the smudgy black print again. Still said the same thing. Twenty-three dead. And only a couple of weeks ago, Canadians rioting in Montreal had burned down their own Parliament buildings. Were all people who lived in big cities crazy?

The true cause of the riot can be found in the New York City newspapers of May 10. The morning editions were crackling with the news of Great Britain's response to American sabre-rattling and fulminations over the boundary between American territory and British Columbia. It is one thing to ride roughshod over the territorial rights of poor, backward Mexico, and quite another to fling threats at The British Empire. Great Britain's official response to the threats was the same answer that should be given to all swaggering braggart bullyboys. The British Lion roared.

The oatmeal clotted in Seana's mouth. That news from London that was printed in the New York newspapers would've been what she'd handed to Mr. Craig at Granville Point the day before.

By evening the New York mob had worked itself into a frenzy. An impotent frenzy, with no one to let it out upon. But wait – appearing at the Astor Theatre that night was another British Lion, the great Macready. The stage was set for riot and mayhem.

There are those who will claim that the riot was entirely caused by the dispute over whether William Macready or the American Edwin Forrest is the greatest Shakespearean actor of the age...

That gave her a glimmer of hope. Maybe it wasn't because of the news from London after all.

While it is true that the thespian rivalry has swollen to ridiculous proportions – to the point where Forrest's supporters recently hurled a dead sheep onto the stage where Macready was performing – that was only the priming for a buried keg of gunpowder waiting to explode. The great Macready has come to represent Great Britain in American eyes. The fury of the mob was the result of Great Britain's refusal to be cowed by American threats.

A sick feeling rolled through Seana McCann. She looked back at the top of the article to make sure. Astor Place Riots, night of May Tenth... On the morning of May *Ninth* she'd been galloping across Nova Scotia thinking only of getting to Granville Point and proving that she could ride an Express run with the best of them, thinking only of herself. And in the dispatch case over her shoulder had been the fuse for that keg of gunpowder. Twenty-three people dead. And God knows how many crippled or badly injured.

IX

S AM DECIDED IT was officially summer with the appearance of new potatoes and green onions beside his roast beef. He said as much to John Thomson, sitting across from him after yet another exercise/ practice gallop from Kentville to Windsor. John Thomson just nodded absently, like she had something else on her mind. Sam said, "You still mopin' 'bout that New York Astor Place thing?"

"T'ain't hardly something to just 'mope' about – twenty-three people killed."

"T'ain't hardly our fault – the news woulda got there without the Halifax Express, just a couple days later."

"Yeah but maybe on another day things wouldn'ta boiled over like they did."

"And maybe there was other days, other times, we carried news that got 'em dancin' in the streets."

"That was other days. Anyway, I wasn't moping about – *thinking* about that, till you brung it up. I was thinking about something else."

"Don't strain yer brain." He took another forkful of supper and shifted chewing to the right half of his mouth so he could politely say out the left, "Thinkin' 'bout what?"

The dark eyes under black, side-swept bangs went slitty and peered around. She whispered, "Can't tell you here." He found it a bit annoying that she had to make everything a big secret, like anyone would bother listening in on what they were saying. But then again, it would only take one slip-up or suspicion to send them both back to places they didn't want to go. So he just kept on eating, biting off a chunk of green onion to flavour every mouthful of juicy beef and thin-skinned baby potato.

After supper they would usually have another half-pint of small beer to lubricate digestion. But tonight, given John Thomson's *Can't tell you here*, Sam asked Kate the barmaid to fill up a quart bottle and put a cork in it.

Kate said miffedly, "Put a cork in it, you tell me?" but she was just playing around. From slow-hours conversations, Sam knew her real name was Hortense but that hadn't sound barmaidy so she'd taken the name with the job of a previous barmaid who'd married a farmer.

Up in Sam's room, they sat on the bed and passed the bottle back and forth for sips. Thomson began to tell him what she'd been thinking about by saying, "We both know the Halifax Express ain't gonna last forever, not even till next winter. I keep putting away as much money as I can, and I'm sure you do too, but even with room and board paid, 'tis hard to scrape much savings out of one shilling a day." It seemed she couldn't shift immediately out of John Thomson like flipping a card, but by the time she'd done saying that she was back to her natural voice and way of speaking, or what Sam had come to think of as her natural voice.

Sam said, "Gettin' real rider's wages now and then helps a lot. Even if it ain't what they're payin' to Corey O'Dell and them." What Sam was going to *do* with the money he saved from the Halifax Express was another question. The traditional way for runaway boys in Nova Scotia was go to sea, but that didn't hold much appeal for him. A canoe out in the middle of a lake was one thing, but a ship in the middle of the ocean just seemed like a big wooden trap with no way to get out of it for months on end. And from some stories he'd heard, being a boy in a ship's crew wasn't all that different from being a boy in an orphanage with Father Gomezes lurking about.

"I think I might know of a way to make our money – yours and mine – grow double its size, maybe triple..." She paused to take a pull off the bottle and handed it back to him. "Me Da used to while away spare hours at the Windsor Turf Club, and bring me along betimes. Some summer Saturdays they run horse races from Windsor to the Newport ferry, turn the High Road into a racecourse. The farmers and other folk who live along the road don't much care for it, kind of in-conveniencing, but what can they do when all the swells of Windsor are out cheering and placing bets? And there's the point of it, for us. There's a prize purse that comes out of the entry fees, but the real money's in the betting."

Sam waited for her to tell him what the point of it was, "for us," but instead she fanned her face and said, "It's hot in here."

It was. Up in the gables where his tiny garret room was, all the heat of the floors below rose up to gather. Cozy in the winter, a bit *too* cozy with summer coming on. But if he opened the window with a candle burning, the place would've filled up with fat June bugs buzzing and bouncing and crunching.

John Thomson untucked her baggy, off-white cotton shirt to let some air in. The skin of her belly, or at least the narrow patch ex-posed above her waistband before she let her shirttails fall, was a few shades paler than her face, more of a dusty golden than brown – cer-tainly not as brown as Sam's skin under his shirt, but not pasty pink like most white folks. She thrust her long-fingered hands up under her shirt, did some squirming and tugging, then sighed and took in a deep, deep breath like it was the first one she'd been able to take all day, now that the cloth band that bound her bubs flat was down loose around her waist. For an instant Sam could see the tips of her breasts pushing out against the cream-coloured cotton, then she exhaled and it was just a shapeless, puffy shirtfront again. He guessed the breastband sort of hung around her hips overnight and then she'd wrestle it back into place in the morning. Probably in her own room she'd unknot it and take it off for the night. He didn't precisely understand the mechanics of it, but decided it was probably best he didn't think too much about the details.

John Thomson – Sam suddenly wanted very much to ask her her real name, but reminded himself that if he didn't know it he couldn't slip up in public – said, "From what I recall of those races to Newport Ferry, the ones I watched with me Da, there's never been a horse in Windsor could outrun Wellington. Maybe on a short course, but never over five miles. Mind you, though, I've not seen one of those races for a couple of years now, there's sure to be some new horses in town. I would come in from Kentville to take a look, once this year's races get started up again, but there's too much chance I might get recognized. Slim chance, maybe, but still too much.

"But you – nobody'd think twice if you came out to watch the races, just for curiosity-like. But your idle curiosity would be giving you the chance to have a lookover of the field."

"The field? I thought you said these races was run along the road," thinking of the fallow field the Halifax Express tryouts were run on last winter.

"Oh, sorry..." A dusting of rose crept into her cheeks. "In horse racing circles – at least the ones I knew, a little – the field means all the horses and jockeys enlisting for a race. It's just a feckless word I heard once or twice, it was silly of me to think anybody else would know that meaning." A lot of people Sam had known would've taken his ignorance as an opportunity to make him feel like an idiot, but she seemed to feel like it was her fault, not his. She brushed past it and went on, "Nobody'd have any reason to suspect your curiosity about these horse races isn't idle. You could rent one of the Shipyard Inn's horses-for-hire to get you out to a good viewing spot – there's a hill about three-quarters along the racecourse that gives you a long look coming and going. I'd split the horse rent with you, since it's kind of an investment."

"Or I could just take Wellington – Express business never laps over to a Saturday, or just about never."

"No, we don't want those we'd want betting against us to get too good a look at him."

"They seen Wellington already, lotsa times."

"Not really. They've just seen him galloping out of town, or trotting back the next day – they ain't seen him like we have, galloped ten miles and still plenty of steam in him. And they ain't seen how rip-fire angry he gets when other horses pass him by, sparks shooting out of his eyes. Out of all the Halifax Express horses, Wellington's our best bet. Well, if it were a twenty-mile race I'd say we should run Big Red, but probably scouring all Nova Scotia wouldn't get you a field for a race like that."

Sam took another gurgle on the bottle – getting low now – and pondered on what Miss John was proposing. "I dunno..."

"All it'll cost you is a few pence for half a half-day's horse rent. And give you something to do on a Saturday afternoon."

"All it'll cost me at first. But then if we goes ahead there'd be half the entry fee, and half whatever we might bet – to make any 'real money,' like you put it. But the money we got now – I got now – that's real money, I mean not maybe-money. Yeah, it's only a few pounds sterling, but I got it in hand, or in the ground. I know you know more about this kinda horse racing nor I do, but still, there's a reason why they call it gambling."

As he was saying that he was realizing that he wouldn't – couldn't – talk to any other girl like that; somehow the time he'd spent kicking around with John Thomson had taken the curse off the great male/female divide. Or maybe it was just who she was – who-ever she was – that made her as much a friend as a girl. But he still couldn't say to her, *If any horse race was a certain-sure thing, yer old man wouldn'ta had to go join the U.S. Army to scrape some money.*

"Maybe you've not seen as many horse races as I have," she said back to what Sam had said out loud, "but you do know horses. Won't cost you much to take a look at one of the Windsor Turf Club's long races, once they get going again. In fact, it needn't cost you a penny – I'll pay for the horse hire."

"No, no, I can chance a few pence – and like you said, it'll give me something to do on a Saturday afternoon. Least I can do is take a look, and then we'll see."

"And then we'll see." She rubbed her eyes with the heels of her hands, then scrubbed her hands back over her ears. "You'd think, now as I've ridden a full Express run for real, just galloping from Kentville to Windsor wouldn't wear me out, but still…"

"Yeah, me too – and I didn't gallop nowhere today." They both stripped to their dayshirts and she pulled out the trundlebed. When they were both snugged into their beds, Sam leaned over to blow out the candle and paused halfway to look down at her: long dark eyelashes closed together, pink lips closed too, breathing through her nose – a lovely little snub of a nose, not a beak like his. He thought of leaning down to kiss her good night, and not just good night. But he wondered if he would seem like, or be like, Father Gomez or her Mr. MacAngus: hungry eyes and grasping paws. So instead he just blew out the candle and rolled over.

In the morning he watched her willowy self – kinda willowy-tall for a girl, kinda willowy-thin for a boy – saddle up the skewbald and ride off. Two Saturdays later the Windsor Turf Club held its first long race of the season, so Sam rented one of Clifford's nags and went looking for the logged-off hillock she'd mentioned, along the road to the ferry across the St. Croix River to the village of Newport. The mouth of the St. Croix River was actually right beside Windsor, just the other side of the hill Fort Edward stood on, but it was too wide and tidal for a ferry there, and from there it curved away from Windsor and snaked inland in such a contorted way that the best place to cross over toward Newport was five miles up a hilly road that did a lot of bending and twisting of its own. Some called it Wentworth Road, some Winkworth Road – damn confusing.

The hill John Thomson said to look for wasn't hard to find: about three-quarters of the way along the course and already buzzing with top-hatted and straw-hatted men – and some fellas wore round-topped, wide-brimmed felt hats instead of toppers – waiting to place last-chance bets. Sam found a spot that gave him a good view of the road and waited. When that last chance came, it all happened so fast Sam couldn't figure it out the first time. The strung-out pack of galloping horses came around a bend and past the hill, and there was a flurry of activity around a tall man made taller by a stovepipe hat.

It took watching three or four Saturday race meets for Sam to sort out the two simple rules of this mid-race betting. The first was that you couldn't change the bets you'd made before the race. The second wasn't so much a rule as a fact of basic arithmetic. If the horse you bet on to win turned out to be running far back, there was no use betting on the front-runner now, because now the odds were so much in favour of the front-runner winning that you'd hardly make anything back.

The field changed a bit from Saturday to Saturday, as new horses came in to replace ones who wouldn't be running next week, and some ran two or three weeks in a row. One thing that didn't change, though, was that even the front-runners looked to be just about out of steam as they passed by the hill, while Wellington after four miles would be just getting loosened up. But Sam knew there were two problems with taking that to mean Wellington would for sure win one of these races. The first problem was that nobody could say for sure when a given horse was going to have a good day or a bad day, sometimes extra good or extra bad. The other problem was that the "fact" of the Windsor horses running out of steam was just how it looked to him, from a hillside set back from the road and often through a cloud of kicked-up dust.

In between two of those Saturdays, the chance came up for another Express run by "the young fellas," as Walrus Carstairs put it. R.M.S. *Caledonia* didn't steam into Halifax until after suppertime on Thursday, so by the time Sam got to Spencer's Inn night had come down. And by that time Barnaby's rider had got ahead of him, though how far ahead Sam didn't know. There was a half moon, theoretically, but in a sky so clouded over there might as well have been no moon or stars up there. A couple miles out of Spencer's Inn the moon poked out to shine up a wide band of gleaming white ahead and to the right – the gypsum cliffs beyond where the road swung to the left – but then the cloud curtains closed again. Fortunately, Brown Bess knew this road blind and Sam could guess where they were by sound and feel and vague shapes: hoofbeats turning hollow-wooden meant the bridge over the St. Croix River, back-slanting saddle meant the steep hill after the bridge, a blacker shadow pointing into the dark sky meant the Windsor Anglican parish church and time to blow the horn...

The road grew into streets with lighted houses. As Sam swerved Brown Bess through a wide turn onto Water Street, he could see by the innyard light Clifford bringing Wellington out to stand by the side of the road. Brown Bess seemed more than happy to be reined to a halt, Sam couldn't blame her. As he slid down off the saddle and made a jump for Wellington's stirrup, he gasped out, "Barnaby's?"

Clifford barked back, "'Bout five minutes, Sammy," then Wellington was off almost before Sam could pick up the reins.

The house lights along the roadside got few and far between, as farm families settled in for an early rooster. The moon peeked out through a seam in the clouds for about half a minute and then disappeared again, leaving Sam even blinder for a moment's blue light. There was nothing in the whole dark, lonesome world but him and the breakneck triple-rhythm of the galloping horse: *ba-da-bump* and then a fraction of a fraction of a second's echo-y silence, *ba-da-bump*, fraction, *ba-da-bump, ba-da-bump, ba-da-bump*...

The road wound up and down so many hills he lost track. When it levelled out again he wasn't sure if it was the flats before the Gaspereau River and Lower Horton, or some piddly plateau he wouldn't've noticed if he weren't riding blind. The feel of Wellington beneath him suddenly changed – still galloping, but the muscles bunching together and tightening. Then the sound of hoofbeats stopped like it was chopped off by an axe. The only sounds were Sam's breathing and Wellington's, and the air rushing past Sam's ears – the only way he knew they were still moving forward. A few seconds later came a thud that almost jarred him off the saddle, and Wellington was galloping again – or galloping still, like he hadn't lost any momentum since his hoofbeats stopped. Sam righted himself in the saddle and held on.

When he got to Upper Horton he found another mystery. As he switched over to the skewbald, he rasped, "Barnaby's?" and then, "Barnaby's rider?" since the Hortonville ostler seemed a good deal dimmer than Clifford.

"Aren't seen him yet."

"Huh?"

"Aren't seen him yet!" louder and slower, like Sam had shown himself to be the dim one, and maybe deaf as well. As the skewbald carried Sam's battered butt out of Hortonville, Sam decided the ostler must've been dozing or thick-eared when Barnaby's rider went by, since Barnaby's man had definitely been ahead of him in Windsor and Sam certainly hadn't passed him on the road. But in Kentville, after Sam had handed off the dispatch case to John Thomson on Big Red – she had a long, dark ride ahead of her – the stableman told him there'd been no sign yet of Mr. Barnaby's Wall Street Express. As Sam was sipping a mug of ale at a seat by the Stage Coach Inn's night-black front windows, he heard a horseman gallop by, heading southwest.

Maybe it was some farmboy galloping to fetch a doctor. But the only bigger town even remotely within galloping distance was Windsor, and that was in the opposite direction. Didn't make sense.

Like several things tonight. But Sam was too tired to try and make sense out of anything. He just finished his ale and went up to bed – John Thomson's bed; Carstairs had pointed out that there was no sense in the Express renting an extra room overnight when "young Johnny's" was going to be empty. Once Sam was stripped down and cozied in and drifting off, he noticed something odd that did make sense. The bed smelled like a girl. Not perfumey or anything girly-girl like that, but didn't smell like a boy. Maybe he wouldn't've noticed if he hadn't known John Thomson's secret, but he did and he did.

Next morning was the easier ride ambling the relay horses back to their home stables. Easier but harder, shifting his position on the saddle to try and take the weight off places that'd got pummelled last night. When Sam and Wellington got to the swing bridge over the Gaspereau River they had to stop. The bridge wasn't over the river but was swivelled back onto the near bank and there were two men hammering on it: a wiry old fella with yellowing white hair, and a younger, bigger version of himself. The older man pointed his hammer south and said, "Ye'll have to go 'round. There's a ford a couple miles upstream, should be easy crossin' this time o' year and tide. Me and the young fella won't be done for another hour or two leastwise."

Sam stayed where he was, patting Wellington's neck and pondering. Standing at either bank were the bases for the bridge ends, earthed-over, heavy-timbered cribwork jutting into the river and making a built-up bottleneck choker before the Gaspereau widened out again to empty itself into the Minas Basin. After a moment of studying on the picture, Sam said, "How long's the bridge been out?" raising his voice to be heard over the young fella's hammering.

The old fella said, "Since yesterday. Coupla rotted out planks, but once we got started, turned out to be more'n a couple. Had to leave 'er overnight."

"Dangerous, for someone comin' along in the dark."

"Nah – we left a lantern burning on the road on either side."

"I ride for the Halifax Express – "

Whitehead interjected an inhaled, "Yeah," like: *And the grass is green and the sky is blue.*

"... and when I came through here last night there warn't no lantern, least not on that side," pointing at the Windsor side of the river.

"Yeah, when we got here this mornin' that one was out, but still plenty o' oil in 'er. Musta blowed out."

"Not our fault," the young fella put in.

"Yeah," the old fella nodded, "somethin' musta blowed it out."

Something or someone. Sam could picture Barnaby's rider dismounting to blow out the lantern, then mounting up again to detour to the ford, leaving the Halifax Express rider to... what? A dunk in the river, or maybe break his neck and his horse's too, depending whether the tide was in or out. Sam said, "I couldn't see a damn thing, but my horse could – or smelled it. He jumped the river," waggling two fingers at the space where the bridge was supposed to be.

"What? Nah, that's twenty feet."

"Eighteen," said the young fella. "We had to measure out the span, remember?"

The old fella waved away such piffles. "Eighteen, twenty, it's still a helluva leap in the dark, comin' up outta nowhere."

"Well, I ain't drowned and got no broken bones, so my horse musta jumped it."

"Huh. Then that's some miracle horse ye got there. But we ain't got time to stand around jawin' with ye, got work to do," though it looked like the young fella was doing most of the work.

Sam turned Wellington upstream toward the ford. Funny, the only upshot out of Barnaby's rider's clever trick – if it wasn't a one-sided gust of wind that blew out the one lantern – was Barnaby's rider lost his lead. Thanks to Wellington. But that didn't mean big-hearted Wellington should be loaded down with every wish and expectation in the world. Not even a miracle horse can guarantee a horse race.

X

A s THE SOUTH edge of Middleton hove into view, Seana slowed the Middleton horse from a bone-bruising trot to a walk. It was partly to allow herself relief with a more comfortable gait – the slow rocking back-and-forth almost a massage – and partly stalling what she might have to deal with in the stables in Middleton. Stopping trotting also stopped the shoulderbag from bouncing against her side. It wasn't much of a shoulderbag, just a flap-over pouch she'd sewn together from a scrap of sailcloth, and she'd cursed it several times the night before last when it got tangled with the straps of the dispatch case and her horn. Maybe she was an idiot for lumbering herself with another bag on the Express run, maybe not – but probably was.

She also felt like an idiot for buying what they called Full Seat riding breeches, instead of the kind with leather overlay just on the inside of the knees. The leather piece that ran up and down the inside of both her thighs and across her bum did give a better grip on the saddle, would make her breeches last longer and did give a wee bit of extra padding, but it was bloody sweaty hot on a steamy summer day.

And summer days in the Annapolis Valley were like the inside of a hothouse greenhouse.

As Seana dismounted and led the Middleton horse into the stables, Charlie Whatsisname – the Valley's other asterisker – came out of the ostler's room. Charlie said loudly, "Well, well, if it ain't Fancypants Johnny Thomson, the Haly-fax Express rider," and stepped in front of her. "You'll unsaddle that horse and give him a rubdown before you saddle Finbar."

"That's not my job."

Charlie's backhand came up so fast it hit the side of Seana's face before she saw it coming, spinning her sideways and knocking her to the ground. Sprawled and dazed, it took Seana a moment to focus. Charlie was standing with his fists balled, waiting to see if Fancypants Johnny would jump up and make a go for him. Seana rose slowly to her feet, reached into her canvas shoulder-pouch and pulled out the revolver. She heard in her memory's ear Da's sombre advice on handling firearms: *Never point a gun at someone you don't intend to shoot.* She pointed the pistol at Charlie's chest and brought her left hand up to pull back the hammer one click. Blood pounding in her eardrums, she said in a voice whose steadiness surprised her, "Just pick up that pitchfork so I can say it's self-defence." One part of her was laughing behind its hand at her ridiculous desperado imitation, but another part was kind of hoping he'd pick it up.

Charlie didn't seem inclined to move toward the pitchfork or anything else. Seana said, "Just do your job and leave me the fuck alone." Charlie nodded very slowly, making no sudden moves. Seana gestured the pistol towards the still-saddled horse, to remind Charlie that was part of his job. Charlie shuffled sideways to take the horse's reins and led it toward its stall. Seana noticed an odd, ammonia-y smell that didn't belong – Charlie had pissed himself.

As Seana trotted out of town on Finbar, revolver bag bouncing against her side, a nunly voice in her head intoned, *How many problems do you think you can solve with a gun?* Seana replied: *Solved that one.*

By the time Seana draggled into Kentville and put Big Red to bed in his own stall with his own manger, she was only interested in slumping into the Public Room and begging Megan to scrounge her a late supper. The journey that'd taken her five hours yesterday had taken fifteen today, and the Sinclair Inn rolls and cheese she'd bought to nibble on the road had given its last nibble many miles ago. But first she went up to change out of tight riding boots and breeches. In the Public Room, Megan approached grinning at "her boy" come home safe from another adventure. But Megan's broad face stopped beaming as she got closer, and she wailed, "What happened to you?"

"Huh?"

Megan pointed to the right side of Seana's face. "You been scrappin'?"

Seana reached up to her right cheekbone and felt a bit of puffiness, and a bit of pain when she touched it. "Oh, no, I..." The real story was too complicated, and opened far too many questions. "One of the horses shied when I was putting him in his stall. Banged m' head against a beam. Musta been more of a whack'n I thought."

"Well, if it was broken you b'God woulda knowed it. I bet you're hungry as well as thirsty – saved you a meat pie."

There was a long, oval mirror set into the coatstand in the lobby, for guests to make last-minute adjustments before venturing out. Seana paused on her way up to her room to have a look, and found a purple and yellow bruise on her right cheek. She'd had worse, wouldn't last long and – like Megan said – nothing was broken, except a few tiny blood vessels. But Seana saw something else in the mirror: a snub-nosed, ragamuffin boy with ratty tufts of chopped-off black hair poking out from under a beat-up old corduroy cap. Why would Sam Smith or Corey O'Dell or any male look twice at a girl in grubby baggy boy's clothes? Like Mr. MacAngus had said, *Pretty girl like you shouldn't be wearing men's castoffs from the Poor Box.* Well, she wasn't a lacy frilly pretty girl, never had been, never would be. So bugger MacAngus, and Sam Smith and Corey O'Dell. Bugger the lot.

By the next time she saw Sam Smith, after another practice gallop from Kentville to Windsor – keeping the horses and herself in trim for further Express runs – the bruise had shrunk too small to be noticeable. He noticed it, though, and asked her about it. She just shrugged, "Bumped m'head. Clumsy." What she really wanted to talk to him about was the plan to run Wellington in one of the Windsor Turf Club's long-distance races. He didn't seem to want to talk about it, though, and kept offering up excuses.

His most prominent excuse, and the hardest to argue, was, "What if the steamer from Liverpool gots a slow crossin', don't make it into Halifax till late Thursday? It's happened before. That puts the run into Friday. Even if we could get Wellington back to Windsor by Saturday noontime, he'd be too wore out for racing. So whatever we'd had to put down for an entry fee'd be forfeit. We got no way of knowin' one week to the next when the mail ship's gonna make port."

In early August, though, that argument went out the window. Mr. Carstairs, on his semi-regular every-other-week tour along the Express route, told Seana, "I won't be seeing you again on my regular schedule."

Seana felt her heart squeezed like a sponge. "They finished the telegraph already?" All her plans – such as they were – depended on the Halifax Express lasting into the autumn.

"What? Good Lord, no – the rate they get things done in Nova Scotia we'll be lucky if it's up and running by Christmas. But Mr. Craig informs us that there's no one in New York City through the stifling mid-August – at least no one of consequence – so The Associated Press sees no percentage in paying the Halifax Express to rush the news there. So, not next week but the next-next week, the Halifax Express will skip a week and take it up again the week following. And so shall I."

When she rode to Windsor to tell Sam Smith that, Sam said, "Yeah, I know. Carstairs told me, too."

"Well... ?"

"Well..." He left that hanging so long, Seana wanted to reach across the skewbald's back and strangle him. They were giving the steaming, lathered horse a cool-down, dry-down rubdown after the gallop from Horton on another of those hothouse inland summer days, each taking a side. Fortunately, the skewbald's back was too high for Seana to actually get her arms across to throttle Sam. Eventually Sam said, "Helluva chancy thing. No way we can know for sure Wellington can beat all them other horses."

"There was no way we could *know* we could ride an Express run, till we done it."

"Well... Maybe it'd be better if *you* rode Wellington in the race. You're a better rider nor I am."

Seana decided not to argue that last part, but, "You and Wellington know each other better'n him and me. And everybody in Windsor knows you're an Express rider, that'd make it harder to sneak up side bets – me, I'm just an anonymous nobody." At least she fervently hoped she'd be anonymous, especially the "she" part.

The entry fee was one guinea, which was twenty-one shillings, one more shilling than a pound. Besides her half of the entrance fee, Seana asked the bank clerk for four gold guineas, just about cleaning out John Thomson's savings account. The plan was that the day before the race Seana would take the stagecoach from Kentville to Windsor and rent one of the Shipyard Inn's horses-for-hire to get around on race day, since showing up on one of the Halifax Express's splendid thoroughbreds would be a dead giveaway.

But on race day morning Clifford said, "T'ain't likely anyone'll want to rent Ol' Molly spur-of-the-moment, so why don't you just take her out for the day? If somebody *do* show up and we're outta horses, I'll tell the boss I thought a day's free exercising for a stall-bound horse was a fair trade and how was I to guess a last-minute customer'd come knocking?" and Clifford handed *her* money, instead of the other way around – two shillings and sixpence. "I know there ain't such a thing as a sure thing, Johnny, but a fella's gotta take a fair chance when it comes along."

Seana knew that two and a half shillings meant a lot more to Clifford than to footloose kids like John Thomson and Sam Smith. Sam had mentioned to her that stable talk had told him Clifford had a family to support in Three Mile Plains – not just a wife and children, but a very aged mother. Seana said, "Want me to bet it at the start, or take a chance the odds'll rise?"

"You do as you think's best – Sammy told me you grew up in the horse race game." Well, maybe Sam had exaggerated a little. Or maybe she'd exaggerated a bit to Sam. Her best guess was that they were better off not betting a lot of money at the start and flattening out the odds, but waiting until the race passed the three-quarter hill when they'd be set up for a bigger payout – if everything went as planned. It was piling chances on chances, but may as well be hung for a sheep...

Clifford had been exaggerating a bit when he called Ol' Molly stall-bound. There was a small paddock on the southeast edge of town, just a couple of streets over from the Shipyard Inn, where the livery horses by turns got a bit of fresh air and green forage. Sam said that when it was Molly's turn, she would sometimes get out of the paddock and go wandering the town. Clifford couldn't figure it. He'd checked over the fence again and again and found no broken rails. And if the young and spry horses didn't jump that fence, surely creaky old Molly couldn't. Then one early morning Sam happened to be out walking when there was no one else about. When he came in sight of the paddock, he noticed Ol' Molly doing something odd, so he stopped and watched from behind a tree.

What Ol' Molly was doing was lying down on her back like rolling in a dust bath. Except there wasn't any dust bed there, just trampled sod. With her legs tucked up, she rolled under the bottom fence rail, got back on her hooves and went ambling down the road, sampling the greener grass and flowerbeds. Creaky and crotchety she might be, but there was a dance in the old dame yet.

Seana and Sam left the Shipyard Inn separately, Seana waiting a few minutes and then heading Ol' Molly up Gerrish Street while Sam and Wellington took King Street. The crowd at the Exhibition Grounds looked like the Hants County Exhibition had started early, more of a crowd than Seana remembered from Windsor race days a few years ago. Among the crowd were a number of red-coated, gold-braided army officers and more fancy-dressed ladies than usual. Scraps of overheard conversation told Seana why for both. Some officers from the Halifax garrison had come to enter a horse in the race: a big, long-legged chestnut with three white stockings, named King's Ransom. In a way, that was good because a second new horse in the field took some attention off Wellington. In a way not so good, because neither she nor Sam had ever seen the military horse run, so had no idea if Wellington could take him over the long haul or any kind of haul.

Too late for second thoughts. Seana just tarried long enough for a quick lookover of the field, then headed down the road – a very quick lookover, given that Ol' Molly was going to take some while getting up and down the hills before the hill Seana wanted. Every half-mile or so there was a man standing by the side of the road, some looking at pocketwatches, waiting to wave off traffic when the time came. For some stretches of the road there was no likely traffic to worry about, unless a spruce tree chose to disentangle itself from the thickets and go wandering. It was a hilly, wind-y, bendy road, but Seana knew it flattened out for half a mile before the river, good for a last sprint if a horse had any juice left in him.

Carriages and saddle horses passed by poor plodding Ol' Molly, heading for the finish line or for Three-Quarter Hill. By the time Seana got to that hill, there were a couple of dozen men gathered on the slope, gentlemen with silk waistcoats, farmers with well-manured boots, sailors with salt-frosted trousers. The long horse races were a rare time the Windsor gentry and the hoi polloi got together, or at least were in the same vicinity. The damp ground at the base of the hill was churned up a bit where they'd hitched their horses to low branches. As Seana dismounted, she stooped and scraped a fingertip through the mud, then rubbed it down her right cheek from the side of her nose. Just another dirty-faced farmboy, nothing to look twice at.

Seana ambled up to the edge of the crowd and sidled around to get as unobtrusively close as possible to the man with the stovepipe hat. She knew the stovepipe man was known around the Windsor Turf Club as Evenodder, but John Thomson wasn't supposed to know that. The men stood around smoking pipes or cigars or suck-ing on long grass stems, trying to talk about the weather or sound ca-sual about who they fancied in the race, but there was an underlying throb of anticipation. Ireland or Nova Scotia, men waiting on a horse race were all the same.

There hadn't been any kind of traffic on the road for some while when someone called out, "Listen!" and everyone went silent. Seana began to hear a low, thrumming drumming that grew louder and louder, almost shaking the ground. Around the bend and past the hill came King's Ransom, the chestnut military horse, white stockings flashing in a blur, whipped on by a smallish man in red and white – a professional jockey – followed about three lengths behind by Sam Smith on Wellington, and then about five lengths behind the big grey came the first of the other half-dozen horses.

A lot of contradictory thoughts passed through Seana in an in-stant. The plan had been for Sam to hold back Wellington as they passed the hill, to let Wellington get a look at at least one other horse's tail and let the punters get a look at Wellington trailing. But three whole lengths was a lot to make up for this late in the race, es-pecially against a damn swift horse like the white-stockinged chest-nut was showing himself to be. Maybe Sam wasn't holding back at all, maybe Wellington had met more than his match? In which case, if she didn't lay down a bet they'd only lose the entry fee. But if she was going to bet she had to do it now, and fast. Screw it, have a little faith and stick to the plan.

Seana stepped toward Evenodder but someone else pushed in front of her, a wide man with grizzled whiskers and pork sausage-fingered hands. Mr. MacAngus. Last time he'd laid eyes on Seana McCann – and hands – she'd had mud on her face too and was wearing boy's clothes, and her then-long hair had been bound back under her hat, looking not that much different from her short-cropped hair now. If she just took a couple of quick steps back and turned away, she'd be lost in the crowd. Instead she held her ground and lowered her head so he wouldn't see much but her chin and the brim of her cap – luckily, not the beat-to-death old felt hat she'd been wearing then – and tried to be a fencepost.

Mr. MacAngus barked, "Odds on King's Ransom?"

Evenodder blinked a few times, calculating behind his eyes, and pronounced, "One to five."

"One pound on Ransom," handing over a one-pound note. At those odds he could only make fourpence on his bet, but maybe squeezing pennies was how he got to be rich.

As Mr. MacAngus turned away – fortunately in the other direction – Seana stepped forward and said in her best John Thomson guttural, "Odds on Wellington?"

Evenodder blinked twice. "Five to one."

"Four guineas on Wellington to win." As soon as the words had blurted out of her mouth, Seana wondered what possessed her. Losing four guineas would mean she'd come out of all the months with the Halifax Express with only a few shillings. But she heard Da speaking in her memory's ear: *If you don't believe in your own horse, who will?*

The stovepipe hat slanted sideways, like it seemed doubtful this muddy-faced ragamuffin had four guineas to bet. Seana scooped the four gold guineas out of her pocket and held them out in her palm. Another blink and the stovepipe hat nodded. As Evenodder's long left hand was reaching out to put the gold in a side pocket, his right hand was reaching to an inside pocket and coming out with a black leather notebook and a pencil stub. Seana said, "Wait a minute," and dug out the other coins her fingers had clinked when she reached for the guineas – Clifford's betting money – plus the one-pound note Sam had given her to bet. "Four guineas, one pound, two shillings and sixpence."

"Name?"

"John Thomson."

After the last horse had passed, Seana and everybody else scrambled down the hill and headed for the finish line. The race might not even be over yet, but would be by the time they got there. On the long ride to the end of the road, Ol' Molly trailing the gallopers and smart carriage-trotters, Seana kept hearing a haunting, keening voice, *What've you done, what've you done... ?*

She heard the crowd on the flats at the Newport Ferry landing before she saw it, the typical bright bubble of babble at the end of every horse race, regardless of winners and losers. As she rounded the bend to the riverbank she saw a swirl of colours: bright dresses and parasols, gentlemen in summer whites and brocade waistcoats, aproned waiters with trays of iced cordials. At one edge of the swirl was a static picture that told Seana what she needed to know. Two red-coated, red-faced officers were standing stiffly with arms tightly crossed across their chests, lips rolled back between their teeth so far that their magnificent mustaches seemed to join their chins. Their horse had lost. And only one horse had been close enough to even dream of catching him between Three-Quarter Hill and the finish line.

Seana wasn't sure if she stood in the stirrups or was pulled up like a marionette with her strings in the clouds. She could see Sam Smith standing a bit wobble-legged, left hand holding Wellington's reins, right hand reaching out to take the winner's purse from the President of the Windsor Turf Club. Seana felt an overwhelming urge to run to Sam, throw her arms around him and kiss him, but several things held her in the saddle. One was that the sight of two lads kissing probably wasn't a Windsor commonplace, even on race days. Another was that it wouldn't be a good idea for the come-from-behind winning rider and the big bettor to be seen too close together, give people suspicions of conspiracy.

Standing in the stirrups, though, gave Seana a view of where she *should* go. Evenodder, still wearing his signpost stovepipe, was sitting behind a folding table with a hard-sided black valise opened in front of him. The lineup at the table wasn't very long, just a few who'd bet on Wellington at the start, when the odds weren't so high. Seana tied Ol' Molly's reins to a tree – not that she was likely to go cavorting off anywhere – and wove her way toward the tip of the black stovepipe showing over the shoulders in front of her.

When Seana got up to the table, Evenodder stared across at her with a stony set to his long face and spade jaw. "Ah yes, John Thomson." Seemed John Thomson and Sam Smith didn't have to be seen close together to arouse some people's suspicions. "The Windsor Turf Club owes you..." glancing in his notebook, "twenty-four guineas, five pounds and fifteen shillings." Seana managed to keep from jumping up and down and whooping, barely. She hadn't allowed herself to do the actual arithmetic before knowing who had won.

The thick half of the valise, the side lying on the table, was separated into various-sized compartments with snap-flap leather lids. Evenodder's long, bony fingers began to count out gold guineas and crowns and silver shillings. As the piles grew, Seana said before realizing her voicebox was still hooked up to her thoughts, "Don't got room in my pockets. Not without some bouncing out."

"You weren't expecting such a haul?"

"Ain't nothin' certain in a horse race, mister."

The grim-set, long face softened slightly. He reached back to rummage in the long pocket in his coattails and came out with an empty canvas drawstring bag with 1d stencilled on it, saying, "The bank won't miss one less coin sack, and if they do, the Windsor Turf Club can afford it more'n you do." Mr. Stovepipe actually winked, not blinked. "Despite your little windfall, we took in a lot more'n paying out, thanks to some military bettors." And Mr. MacAngus, which made it even sweeter for his would've-been stepdaughter.

Seana wasn't surprised she got back to the Shipyard Inn before Sam, even on Ol' Molly and even though he'd be coming on a more direct route: there was a scraggly back road that made a straighter line to Water Street than the elbow of the Wentworth/Winkworth Road and King Street. But Sam would be taking it very slow and easy on surged-out Wellington, and it would've taken him a while to politely extricate himself from the after-race hoopla. Clifford came out of the stables before Seana'd had a chance to dismount. All she had to say was, "Yup," and his face blossomed.

"Was it close?"

"Bit too close for my comfort, but it upped the odds. Yer gonna need both hands."

Clifford held both big brown hands out cupped and Seana filled them with fifteen silver shillings. "Holy Jesus Murphy, Johnny. Just from two shillings sixpence?"

Seana shrugged. "Odds against us."

"I'm gonna have to dribble this out careful-like so the wife won't wonder. She's right churchy and gambling's a sin."

"T'ain't gambling to bet on Wellington."

"Not on Wellington with Sammy on him." Clifford funnelled the coins into pockets and took hold of Ol' Molly's reins. "You go on in and get yerself a victory ale, I'll take care of the old girl."

The Public Room only had a few customers, and none of them were sitting near the booth in the far corner. Even just sipping, Seana was halfway through her half pint of small beer when Sam came in, walking a bit stiffly and still wearing his riding boots and breeches. Two regular lads couldn't very well throw their arms around each other and dance around the room, but they could grin till their cheeks cracked. As Sam came towards her table, Seana called out, "Two pints of ale please, Katy. And pour one for yourself." She'd heard farmers and fishermen call that out if they'd had a good market day or full nets. It sounded a bit big-for-britches coming out of John Thomson's mouth, but Kate didn't seem to mind. This tab was going to be on John Thomson – better to not put it on the Express account and start

Mr. Carstairs asking what they'd been celebrating – but it'd be a tiny bite out of the winnings.

As Sam plunked himself down in the booth and plunked the winner's purse down on the table – four more guineas to split down the middle – Seana pushed the remnant half of her half pint across the table at him. He took a deep guzzle while she said, "That was one helluva lead when you passed the hill. Was it close at the finish?"

"Damn close, feared I held him back too long – but Ransom ran outta steam, didn't have a final kick left in him. His handlers prob'ly knew that was likely, but figured he'd be so out in front by then it wouldn't matter."

Kate set their pints down on the table, saying, "Won your horse race, then?"

"*He* did." Seana pointed across the table.

"But he," Sam pointed back, "hatched up all the plannin'."

Once Kate was out of earshot and Sam had glanced around to make sure no one else was in, Sam said, "Well?"

Seana leaned across the table and made her John Thomson voice even huskier and lower. "Twenty-four guineas and five pounds." Sam's mouth and eyes fell open, gobsmacked, blindsided and dumbfounded. "Best we don't divvy it here, out in the open, but it easily splits even, except the fifth pound, and that'll wait till the banks open."

"Uh... what the hell were the odds, then? Like twenty to one?"

"Five to one, when you rounded the hill."

Sam shook his head slowly. "Calc'latin' odds and multipliers ain't my strong suit, but five to one on two pounds don't make..." He rolled his hand to indicate the gobsmacking amount she'd named.

Seana shrugged. "I took four guineas out of the bank, just in case, and things looked good, so..."

"That was *your* four guineas you laid on the line."

"You did the riding."

"And what would you've done if we'd lost?"

"But we didn't, *we* won and *we'll* split the winnings."

"Well, if it'll make you happy."

After another pint of ale and a couple of pickled eggs – dinner had got forgot with all the agitation and anticipation – Seana felt woozy and dozy. A walk around in the fresh air seemed a good idea. Sam first went up to change out of his riding gear, then rambled with her on a circuit of the up and down streets of Windsor, pointing out things he'd learned about the place.

In her life before the Halifax Express Seana hadn't seen much of Windsor except the Turf Club and Exhibition Grounds. Windsor was a long ride from home and Da hadn't had money for taverning – his rare chance for a drink was local backwoods stuff bartered for a bit of work on a neighbour's farm or someone else's horses. So most of what Sam pointed out was new to her.

On the ridge above the bridge side of Water Street, the tall houses were where the wives of sea captains would keep watch from high windows or widow's walks, hoping to see their husband's ship come home safe. A bit further along, stone gateposts marked the entranceway to Judge Haliburton's estate – Seana had read one of his flinty-funny *Sam Slick* books in a dog-eared copy at the Stage Coach Inn, though she suspected all of Judge Haliburton's money didn't come from writing books. An iron gateway down a treed lane marked the driveway to King's College, where rich boys from all over Nova Scotia and beyond came to learn how to be rich men. The circuit back went past the hill topped by the sprung-shingled blockhouse of old Fort Edward, where cows grazed the parade ground that redcoat soldiers used to march back and forth on, and squirrels nested in old cannons.

Sam pointed at the blockhouse tower on Fort Hill and said, "Ninety-four years ago, in my great-great-grandfather's time, all the Acadian men hereabouts got called to Fort Edward for a meeting. Once they was all inside, the gates were locked and the English governor told 'em they were gonna be shipped away to Massachusetts and Georgia and such. With the men trapped, their wives and children got no choice but go with them. Same day, same thing was happening in Grand Pré, Annapolis Royal..."

"Why?" As soon as that was out of her mouth, Seana realized it was a foolish question for an Irish girl to ask.

Sam Smith said pretty much what Da would've said if asked about some things that had happened in Ireland: "Lots of fancy-soundin' reasons, I bet, but in the end, the men who can tell soldiers what to do can tell everybody else what to do. But my great-great-grand-père didn't get trapped – he lit out and hid out in the woods. Most of Nova Scotia was wild woods where nobody goes – nobody official. Still is – all these towns and roads and such, they're just on the skin, around the edges. All the inside's still wild and free."

By that time they were back to Water Street and turning left toward the Shipyard Inn. The long, hilly walk had stretched out Seana's stomach as well as her legs. By the time they got back to the inn she was wondering what was for supper. The angle of the evening sun across the Minas Basin cast a golden light on what had been a golden day – pocketsful of golden. Seana still wasn't sure what she was going to do when the Halifax Express came to an end, but the day's winnings gave her a lot more leeway to think about it. After a good feed of beef stew – with raspberry custard for dessert – Sam asked the barmaid to again fill up a quart bottle with ale. Kate said, "Hatchin' out new plans you don't want anyone else overhearin', eh? What's it gonna be this time – dory races?"

Up in Sam's room, the first thing Seana did was reach up under her shirt and wrestle the breastband down to her waist, feeling like she could breathe again. The breastband seemed more of a constriction now than when she'd first started wearing one, as though her chest had grown harder to flatten. And the last time she'd worn her riding breeches they'd seemed a bit seam-stretching over the hips, only two months after they'd been tailored to fit her tight but not that tight. It seemed that girls started growing into women whether they wanted to or not, especially with three hearty meals a day courtesy of the Halifax Express.

With her ribcage her own again, Seana plunked down on Sam's bed to pass the bottle back and forth and talk. Logically maybe they should've been talked out, after spending all afternoon together. But that had been as John Thomson; now she could be herself. And although Sam Smith couldn't talk to her in Mi'kmaq or Acadian French, not if he expected her to follow, now he didn't have to pretend he wasn't a half-and-half orphan. About halfway down the bottle, he leaned forward to brush her hair out of her eyes – not the first time in the times they'd spent in his inn room or hers; her self-chopped hair did have a tendency to sneak down a few strands to try and poke out her eyes. But this time instead of leaning back he hung there, hand still beside her face. His dark brown eyes, almost black, seemed poised between wish and fear, just as his body seemed poised between sinking back where it came from or moving further forward. His hand cupped the side of her head and he leaned forward and kissed her.

She'd seen it coming and let her eyes fall closed at the last minute. Her right hand came up to the back of his neck as her lips moved with his, but it was an awkward and straining position for both of them. Her legs straightened themselves and she slid sideways. They were lying face to face still kissing – or again, she wasn't sure – each with their free arm over the other's back and their trousered legs entangling. His arm pressing her back squeezed her breasts against his chest, in a very different way than the breastband squeezed them. The world outside of her and him was whirling, but not in a queasy way. She let it whirl.

Of a sudden he broke away and sat up with his back to her. She felt like she'd been thrown in a tub of cold water. She'd had it in the back of her mind, way back, that they'd have to stop eventually – though not so abruptly nor so soon – but hadn't expected him to do the stopping. Even besides priest-frowning sin, a girl had more reason to think twice and pull back than a boy. The front of Sam's trousers, when he'd been pressed against her, had seemed to say very clearly that he didn't want to break away from her.

Her left hand started to reach for his back, but she stopped it – there seemed to be a kind of shudder in the air between the palm of her hand and his back. Not looking at her, head slumped forward, he growled like it was being ground out of him, "Sorry, I... It's not you..." He clamped a hand on the top of his head. "There's a lot of snaky... *things* in here, bad stuff..." He reached for the bottle on the nightstand, still not looking at her, and gurgled out a couple of swallows.

Now she did put her hand on his back. He kind of jerked away but not quite. His back felt like the muscles of a spooked horse, mus-cles twitching under the skin. She said, "If I did do something wrong, you'd tell me... ?"

"No," turning toward her. "I mean you didn't do nothin' wrong. Like I said. It's got nothin' to do with you. I mean acourse it does, but not... There's just some sick... *things* get in the way. It's not you."

"Well then quit hogging the bottle."

He laughed and handed it over. She sat up to take a sip – not much left. She very much wanted to ask him what kinds of "things" he was talking about, but if he wasn't going to volunteer, it wasn't up to her to stick her fingers in. So instead she just said, "It's get-ting late, maybe we should get some sleep. There'll be other nights." She hoped. Or maybe she feared, she wasn't sure. It had turned into treacherous ground, in so many ways.

"Yeah. Yeah, you're right."

She climbed down off his bed and pulled out the trundlebed, then stripped to her dayshirt – she could hear him doing the same on the bed above and beside hers. Before she'd quite got settled in, he blew out the candle. She said, "We can at least kiss good-night." *Can't we?*

"Yeah, sure we can. If you like."

She reached up to find his face in the dark. Her thumb found his eye. "Ow! No, it's okay..." His hand took hold of her hand and she could feel him leaning down toward her. The kiss was partway be-tween a nighty-night peck and a real kiss, but she could feel at least some affection in it.

Seana lay back down and closed her eyes. But sleep and dreams-capes didn't come quickly; factors of real life kept getting in the way. Like what kind of idiot would she be, getting tangled with another young runaway who'd only double her problems? The only thing they had in common – the Halifax Express – was only going to last anoth-er month or two at most. On the other hand, Sam Smith – or what-ever his real name was – seemed to want her when he only knew her with short-chopped hair and boys' clothes, so whatever he felt for her wasn't just a passing fancy of lilac water and lip rouge. But what-ever he felt for her hadn't been deep enough to keep him from pull-ing away like he was kissing a snake. But no, that'd had nothing to do with her, he'd said. Likely had more to do with a priest or priests back at the orphanage, and whatever had gone on in the stables there.

From the bed above and beside her came a couple of gen-tle snores, so whatever was troubling Sam wasn't enough to keep him from sleeping. Soon, though, the snores turned into grunts and barked-out, formless, snarling syllables. Sam had made noises in his sleep before, but never this angry and scared – and *loud*. If it went on much longer and louder, other people in the Shipyard Inn were going to think someone was being murdered.

Seana sat up and opened her eyes. After so long with her eyes closed hoping for sleep, moonlight through the window seemed as bright as the candlelight had been. Sam was curled up on his side fac-ing away from her, with just the rough sheet over him. His legs were twitching, and one elbow jerked upward in time with another word-less shout. Seana levered herself up to perch on the edge of the bed, then swivelled sideways and lay down spooned against Sam's back with one arm draped around him. That usually worked when one of her brothers was having a bad dream. But Sam kept flailing and shouting. She tightened her arm around him and whispered in his ear, "Sam," then louder, "Sam!"

"Huh? Wha'... ?"

"It's all right. You were shouting in your sleep."

"Oh. I was? Sorry."

"Nothing to be sorry about. It happens. Percy had bad dreams, too."

"Percy?"

"My dog. His first owner treated him cruel, he used to whimper in his sleep."

There was a moment's pause, then Sam asked like he cared, "So what became of Percy?"

"Um, I shot him."

Another instant's pause, then Sam bolted upright and away from her, planting his back against the wall and holding his hands up beside his shoulders. "I'll never do it again, I promise! I won't even snore!"

Seana laughed so hard she had to cover her mouth with a pillow to keep from waking the rest of the inn.

XI

"WELL, SAMMY," CARSTAIRS said across the table as Katy left to fetch their beers, "you've been making good use of the respite 'twixt Express runs, ain't ya? *Lucrative* use."

"Howzat, sir?"

"Siphoning a bit of ready money from the Windsor Turf Club's coffers to your own pocket. Pock*ets*, I should say – yours and Johnny Thomson's, I'd wager. Clever lad, our Johnny, wouldn't you say?"

"Um, I guess so, sir."

"Problem is, you see, Sammy-lad, Wellington ain't your horse. Not yours nor Johnny Thomson's. Ran a Jim-dandy fine race I'm sure, but he ain't your horse to run."

Kate arrived with Carstairs's pint and Sam's half-pint. Sam took a sip to moisten his mouth, then said carefully, "But it didn't do Wellington any harm, Mr. Carstairs. He'd missed out on his reg'lar run that week anyways. And runnin' that race weren't all that different from a station-to-station gallop we'd give him for exercise, to keep him in trim for the next run."

"Maybe not all that different, but not the exact same."

"I guess not, sir."

"Some might say that since the horse belongs to the Halifax Express, so do the winnings." Carstairs took a long slurp of ale and wiped the foam off his mustache with the back of his hand. "But I guess I don't. You pay for these beers and my lunch, instead of put-tin' them on the Express account I gotta account for, and we'll call it even."

About ten or eleven pence out of fourteen guineas, two pounds and ten shillings wasn't a big bite. Sam said, "Sounds fine by me, sir."

"More than fine, I bet. But a couple of orphan lads like you and Thomson will need as much of a stake as you can scrape together when the Halifax Express leaves you high and dry."

"When's that gonna be, sir?"

"Your guess is as good. The telegraph line from Halifax to Amherst still progresses – slo-o-owly. But in the meanwhile – next run's you and Thomson again."

R.M.S. *Caledonia* didn't make Halifax till after 2:00 Thursday morning, and sunrise wouldn't come as early as a month ago. Barnaby's rider got ahead of Sam on their night-blind, winding way out of the city and – from what Sam heard barked by the stablehands at the relay stations – the lead kept growing. The sky was finally lightening by the time Sam got to Windsor, but Wellington couldn't very well get ignited by the sight of another horse ahead of him if the other horse was too far ahead to see. All Sam could do was ride as hard as he could, hand the dispatch case off to John Thomson in Kentville and wait to hear how it all panned out. He thought of waiting in Kentville till John Thomson got back and told him what she got told on the wharf at Granville Point. But an easy ride the day after a hard gallop was the prescription for keeping a horse's muscles from knotting up, and the Halifax Express wasn't paying him to rearrange schedules to suit his curiosity – especially curiosity about something that wasn't going to change if he heard it today or next week.

Besides, he didn't really want to have another long talk with her self until he'd thought something through. He hadn't had time alone with her – which meant he hadn't had time with her – since the night after the horse race. It'd been a strange night. Some moments of it made him shrivel up inside, but other moments had opened up a possibility he hadn't thought of before. Or at least the possibility of a possibility.

The possibility had to do with what the hell was he going to do when the Halifax Express shut down? The question had been poking at him ever since John Thomson told him that not only was the Express not going to last forever, it wasn't even going to last out the year. The Halifax Express gave "Sam Smith" a hidey-hole and an identity; without it, he was just kicking around the roads and streets of Nova Scotia with no disguise except a made-up name. If anybody recognized who he really was, the law would pack him up and ship him back to the orphanage, just like a runaway slave or indentured servant sent back to his master.

There was a wider world, though, west of Nova Scotia. You didn't have to read the papers to know there was a monster gold rush going on, people from all over the world stampeding for the far west U.S.A., so Sam had been sorta thinking about the California goldfields. Not that he was fanciful enough to imagine himself staking a claim and striking it rich, but there must be lots of work there for someone who could wash dishes or chop wood or muck out a stable, and no one there would care about the laws of Nova Scotia. A funny little thing Sam wouldn't've thought of if he hadn't heard John Thomson's story about her father, was that if the huge California gold strike had happened just a couple of years earlier it would've been in Mexico. But that was no skin off Sam Smith, except he wouldn't have thought of escaping to a place where people just spoke Spanish.

The second sorta-maybe possibility for life after the Halifax Express had been seeded by the Halifax Express – in particular by the woolly buffalo pelt sleigh-rug Carstairs wore across his legs for winter inspection tours. The buffalo robe had come from the western part of the Hudson's Bay Company territories, called Rupertsland, way off the other side of Canada. There was a place there called Red River, where most of the population was halfbreeds – or so he'd heard tell – so nobody would look twice at Sam Smith. Best of all, the western prairies was horse country, so someone who knew his way around a stable broom and a saddle could probably find work there.

Both those possibilities needed travelling money, and so did the third possibility he'd just started thinking of. But with what he'd stashed away from his Halifax Express pay, and his horse race winnings, he had a pretty good stake. And there was still at least a few more weeks of a shilling a day coming in – even more coming in if he rode another run or two. But that was now a big if: how much was the Halifax Express gonna trust "the lads" if Barnaby beat them badly on that last run?

When Carstairs next plunked his brown-leathered bulk down in Windsor, he said, "Well, Samuel..." then took a mouthful of ale and mulled it around for a moment before swallowing. "Barnaby's riders left you lads in their dust, didn't they?"

Carstairs seemed kinda jovial about it, though, which was unbalancing. Sam said warily, "How much'd they beat us by?"

"The news dispatch for The Associated Press didn't get onto the telegraph wires until fourteen hours after the news for the Wall Street speculators."

Sam almost burst out, *Fourteen hours? The whole ride only took nine hours!* but managed to rein himself in, given Ol' Walrus's strange mood of delivering bad news like it was good news. When people with power over you are being confusing, better you don't go stomping around with your mouth open.

"Well, our Fundy steamboat was running a little slow that day." That still couldn't come out fourteen hours, unless they rowed across. "Then when our runner did get to the Saint John telegraph office, he discovered that the line was dead. It'd gone dead just after Barnaby's message went out. Nothing the telegrapher could do but send a party out to look for a break in the line. But that'd barely got started when the sun went down – nothing for it but to wait till morning.

"Next morning they found the break in the line soon enough, just the other side of the Saint John River. Not a downed tree or any other kind of accident, the line'd been obviously deliberately cut. No way to prove who by, though. In the meanwhile the telegrapher had handed Mr. Craig a copy of the message that'd gone out to the Wall Street syndicate the night before. Wasn't long, lemme see if I can remember it." Carstairs scratched his mustache, looked at the ceiling as if the message was carved there, and recited: "'Consignees of Neptune write Boards advanced one fourth penny, Shingles two to three shillings per quarter, lower qualities Fish six pence lower.'"

The hounddog eyes lowered to Sam again, and the mustache-masked mouth said, "You wouldn't think there'd be much world-wide trading in vast quantities of boards and shingles, would you? And you'd be right. But if you substitute Cotton for Boards, Corn for Shingles and Flour for Fish, you have the exact precise same figures from the London Stock Exchange that were in our dispatch for The Associated Press.

"So that little cabal of Wall Streeters got a full morning's stock exchange trading – plus the night before to plan it – with knowledge their competitors did not have. I'd guess Barnaby's employers made a few million dollars that day, at least a few hundred thousand."

That still didn't explain why Carstairs seemed so cheerful about it all. Sam chewed his underlip and waited. He waited while Carstairs thanked Kate for bringing him a bowl of chowder – Sam had already eaten – and took a slurp and pronounced it edible, then another sip of ale.

Between mouthfuls – white soup drops spattering his mustache and stubbled chin – Carstairs went on, "Any rate, next link in the chain of events is the new President of the United States of America, Mr. Zachary Taylor – *General* Zachary Taylor, I should say, hero of the Mexican-American War." Sam wondered if that hero general had been in command of the cannons firing at John Thomson's father and the San Patricio's last stand. Strange how things always came back to her.

"President Taylor has not been pleased that the European news has been appearing in the New York City newspapers before it reached the White House. But at least he got it eventually, and a lot sooner than if the Halifax Express did not exist. But this time he got it fourteen hours later than he should've, and he knows the reason why. Not to mention that a few more Wall Street tricks like that could totally bugger the national economy. Why would capitalists venture money on the New York Stock Exchange if the game seems to be rigged?

"The President was not amused. In fact he reared up on his hind legs and roared. So the Wall Street brokers have decided to keep their heads down lest they get chopped off, so Barnaby's Express is out of business. Toot fini. So there will be no more sawed-through saddle stirrups, no more blowed-out warning lanterns... just our riders, our horses and the road. Still be a race, mind, but against the clock, which is unforgiving but don't play tricks. Still just as important that we win. Speakin' of which – not this run but the next-next run, you and John Thomson are up again. Think you're up for it, running fast without somebody to chase?"

"Guess there's one way to find out, Mr. Carstairs."

The morning after Carstairs passed through, Sam took the bit in his teeth and took another practice run to Kentville. It was too spur-of-the-moment to've sent a message ahead by stagecoach. When Sam walked into the Public Room of the Stage Coach Inn – not near as stiffly as he would've after a two-stage gallop two months ago – John Thomson was just finishing her lunch. She ordered a pot of tea and sat sipping while he decimated his dinner. They talked a bit about what Carstairs had told them both, and this and that, but only in dribs and drabs – and not only because Sam was shovelling food into his mouth. In fact, once the worst after-gallop famishment was filled, he didn't feel much like eating. He leaned across the table and murmured low, "I gotta talk to you private."

Up in John Thomson's room, Sam sat down on the foot of the bed, then stood up, then sat down again and tried to start off the way he'd worked it out in his head: "You and me, we got the same prob-lem, about what to do when the Halifax Express goes out of busi-ness. We're both still underage runaways, got legal guardians who can rope us back – me the Church, you your mother and maybe that MacAngus fella now. And the way you been, uh... fillin' out, you won't be able to pretend to be a boy much longer. Not unless you get awful fat." As soon as he'd said that last sentence he wondered if maybe he shouldn't've, if he wanted her to hear the rest he had to say. Too late now. "Another few years we won't be cattles anymore – "

"Cattles?"

"You know, uh, like somebody else's sorta possessions."

"Chattels."

"Okay. But anyway, maybe in just one more winter we will've changed so much that people who aren't seen us since '48 won't rec-ognize us, at least not just passin' on the street. Now, I been thinkin' some pretty far-fetched ideas 'bout what to do when the Express shuts down, how to keep outta sight. But a while ago somethin' come to me, somethin' I wouldn'ta thought of if I'd been thinkin' alone, of just me.

"You remember what I said back when we was lookin' at Fort Edward?" As if she'd remember every bit of blather that came out his mouth. "That most of Nova Scotia is still wild woods where no-body goes – nobody official? That all these towns and roads and such, they're just on the skin, around the edges? My old man had a trapline, and a cabin, where we used to spend the winters.

"In the olden days somebody surely woulda took it over when he died and I was still too young to take over. My mother told me her grandmother told her that in the olden days the sagamos could tell the tribe which family would get which hunting grounds, and it was a big deal. But back then there was a helluva lot more Mi'kmaq than there is now. Most likely that cabin's still sittin' there just as empty as the last time we left it, and the trapline that I been around enough times with mon père to remember the trail, once I get there to see it again.

"Now I never woulda thoughta this if it was just me, I couldn't never do it by myself. But if there was two of us... And I don't mean just any two, you and me seem to get along pretty good... I know I'm pretty loony in some ways, but you seem to be able to put up with that." He hoped. "So, uh, whattaya think?"

He looked straight at her for the first time since he'd started talking. Her face was hard to read – after eight or nine months of pretending to be somebody else, she was bound to be pretty good at holding up a neutral mask – but there was definitely some suspicion there. What she said wasn't necessarily the first thing she was think-ing: "But just two of us, out there in the middle of nowhere – bears and blizzards and the long, long winter... People starve to death in the woods in the winter."

"Yeah, people with real bad luck or don't go in prepared. More so in the old, old days when there wasn't things like flour to get you through a stretch of bad hunting. We'd pack in as much as we can float in one canoe. Far's I can recolleck, there's only two portages."

"Portages?"

"Places where you gotta unload the canoe and carry everything around a waterfall, or from one river to another. As for bears and such, if we was to have the bad luck to wake up a winter bear, you got yer revolver and I'm gonna have to buy a gun anyways, I think we could handle a bear. We prob'ly stood more chance of gettin' killed gallopin' down dark roads on tall horses."

But her eyes had gone more sceptical. She said, "As far as you can recollect the route in?"

He waved that away. "It's only been two years. Was more'n *ten* years I went back and forth that route two times a year, in in the fall and back out in the spring. I'll see it as it comes up in front of me, and the trail's marked if you know what to look for."

She looked at the wall and ran a hand through her choppy hair. Out in the woods there'd be no reason she couldn't grow it back long like a girl, if that's what she wanted to do. But there was a much bigger *if* in front of that, a mountain of an if. He took another stab at getting around it. "Your horse race plan sounded crazy to me, but that turned out not too bad. Maybe this plan ain't so crazy as it sounds."

"But think about it for a minute," shaking her head. "We're still just kids. Maybe a full-grown man and woman could make a go of it out in the woods all winter – many do, I guess – but we're not. If we were a full-grown man and woman we wouldn't have to be thinking of ways to keep ourselves hidden."

"But look what we done already. A year ago, could you see yerself bein' a rider for the Halifax Express? Scarin' off road robbers with a revolver? Carryin' the news that New York City and the White House depended on? That was *us* – we did that. And we can do this." Something caught in his throat and he had to swallow. This was supposed to be just a sensible proposal, not something to get all choked up about. "We can."

John Thomson blinked a few times, like something was surprising her as well. Her eyes had gone glossy and gleamy, mist-sheened. She said, "I have to think about it. But I *will*, Sam – think about it."

So there was where he had to leave it, for now. But it wouldn't be healthy for the skewbald and Wellington to do another long ride after a hard morning's gallop, so John Thomson was stuck with him till tomorrow. They walked around Kentville for a while, trees and storefronts shimmering in the hothouse Valley haze. The hay on the dykelands along the Cornwallis River looked ripe for cutting, keep a lot of horses happy this winter. As they ambled down Cornwallis Street they passed by a flat-fronted brick building with a sober wooden faceplate: Kentville School. Across the street was a growing pile of stone and beams and scaffolding. Thomson said, "That's gonna be the new courthouse and jail."

"Huh. Guess it's only fittin' to put the school and jail face to face. Kissin' cousins."

"Oh, I dunno, I always kinda wished I could go to school."

That took Sam by surprise. "Didn't you never?"

"Schools cost money. And in Ireland we moved around so much..."

"But you talk so educated." Sam glanced around to make sure there was no one in easy earshot, then lowered his voice anyway. "I mean when yer talkin' like yerself, not John Thomson."

"When we moved to a country where everyone spoke English, Mam made damn sure we learned to speak it proper, like she did growing up."

They both dropped the subject as another clutch of pedestrians came toward them. The streets of Kentville weren't chockful and bustling, but fairly active. People nodded at John Thomson as they went by, or tossed off how-d'you-dos like: "Can't be many hot summer days left, eh, Johnny?"

Two chest-high boys stopped in front of them and one said, "We're goin' swimmin', Johnny, wanna come?"

"Don't be daffy," said the other. "John wouldn't go to the Little-boys-damn." Maybe some kind of Kentville code for a nasty place on the river? Before Sam could ask and look ignorant, the don't-be-daffy boy angled his face back up toward John Thomson. "Is yer friend a Express rider, too?"

"Yep, he is, some days."

Sam said, "Sam Smith," and stuck out his hand. Both boys shook his hand like they meant to brag about it, then jogged off down the road. "Little-boys-damn?"

"Upstream of Mill Bridge," came back John Thomson's throaty, word-miser mutter, "two mill dams for two ponds – one's deep, t'other's not so. The Li'l Boys' Dam and Big Boys' Dam."

"So you swim at the big boys' dam."

"Ha ha."

The how-d'you-dos on the street, and the familyish way the
Stage Coach Inn's staff treated "our Johnny," made Sam wonder if
that might point up a reason why she was hanging back about his
plan. She might be wondering about spending months in the woods
alone with no company but him. Of course no one's really alone in
the woods, not if they have eyes and ears and a sense of humour, even
in the winter. There's plenty of birds and evergreens and tiny paw-
prints in the snow. And if you hope to have any luck trapping, the
animals you're after have to become real to you, even if you can't see
them – you have to learn to feel their habits and the way they think
and smell. But he couldn't say that to her uninvited. Once she'd said,
'I have to think about it,' he shouldn't go sticking his boots in.

That night he lay awake on the trundlebed beside her bed, wondering if she was sleeping. He thought of asking her – softly – if she
was awake and if yes what she was thinking. He had to remind himself again that until and unless she signalled she wanted to talk about
it again, he'd only make it an aggravation. It seemed she still didn't
want to talk about it over breakfast, just John Thomson grunts, and
when he'd saddled up the skewbald there was just a John Thomson
half-wave – *See ya*. Next time he saw her he was handing off the dispatch case from the skewbald's gyrating saddle, then she was gone
on Big Red. Two days later a note came on the stage into Windsor
that John Thomson would be taking a practice gallop east tomorrow
morning.

Sam had trouble sleeping that night. He kept telling himself not
to be so wrought up. It wasn't like he'd asked her to marry him or
something, wasn't waiting for her decision on the rest of his life, and
hers. Himself would reply, *No, just the next six months, and better chances
that you won't get sent back to hell*. He was bleary in the morning, but after a couple cups of strong black tea he was up to taking Wellington
out for an easy exercise trot, then found things to do around the
stable to keep him sort of occupied. By the time Kate and the noontime waitress were setting out dinner, and the foremen and top hats

coming in from the shipyards, John Thomson and the skewbald came galloping into Windsor, slowing down for the traffic on Water Street.

John Thomson was famished, of course. She demolished her lamb chops and string beans while Sam picked at his. Between mouthfuls, she whispered, "After, we should talk."

He muttered back, "Don't have to be up in my stuffy room. I know another place."

On the waterfront there was a sunny spot a ways away from the shipbuilding cribs, but not such a ways away that the noise of hammers and mallets and saws and all didn't provide a cover, so if you spoke just loud enough for someone sitting close to hear, no one else would. Once Sam and Thomson were lounged on the bank watching the docked ships rise as the tide came in – with one eye out for anybody coming up behind them – she said in her natural voice, "If I were to go along with your wintering idea – I say *if* – then I'd be chancing some of my saved-up money on the supplies we'd need, maybe most of it." Sam started to interject, but she intercepted, "But you chanced some of your savings on my horse race idea. Not near so much as I did, but that's neither here nor there."

If it's neither here nor there, passed through Sam's mind, *why'd you mention it?*

"But I'm guessing you're expecting there'd be some money coming back from the furs trapped over the winter. The question is: how much? I'm not just being a greedyguts, Sam. Money buys time, and freedom. The more money I've got stored away, the less I must go around trying to find work to keep body and soul together, the less chance people will look at me close and ask questions. So... ?"

"Well, trapping's a bit like gardening – you set up as best's you can, but no one can say for certain sure what's gonna come up for harvest."

"But you can make a guess? I'm not going to make a decision today depending on what you answer, it'll just give me more information to think upon."

"Well, I guess at the least it'll pay back what we paid out for supplies. Or most of it, at the least. Steel traps don't come cheap, and I'm gonna have to buy a few. I mean, I'd make a few deadfall traps, too, all they cost is time and work. But they do take a lot of time to build, 'specially if you aren't had years and years of practice – and I aren't – and they're a bit more iffy nor steel traps."

She looked out across the inlet. Sam followed her eyes to a sail-boat and tracked it skimming across the harbour, running free with its sail belled out like white wings. After a while she said, "There's something I have to see before I can begin to decide one way or t'other. But I can't see it – do it – on my own. If there's two lads on big horses, one won't get looked at more'n the other, just like a pair of candlesticks. It would be a long ride – not a gallop, too far back and forth for that."

Sam very much wanted to know what it was she had to see, but he also wanted her to know that if she could use his help with anything, she had it. So he just said, "Okay."

They set off at first light, heading east along the Post Road, sometimes at a trot, sometimes a canter, sometimes just at a walk. A few miles past Spencer's Inn they turned north along a side road. The country was hilly and scrubby and gravelly, with scruffy little backwoods shanties here and there, and very rarely a large farm with herds of sheep and cattle grazing. At one point when Wellington and the skewbald were ambling along at an easy walk, Miss John Thomson said, "I don't know, you see, if Mr. MacAngus maybe didn't marry my mother after all, without a stepdaughter being part of the bargain." She quickly added, as though that'd maybe sounded like she was the be-all and end-all of everything, "Or maybe some other reason got in the way.

"If Mam didn't marry Mr. MacAngus, then my mother and brothers are still living on potatoes and curdled milk, and not much of that. If that's the fact, then the money I have in the bank would be a great help to them, and so would my hands. I would have to go back."

Sam wondered if it was really "would have to," or "would be able to." If he had a chance to go back to his mother or father and sisters, would he still be planning to rove around as homeless Sam Smith?

Halfway through a bend in the road, she slowed the skewbald from a canter to a walk and sat up straighter in the saddle, stiff-backed. A moment past the bend was a sprung-roofed shanty set back from the road. A tethered, bony milk cow was grazing a yard dotted with stumps and speckled with a few pecking chickens. Near the front of the house, a fair-haired woman was churning butter, and a boy in a ratty straw hat was splitting kindling with a hatchet.

John Thomson halted her horse and muttered sideways, "That's not my mother. Would you – could you please – go ask her where is Elsie McCann?"

Sam trotted Wellington up the dirt driveway, trying to think of what he'd say if the woman said, *She's just around the corner. Elsie!* She saw him coming and paused her two-fisted churning just long enough to bellow, "Hector!" By the time Sam got up to the house, a scrawny man with a raggedy beard was coming around from the back.

Sam reined Wellington to a halt. "Good morning," – or was it afternoon already? – "I'm lookin' for Elsie McCann."

Hector made a head-ducking gesture that wasn't quite a bow and forelock-tug, but close. Sam realized that on their big glossy thoroughbreds, he and John Thomson might look like a couple of rich man's sons out for a scruffy jaunt in the country. Hector said, "She still owns this farm, we're rent-to-own, but she don't live here no more, and ain't McCann no more. Ya go a couple-three miles down the road, ya'll see a big white house with black winda-shutters. That's Mr. MacAngus's place and she's the Missus now."

"Oh. Okay. Sorry to trouble you."

"No trouble at all, young sir."

Sam turned Wellington around and trotted back to the road. As soon as he got close enough for it to be noticed from the skewbald's back, he nodded. She nodded back, then turned her head and kept on nodding, slowly, staring down the road in front of her. When he reined in beside her, she said, "They'll think it strange if we don't carry on along this road, since they told you that's the way to who you're looking for."

"May be. But it's pretty chancy."

From the way she looked at him, she understood both ways he meant that: chancy that she might be recognized if her mother or brothers saw her on the road, and chancy that actually seeing her mother and brothers might be too much for her to just turn and ride away from. Either way, the result would be just slapping her back into the trap she'd escaped from. She said, "You're right. So what what they think?"

They turned and trotted back the way they came. Once they'd rounded the bend in the road, she slowed the skewbald to a walk. Sam could see she was clamping her lips tight together, and every muscle in her face held stiff and rigid. Except her eyelids, which were blinking and blinking. She was holding the reins in her left hand, right arm hanging loose. Sam and Wellington happened to be on her right side. Sam shifted the reins into his right hand, reached his left across and took hold of her dangling hand. They walked on that way for a while, then she gave his hand a squeeze and let go – two lads riding along holding hands might look just a tad bit odd.

They broke into a canter along the High Road. When they slowed again, Sam said, "Might's well stop at Spencer's Inn for a bite."

She just nodded, still keeping her jaw tight. But before they got to Spencer's Inn she said, "There's one thing, though... me Mam doesn't know about the letter from Mexico, what it really says, that Da wasn't a deserter for money and didn't desert us. She should know. But maybe... maybe I'll come back with the letter when all our lives are more settled-in. And maybe it's better for Mam to believe for now as she does."

Sam just grunted like yeah, that was probably true. Anything to keep her from thinking about turning around and going back. They didn't talk much over chicken pot pie and ale, but after they'd been back on the road a while she began to hum and la-la a lovely lilting tune – not loud, but it was there.

Sam said, "What's that, the tune?"

"Oh, it's an old, old song. There's different versions of it – The Whistling Gypsy, The Raggle-taggle Gypsies, Gypsy Davy... – all with different tunes and different endings, but it's all the same story." She began to sing words, loud enough for him to hear – no one around to hear a girl's voice coming out of a near-grown boy, and anyway she wasn't a high soprano:

"The gypsy rover came over the hill,

"Down to the valley so shady,

"He whistled and he sang till the greenwood rang,

"And he won the heart of a la-a-ady...

"Mam knew all the different versions, and would sing them at Da betimes. Well, not so much after we came to Nova Scotia."

She grew quiet again. Sam said, "Yeah, I get the gen'ral idea – but which one of us is runnin' away with the gypsies?"

XII

100 lb flour
1 smoothbore carbine
1 axe
2 A#1 hunting/skinning knives
3 spoons, 1 long wooden
1 cast iron pot
2 lb gunpowder
5 lb pig lead
5 lb birdshot
1 skillet
1 medium-small canoe
2 paddles
2-3 pces sailcloth, 6-8 ft square
5 #1 traps
3 #4 traps
5 lb salt

S EANA SUSPECTED THAT wouldn't be the final entirety of the list, a few other necessities would likely come to mind, but it would more than do for a start. She had a copy and Sam had a copy, and the deal was neither of them would make a purchase without consulting the other. The sailcloth was easy; those size pieces were remnants to the sailmakers in the Windsor shipyard. There was a big new hardware store called Dimock's in Windsor, and Sam would no doubt be checking out their stock, as well as in the other Windsor stores. Seana took her list and a pencil stub and a folded-over old handbill to make notes on, and went around to Calkin's General Store and the Red Store. Calkin's best medium-sized cast iron pots – the biggest you'd want to carry over a portage – looked sturdier that the Red Store's but were more expensive. As if Little Miss Seana McCann had a practiced eye. She felt a bit like she was playing grown-up in her mother's shoes. But since there was no one she could ask for advice, she'd just have to guess the best she could – she and Sam Smith, or whatever his real name was.

The conversations at the tables around her at dinner that day said there was a family band of Mi'kmaqs camped by the river just east of town. Since the last hay had been taken off by now, no one much cared who camped in the fields. Seana sent a message to Windsor on the stagecoach, and the next day Sam rode into Kentville on the skewbald. He said, "It can't be all that far a walk. If we ride in on big fancy horses they'll clam up." So they walked over to Cornwallis Street and along it. Before they reached the bridge they could see campfire smoke off to the right, so struck off across the stubbled fields.

There were a couple of wigwams patched together with bark held down by poles. Pulled up on the shore were three canoes: two big ones and a smallish one. Before Seana and Sam got to the camp, a dog started barking, then a bunch of dogs, including the high-pitched yips of puppies trying to sing with the pack. Three men came away from the wigwams and stood in front of them – an old man and two

younger ones. Sam said, "Kwah-ee, Nikskamich," took a twist of tobacco from his coat pocket and held it out.

The old man looked down, nodded and took the tobacco, then
gestured toward the campfire. They sat down around the fire: the old
man, Seana and Sam, and one of the young men. Sam and the old man
began to talk, and talk and talk, sometimes with long pauses in between. Seana suspected that their conversation in Mi'kmaq was much
the same as bargaining conversations in Erse or English or any other
language: talking about the weather and family relations and how the
fish were biting, only occasionally circling around to the business at
hand and then away again. Though she couldn't understand a word
they were saying, it seemed to her that Sam was kind of hesitant at
first but gradually got his mother tongue back, and the old man was
patient with him.

The young man at the fire got up and left and other Mi'kmaqs
came and went, some sitting for a while and maybe putting in a few
words of their own. Seana couldn't help but notice that they all,
even the women, had rough-looking knives on their belts or hanging around their necks. A girl about Seana's age knelt sideways with
one arm scooped around a baby and the other hefting a pot onto the
stones beside the fire. At one point Sam said something that made the
old man and the others laugh so hard they had to wipe their eyes. So
much for the stonefaced Red Man she'd read about.

Seen up close, the Mi'kmaqs – or at least these ones – seemed
more wiry than sturdy, even though at the end of the summer all
creatures wild and domesticated were supposed to be well-fed and
fattened up to get through the winter. These Mi'kmaqs seemed at
home in the open air, but still wary, travelling through a land that
was their land but wasn't theirs anymore. From what Sam had said
his Mi'kmaq grandmother had said, there used to be a lot more of
them. Disease and hunger and alcohol had wiped out more of them
than their old wars against the conquerors. Which wasn't all that different from how things stood in Ireland these days. Except that the
Irish could escape to somewhere else – like here.

Mi'kmaqs of all shapes and sizes weren't the only ones to come and go around the campfire. Several motley-coloured, scrawny dogs poked their noses in in hopes someone might take to eating something and maybe drop a few crumbs. A couple of still puppy-fat progeny tagged along, still unsteady on their roly-poly paws, and one of them took to chewing on the toe of Seana's boot. Its floppy ears would no doubt grow more upright like its elders', and its black and tan downy fur turn thick and feathery like theirs, good for sleeping in the snow. Seana was busy noticing those things when Sam and the old man abruptly stood up, Sam muttering sideways, "Come on."

Seana went with them to the riverbank, where Sam turned over the small canoe and looked over its insides. Seana had no idea what he was looking for – maybe he didn't have much more of an idea, was just guessing as best he could. She couldn't see any holes in the honey-brown birchbark skin showing between the ribs. Sam said in her direction, "Says he wants ten shillings for it. Sound all right by you?"

Seana half-shrugged. "If it does to you."

Sam took a leather pouch out of his coat and counted out ten silver shillings. Seana wondered why he didn't just give him two crowns – same amount, less weight and bulk – then realized some store clerk would be less suspicious if an Indian paid him with a shilling instead of a crown. Seemed that being an Indian in Nova Scotia wasn't all that different from being a gypsy traveller in Ireland.

Instead of putting his purse away, Sam talked a bit more with the old man, then counted out a few more coins. "Three more shillings buys us a couple of paddles and a bark rogan of spruce gum for sealing seams. I'll cut us a couple sheets of birchbark in the woods around Windsor, and some spruce roots for thread and there's our repair kit. Birchbark pierces easy but it's easy to fix if you got the fixin's."

Something bumped against Seana's ankle. She looked down. The black and tan puppy with the taste for boot leather had followed them to the riverbank. She said to Sam, "Ask him how much for the puppy."

Before Sam could start translating, the old man turned to Seana and said in easy English, "Take him – one less mouth to feed."

Sam lashed the two canoe paddles amidships and hoisted it upside down over his head. Seana was surprised at how light the canoe must be for him to heft it so easy; she knew Sam was stronger than he looked, but still... Then again, maybe it had something to do with practise remembered in his bones, knowing how to swing it up and balance it. Either way, he seemed comfortable walking along with a canoe over his head, though it seemed he likely couldn't see much except his own feet. Seana led the way back toward the Stage Coach Inn, with the puppy cradled in her arms. It fell asleep along the way. As she strode along watching for things a blind canoe might bump into, she reassured her impulsive self with all the practical reasons why a dog at a cabin in the woods was a good thing. A dog would bark to warn you if there were any strange animals lurking outside. And not only cats catch mice – bound to be woodmice trying to sneak into a cabin and nibble on flour or sugar or bootlaces. At the moment, though, what Seana most hoped for from this puppy was that he wouldn't piddle in his sleep.

They stored the canoe beside the Stage Coach Inn stables for now. Sometime in the next few weeks there was bound to be a freight wagon heading for Windsor that could tie a canoe on top of its load. From there Clifford would take it to his home in Three Mile Plains; Sam said a river that would take them where they wanted to go was near to Three Mile Plains.

Seana went into the inn kitchen and scrounged a bowl of chicken noodle soup, making sure the only chunks of chicken were as mushy as the noodles. They sat in the stables watching the puppy slurp and snuffle. Sam said, "Maybe you should name him Patrick, you bein' Irish and all." It was only later Seana realized that made the puppy's name Pat the dog.

It turned out Sam hadn't yet got around to checking out the prices of pots and skillets in Windsor, which annoyed Seana. He promised he would send a message with the stagecoach. Instead, what came was a message that some tinkers were camped near Windsor selling pots and pans. Seana had to wait until the next Halifax Express run was done before riding to Windsor. She was worried that the tinkers might move on before then, but there was nothing she could do about it. Turned out she needn't've worried, the tinkers had come for the crowds at the Hants County Exhibition and that was still going on.

The exhibition grounds were on the east side of Fort Hill, the same meadow that the Windsor Turf Club long races started from. At different spots around the grounds were ox-pulls, horse auctions, pie judgings... There were mounds of fresh-picked apples everywhere, and apple cider. After her first mug of cider, Seana decided it was sneaky stuff and they better go check out the tinkers' wares before they had another mug; Sam didn't disagree. The tinkers' set-up was an old freight wagon with a brightly-painted box built on top, a box tall enough to stand in. The tinkers weren't inside it, though, but sitting on the fold-out steps in back, with a few sample pots and tinware hanging on hooks. When a possible customer said they were interested in one of these or one of those, or maybe something not on display, one of the tinkers would duck inside and fetch one out.

The tinkers were a man and a woman coloured by summers of living outdoors, both ruddy brown and the man's light brown hair sun-streaked with blond. A toddler was napping in the shade under the wagon, and Seana suspected there were other children circulating through the fairground crowds. Seana pointed at a cast iron skillet and said in her John Thomson guttural, "Got one with a longer handle? For campfires?"

The tinkerman said to his woman, "Fetch out a noggy one for the kinchin cove."

As the tinkerwoman was heaving herself to her feet, Seana's memory was ricocheting back through many years and across the ocean to where *kinchin cove* – "little man" – was the kind of phrase she'd hear around the caravan campfire. She said, still keeping her John Thomson voice, "Nay, fetch the best's ya got in yer rolling ken."

The tinkerwoman froze in the doorway like she'd been harpooned, and turned around. "Aye, maybe this kinchin cove's a downy cove."

The man said, "Ya patter Romany?"

"Nay, but I growed up with the canting crew."

"A canting cove," said the tinkerwoman.

"A Romany rye," said the tinkerman. "Where ya growed up?"

"Erin Isle."

"Whatcha doin' here-bouts?"

"Was ridin' the rum prancers, but that gaff's done." Seana was scraping back through her memory for words and phrases, and feeling like she guessed Sam must've when he was speaking Mi'kmaq for the first time in a long time – only it'd been a lot longer for her. One advantage, though, to all the months of trying to get away with being John Thomson, it had got her into the habit of choosing words carefully to use her voice as little as possible. "Now me an' me pardo's gettin' geared for the snowy."

"He a canting cove too?"

"Nay, but a trusty cuffin. And you and yer covi here, yer playing a geachy game, bait 'n switch gaff."

"We ain't respun nothin', just testin' the gadjas' eyes."

"And we ain't here to raise a romboyle or blow the gaff, just lookin' for fair trade."

The upshot was that Seana and Sam walked away with a good cast iron pot and skillet and two steel spoons for a lesser price than any store would sell them. Once they were out of earshot, Sam said, "What was that all about – rumballs and rum prancers and geachy goomees?"

"Not all gypsies got curly black hair and rings in their ears."

"Huh. They weren't very friendly for bein' your people."

"They're not my people." Now as the phrase had come up, Seana realized she didn't have a "my people." And neither did Sam Smith. He could talk to the Mi'kmaqs, but he wasn't really one of them. "Distant cousins at most."

"I woulda thought even distant cousins'd be friendlier, meetin' up in a foreign land."

"That's about as friendly as they get. All over the world they get told to move on, people looking slantwise at 'em, siccing the dogs on 'em. Makes 'em kinda wary of other people."

"But you got 'em tradin' straight with you. What'd you say to them about baitin' something... ?"

"They been playing the old bait 'n switch – the old, old, *old* bait 'n switch. You haggle out a price for an article, then tell the customer, 'I'll just nip in back and wrap it up for you,' or wipe it off for you or polish it up or whatever, then you hand them a different article wrapped up, or one that looks the same at a glance but's cheaper made. For them," nudging her head back toward the tinkers' wagon, "the pots and pans they sell to the gadja only have to hold together for a week or two. By then they'll be long gone."

Sam seemed to ponder on that a moment, then said, "Huh. I bet there's plenty 'honest farmers' hereabouts pull lotsa their own kind of sneaky trickery sellin' cattle and hogs and all, and just call it clever trading."

"Same anywhere. Me Da told me, 'If you come across someone who'd rather sell you a solid piece of work for sixpence profit than a piece of junk for seven pence profit, you've found a rare human being.'"

After parking their purchases at the Shipyard Inn, the next stop was the big new building with Dimock's Hardware & Ship Chandlery across the front. The price for a pair of good hunting knives was better than the Kentville stores, logically: a brand new store trying to attract business, and less far for goods to be freighted inland to the retail counter – in fact, just across the road from the Windsor docks. The same was true of a short-barrelled musket gun-of-all-trades that could be loaded with a bullet or birdshot or buckshot.

When they got back up into Sam's room – beginning to get crowded with piled-up gear – Sam said, "There's somethin' else I got, somethin' what ain't on the list..." He seemed kind of embarrassed about it. "Last time I was in Halifax after a run, bringin' the Express horses back to their stations, I went around to the junk shops – secondhand shops, I mean. I been thinkin', ya see, 'bout how much ya like to read, goin' away to another world betimes, and it's gonna be a long winter, but we can't be haulin' tons and tons of books and magazines and newspapers 'long with us. So I thought if maybe there was one big book with a lotta stuff in it..." He reached down behind his bed, came out with a thick, battered, faded green book and handed it to her awkwardly.

The gold lettering on the cover had almost worn away, but she could still read the inset letters:

The Collected Works

of

Wm. Shakespeare

Vol. II

Sam said, "The fella at the store said it's rip-roarin' stuff once you get used to it, and even though there's some strange words there's little footy-notes to tell ya what they mean. He says it ain't like a three-volume novel where if you ain't got volume one it don't make any sense. And he said it's the kinda thing you can read over and over and still find new stuff."

For some reason, Seana was finding it hard to speak. She managed, "Thank you, Sam."

On the road back to Kentville, some of the trees were starting to turn colour. Next time Mr. Carstairs passed through, he said it would be his last time. "Next run's the last one, least on this route. Of course Nova Scotia hasn't completed its telegraph line yet, not even close, but New Brunswick has. So the Halifax Express'll run to Sackville, New Brunswick, for the next run – top of the Bay of Fundy – save us the steamboat 'cross the bay and one rider can do the whole gallop. After this next run we'll be taking all the horses back to Halifax. You could be one of the herd-riders if you like."

"Thanks, Mr. Carstairs, but I got a bit too much gear stocked up here to carry horseback, so I'd end up just having to take the stage back to Kentville anyways."

"Yeah, I heard you and Sam Smith were getting geared up for life after the Express."

"He's got a uncle's got a trapline, we're gonna go help out. What's gonna happen to the horses after you get 'em back to Halifax?"

"Some we'll use on the Sackville run, some we'll sell off right away. Oh, no need to fret over their fate – nobody's going to pay out what a horse like that costs and not treat 'em well. Any rate, I'll pay you now for up through Saturday, then once the horses are collected we're done and even." He counted out twelve shillings for last week and this, then looked back over both brown-leathered shoulders, lowered his voice and stuck out his hand. "So I guess this is goodbye John – or Jane, or Joan or Julia, whatever your real name is."

Seana's hand froze halfway to his.

"Oh, no need to fret about that, either. Not everyone has five daughters – living in a house full of females makes a fella conscious of subtleties. Your secret's safe with me, and there's my hand on it."

After the last run, the horses were given a day to rest up before the long ride back to Halifax. On the evening of that day, Seana brought a few apples out to Big Red to say goodbye. The Valley was knee-deep in apples this fall, but too many at once was as bad for horses as it was for humans. As Big Red's front chisel-teeth crunched apples off the flat of her right hand, her left hand stroked the wide, flat, furry forehead and bronze forelock – the monster horse of all the Halifax Express's big-barrelled gallopers, he who at any time in the last nine months could've crushed every bone in her body just by leaning sideways in the stall. Pat the puppy had followed her into the stall and was snuffling around those monumental, gleaming hooves, but Seana wasn't worried for an instant he'd get kicked or even accidentally stepped on. She murmured, "You carried me so very far, Eoch Ruadh," – Red Horse – "in many ways."

But, as Mr. Carstairs had said, Big Red would be well cared for wherever he went. And Seana told herself that Sam Smith's goodbye to Wellington was probably even harder – Big Red had carried her a lot of miles, but he hadn't jumped a river blind or won a horse race under her. For that matter, she and Sam Smith would've been saying goodbye to each other if he hadn't come up with this plan about a trapline and a cabin. Though for about the ten thousandth time, Seana wondered if it was a plan or a fit of madness.

The next day Corey O'Dell and a small squad of riders came through collecting Halifax Express horses, some of the horses running riderless with a long bridle line hooked to a rider's saddle. Next morning John Thomson sat on the steps of the Stage Coach Inn waiting for the stagecoach, with all her worldly possessions piled beside her – though some of them were hers and Sam Smith's, since they'd both paid for them. As the coach horses were being changed for a fresh team, some of the staff of the Stage Coach Inn – Seana's home for the better part of a year now – came out to say goodbye. The hug-and-kiss from Ella the chambermaid and from Megan the barmaid were a bit more than friendly farewell, like it was some sort of contest. Seana was glad she was wearing a thick coat and had tied her breastband tight.

In Windsor, Sam was waiting beside a farm wagon already loaded with the canoe and paddles and all their other gear. Clifford drove them to Three Mile Plains, where they spent the night at his home, and then up a winding track through the woods that was barely wide enough for the wagon. They stopped by a deep, clear, wide stream and Clifford helped them put the canoe in the water.

By the time the canoe was loaded with two humans and all their gear, it was riding pretty low in the water. Seana was glad they'd left a canvas sack at Clifford's with her and Sam's riding boots and breeches and a few other things that would be no use in the woods. Not just her riding boots, but also her newly resoled old ankle boots. Last night Sam had told her that hard-heeled boots were a liability in a birchbark canoe and would be no good with snowshoes come winter, and had handed her a pair of Mi'kmaq moccasins. Most of her childhood summers had been barefoot, so she knew her feet would harden up after only a week or so of being tender. She just hoped there wouldn't be any long portages before then.

Sam knelt in the stern and said to her in the bow, "You just paddle as best's you can and try to keep a steady rhythm, I'll balance it out and keep us straight. Lemme know if you see any rocks or snag-heads stickin' up ahead of us."

"Uh, sure..."

"Well, see you in the spring, Clifford."

Clifford said, "God willing," and pushed them off.

Seana struggled with the paddle at first, but gradually found its rhythm. By the time they stopped for a shore lunch, her arms and back and shoulders were sore in places where she didn't know she had muscles. The first thing she did once they were onshore and now safely away from any need for John Thomson was reach under her shirt to take off her breastband and stuff it in her rucksack. All the aches and pains were worth it if she never had to wear a thing like that again, or at least not for a long while. As she nibbled her bread and cheese – Sam didn't have to tell her that once this lot was gone they wouldn't be seeing any more for a long time – she said, "So now as we don't have to pretend for anybody, what's your real name?"

"George."

"George? What happened to Magrufkex... Megorffle... whatever you said before?"

"That's my Mi'kmaq name. Most of the time I got called George, or Georges. What's your real name – besides McCann?" That caught Seana by surprise, and not a pleasant one. "Oh, don't panic, I aren't been snoopin' or nothin'. When you told me at that farm to ask for Elsie McCann, I figured a pretty safe bet yer last name's the same as yer mother's."

"Oh. It's Seana. Seana McCann."

"Seana. That's nice, I like it. Seana."

Seana took another mouthful, trying to savour it, washed it down with fresh, clear river water, then said, "You don't look like a George."

"I've got kinda used to bein' a Sam. You can keep on callin' me Sam if you like."

"Okay. But don't you dare call me John!"

"Do my best. We'd best get back at it. Paddlin' upstream's slower and harder'n down, but a lot easier nor it woulda been in spring and early summer. Come spring we'll ride the runoff currents back."

If we come back, passed through Seana's mind, but she didn't say it. Sam surely knew as well as she did, probably better, how many different kinds of accidents and disasters could happen to people stuck in the deep woods all winter long.

They set off upstream again with Pat the puppy planting his front paws on the bow like a Viking figurehead. Now that she was getting a bit comfortable with paddling – didn't have to concentrate all her attention on it – Seana had room to notice that the canoe's springy ribs and thin skin moved in and out with shifts in the current, like it was breathing. Travelling in a canoe seemed almost as much a cooperation with a living thing as riding a horse. Partway through the afternoon the riverbank undergrowth thinned enough to see the whole slope of a hillside to the right, flares of red and gold and orange among the evergreens. Part of Seana was delighted by the autumn fireworks show, but to another part of her it just showed they didn't have endless time to get where they were going and get snugged in for the winter.

She didn't complain, though, when Sam said they should call it a day if they hoped to make camp before dark. She felt as stiff and sore as after her first Halifax Express run, but different muscles. There was some consolation in the possibility Sam was feeling the same – must've been at least a year or two since he'd last paddled a canoe. After they'd got a fire going with flint and steel – the wax vespa matches were for emergencies – Sam said, "It'll take a 0while for this to build up coals. Meantime I'll try and turn these," taking a few coils of copper wire out of his coat pocket, "into rabbits," punctuated with a mysterious wink.

Seana reached for one of the coils, saying, "I don't have to sit here like a bump on a lump when I could be setting snares, too." The look he gave her was a mixture of surprise and disappointment, like he'd kind of wanted it to be a mystery to her. "Every travellers' child in Ireland knows how to do a bit of poaching by the time they're knee-high to a pony. And I've skinned and tanned rabbit pelts before, and stoats and foxes."

He also seemed sort of disappointed that she already knew how to make campfire bannock. But she didn't know how to tell safe mushrooms from the look-alike kinds that weren't – at least not the kinds that grew in the deep woods of Nova Scotia – and the double handful he picked made a tasty addition to the salt pork they fried when the bannock was done. Pat the puppy licked the skillet clean. When they were leaned back sipping black tea out of tin cups, Seana said, "Now that we've got a start, how many days do you figure from here to the cabin and the trapline?"

She'd expected him to say something like three or four days, or six or seven at the worst. The last thing she expected was, "Dunno, I never come this way before."

"*What?* You said..." she was sputtering, "You said every year for ten years and more, back and forth!"

"Yeah but this ain't the way I'm used to goin'. Clifford told me, though, this river hooks up with the river I'm used to, or pretty close. Them Mi'kmaqs in Kentville said the same."

"*Pretty close?*"

"Don't worry, Seana – " It sounded surprisingly intimate to hear him use her real name, even more than that they'd kissed and twined together for a moment on his bed, or that he'd seen her in the bath-tub. "These rivers've been Mi'kmaq highways for hundredsa years, maybe thousands. There's signposts, if you know what to look for."

When she was rolled up in her bed of canvas doubled over and under blankets – with Patrick snuggled against her chest, and her pouched revolver close to hand – she listened to the tapestry of sounds around her: the burble of the river, long-needled pine trees whispering in the wind, bare branches rattling like dried old bones, the rustle of autumn leaves. Maybe that wasn't the wind rustling the leaves. She was nowhere near a road now, where human traffic might keep bears and wolves away. Maybe this river did used to be a Mi'kmaq highway, but there weren't near as many Mi'kmaqs as there used to be, and even back when there were it could hardly have been the same as a High Road today, not enough constant human presence to scare off wild creatures. The air in her nostrils tasted wild and un-human too, spruce and balsam fir and juniper and woodrot loam and river-licked rock and campfire smoke, so different from the smell of a fireplace or woodstove.

It wasn't the woodsmoke, though, that was stinging tears out of her eyes. She hugged the puppy and the pistol closer to her and tight-ened her jaw so no whimpery sobby noises squeaked out. The tears were as much anger as anything else. Sam – or George or whatever his Mi'kmaq name was – had lied to her about knowing where he was going, or at least hadn't told the truth about this being a new route to him, not until they were already well on their way. What else had he lied about? It wasn't too late yet for her to turn around – they hadn't come all that far in just one day's paddling upstream. She could pack together as much as she could carry on her back and just follow the riverbank back. But back to what? She'd spent away half her savings on the list of what they'd need to get through the winter, and once she'd decided to go along with Sam's plan she hadn't thought through any other plans of what she might do, how she could hide, when the Halifax Express was done. Going back was a dead end.

She tried on the possibility that the tears and the lost feeling were just dizzy panic: now that she finally had a moment when she didn't have to be lifting or paddling or moving, she had the chance to be dizzy at how much change had happened so fast. The night before last she'd been John Thomson sleeping in his bed in the Stage Coach Inn, the same bed she'd slept in for most of the past year. But no, that didn't explain it, she'd been through changes as big or bigger before without panicking: uprooting from Ireland to Nova Scotia, and desperately trying out for the Halifax Express. Why should this time be any different?

There was a difference, though, now that she asked the question. Those other times there'd been other people in it with her, or at least around her. Now the only other person around her for a hundred miles – might as well be a hundred, in this wilderness where other people didn't go – was the boy on the other side of the campfire, who'd never come this way before and made crazy noises in his sleep.

The farther upriver they got, though, and deeper into the wilderness, the less Sam made those troubling noises in his sleep – those snarly, barky yelps like Percy's twitchy-legged nightmares. He seemed to move more loose and easy, and he grinned when his hands remembered how to do something they hadn't done for a few years – maybe do it even better, since they were bigger now. But the farther upriver they got, the smaller the river became; it seemed to be narrowing in front of Seana's eyes. She began to wonder if it was going to shrink too small for their canoe. Partway through the third morning, though, Sam called from the stern, "I think that's it, up on the right."

"What's it?"

"What say we pull into shore and see."

Seana shifted her paddling to the left side of the canoe. As they swerved into shore, she saw there was a patch of riverbank that was miraculously free of rocks, just the river meeting a band of clay and then low groundcover. As she climbed out to pull the bow up on shore she saw a pile of stones beside the clear patch, as though rocks had been cleared away and piled there – though so long ago there was silt and moss between them.

Sam picked up his gun. "I'll go see if I can follow the portage trail – if there is a trail and this is the right spot. You stay here and make sure no little claws or paws get into our flour and sugar and such, okay?"

"How far is it?" meaning, "How long will you be gone?"

"Dunno."

"Okay."

Once he'd disappeared into the bush, she sat on a rock for a while, watching Patrick stalk the wily water beetle, then decided she should do something. At one of their shore stops, she and Sam had cut a couple of poplar poles and fixed a fish hook on a length of fishing line tied to the skinny end. Nowhere near like the fancy fly-fishing rigs she'd seen in Ireland but should work, although they hadn't worked yet. This time, though, only a few minutes after she'd impaled that water beetle on a fish hook and dropped it in the water, the pole twitched. She jerked the pole up to fix the hook, then flipped ashore a silvery fish that glinted in the sun. Not big enough for dinner for two, but could be part of a dinner, and Pat could get the guts.

As Seana was working the fish hook free, she was startled by a sound that made her almost impale herself. It was a distant gunshot, from the same direction where Sam had vanished into the woods. His muzzle-loader carbine only had the one shot and took time to reload, more time than it would take a charging bear or pack of wolves to get across a clearing. Maybe she should've lent him the revolver to take with him...

She told herself there was no point thinking about it, worrying about it – she was just a typical idiot who'd grown up in a place where there were no large wild animals left so got panicky at the thought of them. Better to busy herself rebaiting the hook and jigging it up and down in the river. Nonetheless, she was relieved when Sam came back out of the woods looking no different than when he went in, except that the bottom half of his pant legs looked darker than the rest. She said, "Are you all right?"

"Huh?"

"I heard a gunshot, or thought I did."

"Oh, there's a fat goose for supper waitin' at the end of the portage, covered over with brush to keep the crows off but won't keep 'em off forever. Had to wade out into the river a little to fetch 'im – the river we want, I'm just about sure."

"Just about... ?"

He just shrugged. She didn't get angry; she was starting to get the hang of this. He was doing as best he could with what he had to work with. All they could do was keep on going ahead, like riding the Halifax Express on a moonless night. She held up her catch, saying, "Roast goose for supper and fish for dinner."

"Huh. You're a better fisherman nor me." He said it a bit awkwardly, almost bashfully. He seemed to be getting more shy with her since she stopped being John Thomson. "How 'bout you cook 'im up while I rig our gear up for carryin'?"

The portage trail turned out to be narrow, winding, up and down and overgrown. In places, she wouldn't've known it was a trail except for pink-white blazes on some trees. Sam said they'd gone almost bark-grey – so long had it been since the trail was last used – so he'd cut the weathered skin off on his way back from the other river, which was part of what took him so long while she and Pat were waiting by the canoe. The portage actually wasn't all that long, though it felt like it carrying heavy, jury-rigged backpacks – Sam called them pièces – with rope shoulder straps. On the last trip, Sam carried the canoe while Seana walked ahead carrying only the two pairs of snowshoes that he said were going to be more valuable to them than guns or firestarters.

Two forked green sticks standing up on either side of a campfire and another green stick laid across them made a workable turning spit for roasting a goose, sizzling and popping as its fat sweated onto the fire. There were a lot of leftovers, but the days had grown so cool

– and the nights so cold – that edibles would stay edible a few days. In fact the nights had grown so cold, and this one coming on even more so than the nights before, that Seana said, "It's foolish for us to shiver in our lone beds when the three of us in one bed would keep each other warm. You don't kick and snort in your sleep the way you used to."

Since they only took off their coats and moccasins to go to bed – coats for pillows, moccasins in the bottom of the bed to keep from frosting over – it was hardly an invitation to do anything else but sleep. He lay on his side and she spooned up behind, with one arm draped across him. Pat the puppy squirmed in against her back. All three were so tired from the day, they were gone as soon as they closed their eyes, or at least Seana was. When she woke, Sam was already up and boiling tea. After breakfast they loaded the canoe into the water and set off again, Sam steering and setting the course while Seana just paddled. This river seemed even narrower and shallower than the shrunken one they'd left behind, this was more like a creek than a river. They did seem to be making good time, though, moving along at a much better clip than before. Maybe she was getting the hang of propelling a canoe. But then she realized the real reason they were travelling faster – they were moving with the current, not against it.

Seana shipped her paddle and barked over her shoulder, "Hey! We're going downstream!"

"Yep. If we went upstream here we'd scrape the bottom off 'fore we got far."

"But you said! You said we'd go upstream in the fall and downstream when we come back in the spring."

"Yeah, the way my family always used to go. Things don't always flow the same when yer goin' from one river to another."

Seana reminded herself of what she'd thought she had learned yesterday: spitting and sniping at each other would only make things worse; all they could do was keep on going ahead. So she closed her mouth and put her paddle back in the water, but it wasn't easy. They didn't talk much when they stopped for a quick lunch of cold goose and leftover bannock, then they were back on the water. A while before she should start looking for a place to pull in for the night, their piddly creek flowed into the side of a real river. As the river approached, Seana saw brown and yellow leaves floating from left to right, so she switched her paddling to the right side of the canoe and they swerved in headed upstream. Seana called over her shoulder, "Is this the river you remember?"

"Think so." It sounded more like *Hope so.*

When they were camped that night, watching the fire sink down to coals, he said, "This is the best time of year to be out here, all the bugs are buggered off – least all the ones that bite ya. No one goes into the woods in summer 'less they're crazy or a white man. Oh, no offence."

"Why would I take offence? I'm not a white man." Though there did seem a good chance she was crazy.

He stared in silence at the dying flames a moment, then said, "Ya know, once we get settled in in the cabin, you won't be saddled with me all the time. The trapline takes two, three days to go 'round, dependin', and I should try to do it 'bout twice a week – don't want critters stuck in the traps for long. 'N fact, soon's we get settled in, even 'fore snow sets in, I should do the circuit and rebuild the lean-tos – overnight stations – that've been sittin' untouched a couple years."

Seana didn't necessarily see why she should do all the sitting in the cabin alone waiting while he was doing all the going around the trapline alone, but she decided to wait that debate till they'd actually got to where they were going. If they ever got there.

Next morning they'd only been paddling for about an hour when he called from behind her, "Seems our goose ain't cooked after all."

"Pardon me?"

"That sorta cliff up ahead – not really tall enough for a cliff, but – that rusty brown rock stickin' into the water, with the twisty pine tree on top. I seen it before. This is the right river."

"You're sure?"

"Yep, that picture stuck in my mind – it meant we were more'n halfway to our wintering grounds. I used to watch for it when I was a squirt and had no patience." Seana wasn't sure if the grin in his voice came from recognizing a piece of his childhood or from plain old relief.

Not long after they'd rounded that rocky headland, though, they began to hear sounds she hadn't expected – something else he hadn't told her about? – the whack of axes and hammers and, as they got closer, the burr of four-handed saws. Seana saw a place ahead where the riverbank had been cleared of trees and brush, and behind it a half-built, long, log barracks – the beginnings of a lumber camp. Sam murmured from behind her, "That wasn't there before."

A couple of check-shirted men were dipping buckets in the river. One of them stood up and called out toward the canoe, "Hey Chief, want-um firewater?"

Sam said, not loud enough to carry over the water, "Just keep paddling, look straight ahead." After the sounds of the logging camp faded behind them, he said like he'd been thinking it over, "We still got a couple days to go, and past some pretty rugged country – I mean rugged inland. They won't come lumbering that far." It sounded like he was trying to reassure himself as well as her.

After two more days and a snowfall that didn't stay, Seana heard a distant, muffled roaring sound between the dip and ripple of her paddle. Whitewater rapids, or maybe a waterfall, around the bend she could see up ahead. Sam called from behind her, "Don't worry, we'll be landed before then. Past this bend you'll see a creek mouth on your left. Too shallow and rocky for us to paddle up, but just before it there's a cleared space we can beach the canoe." There was a thrum-ming excitement in his voice, even though he tried to sound like he was just giving directions.

Beyond the bend there was a lovely, frothing waterfall – or sev-eral, in a series of skewed steps, white plumes against the slate and black spruce. A ways before it was a creek mouth coming into the river, and before that the "cleared" space Sam had predicted – actually a tangle of weeds and reeds, but no canoe-gouging rocks Seana could see. Once the canoe was pulled up on shore, Sam said, "It's not far – what say we leave the carryin' till after we go have a look?"

"Okay."

Sam did pick up and carry his gun, though, so Seana took the revolver. Patrick trotted along on legs already longer than when Clifford handed him into the canoe. After a raggedy path through the woods – so much taller and darker than they looked from the river – they came out into a clearing with a log cabin. A sort of a cabin; Seana had to look twice to make sure that's what it was. The autumn-dessicated, grey-brown goldenrod and grasses crackled and snapped against her legs as she crossed the clearing. She could see now that the cabin's roof slanted from front to back and was made of overlapping slabs of birchbark. She told herself that a birchbark roof really wasn't any more primitive than shingles, just bigger pieces. But there was no "then again" about the height of the place. From the ground up, the tallest wall was barely taller than she was. Was she supposed to spend the entire winter stooped over, or out of doors?

Sam lifted a basketwork square stuck on the front wall, disclosing a parchment leather window, no good for seeing through but probably pretty good at letting sunlight in. Then he pushed the sagging door open and his hand said, *After you.* Out the open doorway came a musty, mushroomy smell of damp earth and things that lived under rocks. As she bent her head and raised her foot to step into the dark, he said, "Careful, there's a drop." There was; the floor of the cabin had been dug down about one stair height. Which still didn't explain why the roof inside was a good arm's length higher than it looked from the outside, until she realized it would be if the dug-out earth had been piled up around the bottom logs outside – for insulation, drainage? – and grass and wildflowers grown themselves on top. Her eyes adjusted to the twilight inside. One of the side walls had a rough – very rough – stone fireplace and chimney. Light from the doorway and window wasn't the only sunlight coming in; one of the sheets of roof bark had a split in it. Sam, stepping in behind her, said, "I'll have to patch that," without Seana having said anything. Then, "Not much to see, is there?"

"It'll be shelter from the winter, that's the main thing, isn't it?"

"Well... guess we better be movin' our goods here 'fore they get et." But when they stepped back outside, he didn't go far before he stopped and stooped. Seana looked to what he was looking down at: a scattering of dark pellets. He straightened up again, saying, "Caribou. Not long ago, neither. Guess there's been no people 'round here so long it's just a sunny place to graze. Be easy shootin', I'd just have to sit in the tall grass and wait. But, ya know, maybe better I wait a few weeks... ? They'd be skittisher by then, but still..."

Seana puzzled at what "ya know" she was supposed to know. It didn't take her long. With just the two of them – two and a half of them – a whole caribou's meat would go bad before they'd eaten all of it, or even half of it. In another few weeks meat would freeze and stay frozen. She said, "Yes, better to wait."

He nodded that he agreed with what she'd agreed with. But he still didn't carry on toward the river. Instead he turned and looked back at the rundown little cabin. Seana realized it was his family home, for half the year for most of his life. She stepped up beside him and said, "It'll be grand and cozy when it's all drifted around with snow." His right arm came up around her shoulders, she put her left around his waist. Her mind's eye saw the cabin as it would be in winter: smoke curling from the chimney, snow on the roof, the parchment window a warm amber eye in all the white and grey, new moss filling the gaps between logs where the old chinking was crumbling away, maybe a lynx or wolf pelt pegged to the wall to stretch and dry... Whatever had to be done to make the place snug for the winter, they would have to take care of themselves. They would have to take care of themselves, and each other. No one else was going to, except for a price neither one of them was willing to pay.

Looking back the other way, she saw herself last autumn, trapped and hopeless and then clutching at the windblown straw of the Halifax Express. Only a year ago but that girl seemed so distant, so painfully unsure of herself in some ways and too sure of herself in others, with no real idea of what she was getting herself in for and how she would handle it. She had a funny feeling that a year from now she'd see the girl standing here now the same way.

Author's Note

WHEN I FIRST heard of what we now call the Nova Scotia Pony Express (1840s people would've been appalled at the name; to them "pony" meant a pit pony dragging coal cars through the mine, or a fat little Shetland for the kiddies to ride), it struck me as a perfect hideaway for a runaway teenager, or two. I figured someone back then could've disguised him/herself to ride for the Express and no one today would know whether such a person had or hadn't existed. But I've been wrong before, occasionally.

First question was whether all the riders were documented and none of them could've been a teenage runaway. Turns out only three are known for certain: Corey O'Dell, Thad Harris and a Hamilton whose first name's a blank. The Halifax Express made thirty-one runs, with two riders per run, so it definitely had more than three riders on call. There is one wider list of riders, adding three or four other names, from the reminiscence of an old fella who was a young fella in 1849. But it's only names: the old fella doesn't say whether they rode for Hyde & Craig or Barnaby and his memory seems a bit hazy, so hazy that he gets mixed up which Express was working for which New York syndicate. Why I said "three or four" other names is be- cause one print version of the old fella's handwritten list says, "Mason and John Pineo..." and another says, "John Pineo, a Mason..." So maybe he meant that two riders were the Pineo brothers, John and Mason, or maybe meant one rider, John Pineo who was a member of the Ancient Order of Freemasons. Welcome to the wonderful world of historical research.

So all the historical evidence that exists still leaves plenty of room for a couple of anonymous riders. But that still left the ques- tion of whether an outfit like the Halifax Express truly would want to hire young, lightweight riders – made sense to me, but just because something makes sense to me... Well, one 19th-century account refers to "a lad named Hamilton," and another says, "Thad Harris... was only twenty years old, and some of the riders may have been younger." When the U.S. Pony Express went into business, ten years after the Halifax Express (out west pony meant a tough and scruffy mustang, so Pony Express was no shame), its ad for riders read: "Wanted – young, skinny, wiry fellows, not over 20... Orphans preferred." Buffalo Bill Cody said he rode for the Pony Express when he was fifteen, but Buffalo Bill said a lot of things, though he was habitually smart enough to not stretch his stories beyond plausibility. All 'n all, the Halifax Express seems to've been tailor-made for a willowy teenage girl pretending to be a boy.

Luckily for me, a few thoughtful and diligent people got busy digging on the 150th anniversary in 1999 – dug up all the histori- cal records of the Halifax Express there is to dig. Which added up to a barebones sketch with a few dabs of colour here and there, like "young Mr. Hamilton's" broken stirrup strap, and an unnamed rider's night-blind leap across the Gaspereau River when the swing bridge was swung out of place. Maybe I did Mr. Barnaby a disservice by saying those weren't accidents, but the cut telegraph wire is defi- nitely factual, so dirty tricks weren't outside his definition of business competition. One account says the cut-telegraph delay was eighteen hours, another said twelve, so I sorta split the difference.

I had to do some guesswork about where the Halifax Express relay stations were, since the only points known for certain are the start and finish and the midpoint/changeover at Kentville. Some accounts name other places, but they contradict each other and don't differentiate between Barnaby's Express and Hyde & Craig's. Some accounts say there were twelve relay stations and twelve horses per run, on the logical basis that the total distance was 144 miles, each leg was supposed to be twelve miles, and 12 into 144 = 12. But a morning-after newspaper article on the second Halifax Express run includes, "A distance of 18 miles, from Kentville, was performed by Mr. Thad. Harris, in 53 minutes." So the next relay station after Kentville was eighteen miles away, which would put it around Aylesford. Seems that Hiram Hyde's original plan for twelve-mile stages got modified a bit by factualities.

A couple of other venerable old towns along the route, which looked like good relay station candidates to me and were even mentioned in 20th-century accounts of the Halifax Express, turned out not to've existed till the railway came through, twenty years after the Express. The town of Kingston, fr'instance, was barely a pimple on the map until the railway decided it was easier to put a station there than build a bridge across the river to the nearest noticeable town.

The "Pony Express" plaque at Granville Point, now called Victoria Beach (don't go there with your beach blanket, it's mostly rocks), says it's 146 miles from Halifax, but most historical accounts say 144. Roads change, so does mileage. The old Post Road or High Road was generally the same as Highway Number One today, but not entirely. Highway #1 – no longer the number one highway – runs outside my front door, but out my back window I can see the ridge where the High Road used to run along the side of the valley. I can also see the horses gambolling in my next-door neighbour's pasture, though they tend to be standardbreds or quarter horses, not thoroughbreds.

Thoroughbreds is another one of those words, like pony, whose generalized·meaning has changed over time. Nowadays a thorough-bred means a highly specialized long-distance racehorse, fine-tuned to the point they have fragile leg bones and generally need to be pampered. 19th-century thoroughbreds were long-distance racers, too, but the distances were a lot longer, and a gentleman's prize thoroughbred was also expected to carry him to church and to the tavern two towns over and the three-day ride to Aunt Matilda's at Christmastime. Kinda like the difference between a modern Formula 1 racecar and the early days of stock car racing, when your competition vehicle also had to be able to handle the back roads and highways.

Place names and landscapes change, too. Upper Horton is now Wolfville, though that originally applied only to that part of Upper Horton previously known as Mud Creek, which the more dignified citizens thought not very dignified.

The inland back-country that Seana and Sam travel through in Chapter XII has been greatly changed by man-made lakes, dammed for hydro power or for recreational use or for I dunno what-all. Many separate towns in this story are now bled together, with houses and parking lots where the old Post Road would've wound through stretches of miles and miles of woods. Southwest of Kentville is now endless, borderless strip malls and 'burbs – it does end eventually, but the tall forests that would've loomed above the Express riders are now spindly birch and scrub spruce. There's now an iron bridge upstream from the long-gone swing bridge over the Gaspereau River, but you can still see the remains of the cribwork where the old bridge stood, and the power lines cross the river where Wellington made his midnight leap.

Many of the places I described in Kentville (the Stage Coach Inn, etc.) have been replaced but are archived more or less as I've described. Windsor was a different story, since Windsor's Great Fire of 1897 destroyed many records as well as buildings. Some inn's names did survive even though the buildings burned, but among the names that didn't, there might maybe've been a Shipyard Inn. I don't know if there was a Windsor Saddlery but there definitely was a Windsor Turf Club, and I don't think they went all the way to Halifax to get their gear.

I've read that no likenesses (photos, portraits, sketches, doodles...) of Express riders exist, but there is an old photograph of Corey O'Dell in an artfully restored Victorian room in Annapolis Royal. He's considerably older than the time of this story and has grown a full beard, but looks like a decent bloke even if his head's one size too big for his shoulders. About ten years after the Halifax Express, he and his young family settled in Annapolis Royal where he eventually built and operated his own inn and did quite well for himself, thankee very much. I found online a photograph of Daniel Hutchins Craig taken about fifteen years after the Halifax Express. He eventually became president of The Associated Press and built a mansion in Westchester County, New York.

Hiram Hyde wasn't near as successful financially, but it doesn't seem to've bothered him much. His main line was the stagecoach business (or main business was stagecoach lines), but he invested the profits in everything from gold mines in Musquodoboit to the Pitch Lake in Trinidad, lost it all and cheerfully resigned himself to running a fuel business in Truro – everybody needs coal and firewood. He got himself elected to the Nova Scotia Legislature but apparently never took his seat. In Chapter IV I made a sideways allusion to the Halifax Express's possible lack of prejudice; Hiram Hyde's stagecoach line was the first in Nova Scotia to hire a black driver. When business was slow or a coach was out of commission, Hyde would drive the route himself in a ratty old express wagon with no one riding shotgun. When people cautioned him about carrying valuable freight with no protection, he said, "Who's gonna rob ol' Hiram Hyde?" and no one ever did.

There is no historical record, though, of Mr. Carstairs or anyone like him, but there wouldn't be – either the Halifax Express didn't believe in keeping records of its inner workings or they all went into the nearest firebox when the Express shut down. Through 1849

Hyde had plenty to keep him occupied in Halifax and Truro, including building the telegraph line between them, and Craig was busy on the west side of Fundy and in the Boston States. Seems logical that neither Hyde nor Craig would take off for days to check the circuit, ignoring other business interests. Someone did the hands-on that kept the machinery well-oiled and every relay station primed and ready to send the incoming rider back on his way without hardly breaking stride. If someone like Carstairs hadn't existed, Hyde & Craig would've had to invent him.

The Astor Place Riots in New York City are a matter of historical record, though historians have varying opinions on the exact cause(s). Any mass mob riot tends to happen for a number of reasons, I just focused on how it might seem to Seana McCann. There's no might or maybe, though, that the riots were May 10 and the Halifax Express run was May 8-9, perfect timing for the news from London in Seana's dispatch case to hit the New York morning papers on the day.

There was an odd coincidence (these things happen) just as I started thinking on this story. I'd decided that Seana's father would've joined the U.S. Army for the Mexican war and been killed there, but it was just a kind of nebulous, generic picture. But right then, reviews popped up about a new album by Ry Cooder and The Chieftains, about the San Patricio Battalion. Like most folks north of the Rio Grande, I'd never heard of the San Patricios, but it looked like a dandy fit for this story. And yes, there were definitely some volunteers from Canada and other British North American colonies in the St. Patrick's Battalion.

But I did stay kind of nebulous and generic about the orphanage school Sam ran away from and Seana goes to visit. There were historically documented orphanage/boarding schools dotted here and there throughout Nova Scotia, run by various religious denominations or the province, but none were charged with abuse in the nineteenth century – back then you just didn't talk about that kind of thing, didn't even think it. I have no doubt it happened in some schools

– sexual exploitation wasn't invented in the 20th century – but I didn't want to pin it on some specific school unfairly.

If you do decide to check out unnovelized information on the Halifax Express, please keep in mind that no single report of a historical incident is the whole truth and nothing but. The Wikipedia entry on Hiram Hyde said he was born in 1837, "came to Nova Scotia in 1841 and was hired by Samuel Cunard to transport mail" which does give a rather charming picture of knee-high Hiram toddling mail sacks around in his little red wagon. The entry's since been altered to "born 1817" but still tells us he died in 1907 at the age of 70. Not to single out Wikipedia, you'll find other discrepancies on other websites, not all that obvious. And not to single out the Internet, either, mistakes and assumptions get printed in books, too. I'm just sayin' that just because one source tells you something don't mean another source might not tell you something slightly different. Ya gotta shop around.

One account of the "Nova Scotia Pony Express" told me the Cunard mail ships anchored in Halifax harbour and a rowboat would charge out and bring back saddlebags to hand up to the Express Rider, which would've made an awfully complicated scene out of the chapter where I have Sam start his first express run from Halifax. But the ships certainly docked sooner or later, so I decided that if they came in at low tide they'd anchor in the harbour and at high tide steer straight for the wharf. As for the saddlebags, I started writing this story with saddlebags (well, I was writing with a keyboard actually, but anyway...) but saddlebags seemed awfully cumbersome for fast changes of horses, and luggage overkill for one telegraph-ready dispatch of 3,000 words.

Saddles brought in some contradictions, too. Some reports say each Express rider's saddle was shifted from horse to horse in the relay, some say the horses were already saddled and waiting, and it's hard to tell if they were talking about the Halifax Express or Barnaby's. So I lumped the contradictions together and had Corey O'Dell keep his own saddle and others not.

If you're more inclined to check out actual three-dimensional history instead of texts, The (Corey) O'Dell House and Sinclair Inn in Annapolis Royal are now museums, thanks to the Annapolis Heritage Society. One of Hiram Hyde's stagecoaches is in the Colchester County museum in Truro, and Truro also has a tree sculpture of Hiram Hyde – much older than he would've been in this story, but still looks like a lively and affable fella. In Halifax the Maritime Museum of the Atlantic has a permanent display on the Cunard steamship line that fed the Halifax Express.

I'll end this little background note where it began, with why this story of 1849 doesn't use the current term Nova Scotia Pony Express. 'Round about 1912 an old man who'd been a young boy when the Halifax Express used to gallop through his town wrote befuddledly, "... but I cannot understand why the service (is) called a 'Pony Express,' as the finest horses were employed..."